Two Billion Enemies

RUTHLESS BILLIONAIRES 2

LYDIA MICHAELS

Lydia Michaels Books, LLC
www.LydiaMichaelsBooks.com

USA | CANADA | SPAIN | EUROPE | NEW
ZEALAND | AUSTRALIA

TWO BILLION ENEMIES
Ruthless Billionaires 2
Billionaire Romance
Contemporary Romance
Copyright © 2023 Lydia Michaels
Lydia Michaels Books, LLC
2nd E-book Publication: © Lydia Michaels 2023
Cover Design by Lydia Michaels Books, LLC

Also for Amy—
A lioness who's not afraid to roar.

Part One

Isadora

Prologue

PEOPLE DRESSED in gowns and tuxedos filtered into the cozy book bar across from the opera house, reminding her of where they were and how long they'd been missing. She reached in her purse to check the time on her phone, shocked to see it was almost midnight.

There were a few missed calls and texts from Toni asking where she was. Some worried ones too.

She couldn't tell her family what happened. Couldn't explain how seeing Sawyer Bishop with another woman absolutely devastated her. They'd never understand why seeing their father's protégé kissing a woman would destroy her. And it actually hadn't.

Strangely, the man sitting across from her had literally crossed her path at precisely the right time.

Guilt slithered through her. She should at least let her sister know she was safe. She didn't want to leave this little sanctuary, but she had to get back.

"Thank you for helping me tonight."

"Please don't thank me. I feel terrible I knocked you over."

She shrugged, glad they bumped into each other. "Accidents happen."

His hand brushed hers and her stomach tightened. As she stared at his fingertip grazing her knuckles, a whoosh of butterflies exploded in her stomach and her gaze jumped to his face.

Other than Sawyer, no one had ever caused her to feel butterflies like that. He gave a shy smile. "I had a great time getting to know you."

Feeling winded though she'd been sitting for some time, she whispered, "Me too. It was sweet of you to bring me here and..." She gestured to the damp napkin. "The ice." If her lip was still swollen from the fall, she couldn't tell. Her face was rather numb as he held her gaze.

"My pleasure." His hand slowly pulled away and the strange feeling faded.

She fidgeted, unsure how to say goodnight

and thank you without seeming awkward. "People are probably wondering where I am."

"Him?"

Her smile fell. "No, he doesn't even know I'm here. My family, though ... I just left without telling them." She gestured to her phone. "My sister texted me about a hundred times."

"Ah. If you want to stay and talk a while longer I could take you home. You could let her know you're safe."

Her lips parted, a curious feeling twisting inside of her. Was he asking her out or just being considerate?

"I should probably go home with her. I insisted she come with me tonight."

"Does she live with you?"

"No, but she's spending the night."

"Then you should probably let her know where you are." He gestured to her phone.

Her hands trembled, her mind protesting that she wanted to stay. She texted Toni letting her know she was at the bar across the street.

Her phone buzzed back and she slipped it inside her clutch. "She'll be here in a few minutes."

"Can I see you again?"

Fear and nervous excitement took hold. She

wanted to see him again, but she was so afraid she was leading herself toward another letdown. He wasn't like the other men she knew, yet she couldn't put her finger on what made him so different.

Her phone vibrated again. "Excuse me."

She pulled it out and read the text from her sister saying they were crossing the street now. Feeling suddenly rushed after such relaxed conversation, she collected her gloves and stood, brushing the creases out of her evening gown.

He stood as well, a pulse of energy beating between them. Though he was just a stranger she'd chatted with in a bar, he looked like Prince Charming in his tux. Her lip twitched as she had the sudden thought that this was how glass shoes sometimes got lost. She wanted some promise that she might see him again.

Her heart sped up as she spotted her siblings working their way through the late night rush at the bar. Lucian's dark hair and broad shoulders were easy to identify in the crowd. He was flanked by Toni and Evelyn's smaller frames.

She wasn't ready to say goodnight, but she was running out of time. "I had a really nice time tonight."

He smiled, his anxiousness seeming to

mirror hers. "Me too..." He laughed and shook his head. "I don't know your name."

She laughed as well. How strange to talk for hours with someone, but never share their names. "It's Isadora."

Reaching into his pocket, he pulled out a plain white business card with a phone number. "It was a pleasure to meet you, Isadora. I'm—"

Evelyn's voice cut through the air. "*Parker?*"

Isadora turned as her sister-in-law stared up at her companion and Lucian scowled.

Toni took inventory of everyone's expression, seeing their brother's clear dislike for the person Isadora had spent the evening with, and a slow silent *ooooh* shaped her sister's mouth.

They knew each other? How?

Evelyn laughed, her expression the absolute opposite of her husband's. "Holy. Shit."

"My sword was all I needed there
It would suffice to right my wrongs;
To cut the knot of all those thongs
With which she'd bound me to despair,
That woman with her midnight hair..."

Madison Julius Cawein
The Black Knight

"SCOUT?"

The man Isadora had spent the last few hours with wore a matching expression of astonishment as he stared wide eyed at her family.

Apparently, he knew her sister-in-law well enough to call her by her nickname.

They knew each other? How?

Isadora hardly had a chance to catch his name once her family arrived. They'd been across the street at the opera house—until her night took a terrible turn and literally knocked her down. If not for her new friend she would have been humiliated, but he escorted her out of the event before anyone could see the disgrace she was making of herself.

Up until this very instant she believed he was a true gentleman. Now, however, her brother's scowl had her instantly questioning her judgment—again.

"What the hell are you doing here, Hughes?" Lucian barked, cutting off all small talk and placing a protective arm around his wife.

At the same time, he managed to insert his body between Isadora and the other man—Parker, was it? She frowned at her brother then turned her confusion on Parker. "You know each other?"

Deep regret flashed in his exotic eyes. "You're a *Patras*?" He spoke her name as if it were a filthy word and she stiffened. "I thought you looked familiar. I should have known."

Though she didn't like the influence her

last name typically carried, it had never earned that sort of revulsion. She looked to Evelyn and her brother then back to Parker. "I'm sorry, could someone please explain how you all know each other?"

"She's my sister," Lucian all but growled. "And she's no one you should be talking to." His glare dropped to the splash of wine that stained her gown and he turned his scowl back on Parker.

Parker hardened his stare, meeting Lucian's glare. "If I'd known she was your sister—"

His words abruptly cut off as he glanced at her, disappointment narrowing his eyes. God only knew the kind of face she was making.

"Go ahead," Isadora urged, keeping her voice calm and low, despite her rapidly beating heart. So much hostility filled the small bar. She was truly curious as to how he intended to finish that sentence. "If you'd known I was Lucian's sister, you would have...?"

His mouth flattened and his gaze measured her from head to hem, eyes apologetic. "I'm sorry, Isadora. I had a great night, but..."

It was silly. He was just some guy she'd met at a party who happened to be nice to her. Her mouth curved into a shaky smile because that seemed more graceful than tears.

She put too much emphasis on the short time they spent together, misinterpreting his kind manners for something more. He was still being polite to her, but their earlier chemistry had twisted into a sort of gridlock. This was just an overall terrible evening.

"It's okay," she whispered, not able to handle one more ounce of rejection. "We should be going."

He frowned and glanced at the table then back to her and her family. "No," he said, brow tight with tension. "It's not okay."

"Quit while you're ahead, Hughes," Lucian growled.

Parker glared at her brother. "Fuck you, Lucian."

She gasped as Lucian lunged forward, halted only by Evelyn's small hand. It was amazing how easily she could reel him in when everyone else feared him. Well, almost everyone.

She turned to Parker to find a challenging glint in his eyes. His gaze softened as his focus shifted to her—ignoring her brother's seething rage.

"I had a great night, Isadora. It didn't start out as I expected and that part could have gone better, but I'm glad I bumped into you. Can I take you to get something to eat, somewhere we can talk so I can explain all of this?"

"Night's over," Lucian snarled. "Isadora, go with Evelyn and Toni back to the limo."

Appalled, she spun and scoffed at her *little* brother. "Just who do you think you're ordering around, Lucian?"

"You don't know him!"

"I've spent the entire evening with him," she snapped.

"Get in the limo," he growled through gritted teeth.

It could have been the wine, but something gave her the courage to hold his threatening stare without blinking.

"I'll leave when I'm good and ready." Her eyes narrowed, silently daring him to give her one more order. She was sick and tired of men deciding what was best for her, putting absolutely no consideration into what she wanted. Her attention shifted to her sister. "Toni, you have your key, right?"

"Uh ... yeah."

"Good."

If she had to, she'd spend the night at the hotel or take a cab home, but there was no way she was getting into that limo, ordered about like some dog. She turned and reached for

Parker's hand, which closed around hers, offering a quick squeeze.

"Isadora," Lucian barked and that was all she could take.

Her head snapped around and she hissed, "*Enough, Lucian!* I don't intrude in your personal affairs, so don't trespass in mine."

His temper visibly boiled as his jaw ticked and clenched, his eyes narrowing with unrefined dislike for her companion—which made her nervous. She had a terrible track record with men and her brother typically had spot on instincts.

Before she could decide if she was making a mistake, Lucian turned and stormed out of the bar.

Toni gaped and chuckled, apparently amused by the family feud. "I better go make sure he doesn't kill someone."

Evelyn rolled her eyes and leaned closer. "Good to see you, Park. Sorry about that. You know how temperamental he gets. You call me tomorrow, Isa." She turned and went after her husband.

Isadora watched them disappear out of the small bar. Once they were out of sight, she tugged her hand from Parker's grip. Her palms were clammy, her fingers shaking.

She had no idea what just happened or if she'd done the right thing. She usually trusted her brother's opinions and listened to his advice. But she was done taking orders from half-informed men.

Something brushed her bare arm—Parker's knuckle. "Are you all right?"

She looked him in the eye. "Who are you?"

"Parker Hughes."

"How do you know my brother?"

"Scout was my best friend growing up."

She frowned. Evelyn didn't grow up like ordinary children. She'd had a terrible life, the sort no child should ever have to endure. "Did you meet her when she lived at St. Christopher's?"

"No. I met her when she lived at the tracks."

None of this made any sense. "What are *the tracks*?"

"A dark place where homeless people go." He barely flinched as he said the words, which made her believe he was telling the truth. Holding her stare, he confessed, "I lived there, too."

She dropped into a vacant seat, blinking as her mind worked to make sense of all this. "You ... lived there? You were homeless?"

"Not always. When I was fourteen my dad was arrested. Then he killed himself. The courts took everything we owned, leaving my mother and I destitute."

Oh, my God. "You're *that* Hughes? *Crispin Hughes's* son?" The Hughes name once had as much clout as Patras's, if not more.

His eyes. She knew why they were so familiar.

"I saw you on television the day they arrested your father. You were just a teenager, a little younger than Lucian. I kept thinking how terrible it was that you and your mother were being exploited for your father's crimes."

"It was a long time ago," he said, blanking his expression.

She studied him, unable to assimilate *this* man with *that* boy—and the one she now pictured living in poverty. "Why doesn't my brother like you?"

"Maybe I don't like him."

Not appreciating his humor, she reminded, "He's my brother."

Parker drew in a slow breath and took the seat beside her. "You're right. I'm sorry. He doesn't like me because the woman I told you about, the one I thought I loved... It was Scout."

"Evelyn?"

He nodded. "We grew up together in a place where there weren't many kids. We sort of looked out for each other. In a way, I *did* love her and probably always will, but it isn't the same as the way she loves your brother. I know that now."

"Are you sure?" If this was some ploy to hurt her family...

"*Positive*. I'll always care about Scout, but I realize now it's more of a platonic affection."

"How come I've never met you if you're friends?"

"I've only been around your family one time and it was probably one of the hardest days of Scout's life. I wasn't there to interfere. She needed the support of friends. Lucian understood that, and I was there for her, but I left shortly after."

It was all coming back to her. "When her mother passed."

They'd all been so concerned for Evelyn, she'd hardly paid attention to the other guests. She did recall Slade being present, which surprised her, being that Lucian and Sawyer's son rarely socialized anymore. Her brother had put all of his personal feelings aside in order to show his wife the love and support she needed to get through that tragedy.

"It was a sad day," Parker murmured. "I couldn't bear Scout facing it alone—even if she had your brother."

"Then this isn't the first time we've met."

"Apparently not."

She tried to recall that day and vaguely remembered going to Sawyer's afterward, the funeral bringing back a lot of bad memories of her own mother's passing.

She looked at Parker—really looked at him—noting how attractive he was, how assertive his features were. She liked the strong line of his jaw and the shade of his hair. Though she couldn't discern the exact color of his eyes, they were so expressive she found them mesmerizing. And his smile was absolutely charming. He was lean yet broad and... How had she not recognized him before?

This was what Sawyer had warned her about years ago. So long as she was with him, she'd be blind to everyone else. Her brow pinched. "If you and Evelyn have this long history, how come you weren't at their wedding?"

"Well, there's the fact that your brother despises me."

"Does Evelyn hate you?"

"No," he said with gentle confidence. "But out of respect for her, I keep my distance from her day-to-day life. I guess it's my way of making amends."

"For what?"

"Let's just say that my judgment wasn't at its best a couple years ago."

Her gaze lowered to the table, unsure if she should be grateful for his disclosure or run in the opposite direction.

"For what it's worth, Isadora, I don't wish your brother any harm. He's good to Scout. I know he loves her."

"Why is nothing easy?" She sighed and massaged her temples.

Parker's slouching posture mimicked hers, as if he, too, sensed the loss of an opportunity.

"I don't know what to do," she told him honestly.

"I know you're probably imagining the worst, but when you grow up the way we did, you tend to guard the things you care about, like a dog protects a bone." His voice lacked the assuredness she'd heard earlier that evening. "Falling into poverty and breaking out of it was like a backward birth. It was painful, ugly, and I lost a bit of my dignity along the way. I can mimic the rest of them and hold my own pretty well, but the truth is, I'll never be like them."

He plucked at his cufflink, then brushed off his fingers as if the tiny accessory was somehow offensive to the touch. The troublesome thing about tuxedos was they really did mask a whole lot. It was hard enough trusting people she didn't know, let alone trusting them when members of her family despised them.

"If you're using me to somehow hurt my—"

"I'm not. I swear it. I didn't even know you were a Patras until five minutes ago. Up until then, you were just a beautiful woman I wanted to know."

She smiled, despite her conflicting thoughts. It was nice to hear an attractive man thought her beautiful—and not for her name. "I think I need some water."

He stood and disappeared for a moment, returning shortly with a bottle. "Why don't I drive you home? We had such a nice night and this isn't how I wanted it to end, but maybe you need some time to think things over. Don't decide anything tonight."

"This might take a while." And it wasn't looking good for him. No matter how much she wanted to weigh her options, she rarely opposed her family. If Lucian honestly believed she shouldn't trust him then she should go with her brother's instincts. His intuition had always been better than hers.

"I can be patient." He gave a half smile. "And you have my number."

She was in no shape to make big decisions at the moment. She wanted to hear Lucian's side of everything before she made up her mind. And what if tomorrow Parker was just some guy who came at the right time when she needed a distraction?

Her head was a muddled cemetery of un-lived possibilities and she wanted to bury the ugly moments of this day far away from where they could never hurt her again.

"I think I need sleep."

He nodded, a polite smile masking his thoughts, as he helped her stand.

The bar was crowded now that the event across the street had ended. Parker never let go of her arm as he guided her through the crowd, his other hand protectively resting on her lower back and she didn't object.

People trickled out of the opera house as he led her through the limos snaking down the street. "My car's with the valet. It should only take a minute."

She waited as he handed the attendant his ticket. They stood at the edge of the crowd as the attendant disappeared to retrieve his car.

"Isadora?"

She turned at the sound of her name and, once again, the breath knocked out of her.

"Sawyer!"

For the love of God, someone get me out of here now!

His gaze shifted over her shoulder to Parker and he gave a clipped nod. "Mr. Hughes."

Did everyone know him?

She turned and Parker made a polite grin, the sort reserved for colleagues and semi-familiar acquaintances. "Mr. Bishop. How are you?"

"I'm well." Sawyer's brow pinched, his expression otherwise blank as his gaze returned to hers. "Did you enjoy the evening?"

Her heart beat erratically, her gaze fastened to his familiar eyes, but not missing the woman at his side. "It was ... unexpected."

Whose words were they? Her brain seemed to be coasting on autopilot.

He frowned and took a step closer only to pause. "Your lip..." His hand lifted as if he intended to touch her but then thought better of it. "Did you hurt yourself?"

Her fingers self-consciously covered the bruise. "I was distracted."

"Are you heading home?" he asked and she frowned, sensing implication in his question.

She glanced at the woman at his side and he followed her gaze.

"Where are my manners? This is Cassandra Birch. Cassandra, this is Isadora Patras, a good family friend."

Friend? "It's nice to meet you," she said numbly, unable to touch the woman as she clenched her own hands in her gown.

"It's been a long time," Sawyer commented, as though thinking out loud.

"Yes." She couldn't blink or push her voice higher than a whisper. "It has."

Parker handed the valet a tip and brushed a hand over her shoulder. "Are you ready, Isadora?"

Sawyer seemed to snap out of whatever trance he was in. He cleared his throat. "Well... It was nice seeing you."

She couldn't say the same. "Goodbye, Sawyer."

Parker held her door and she awkwardly pulled her skirts into the car, some type of sleek white coupe. The door closed and she willed herself not to look back, shutting her eyes to avoid the view in the side mirrors as her heart pounded.

The driver's door opened and Parker climbed in beside her. "Was that him?"

Jarred that he had somehow noticed something everyone else overlooked after only thirty seconds of seeing her in Sawyer's presence, she swallowed thickly. She debated lying for a moment, but the evening seemed to be doomed, with one disaster after another, so she figured why bother?

"Yes. He knows you."

"He used to be my boss."

Opening her eyes, she stared at him. "You worked at Leningrad?"

He nodded. It must have been after she left. Otherwise, she would have read his application.

How had he gotten a job with such animosity between him and Lucian? "Patras owns a portion of that company."

"I know."

It seemed everyone knew everything. She was the only one in the dark. At this point she honestly didn't care to figure out what made men act like boys. "Please take me home."

He eased into traffic and she gave him her address as he plugged it into the car's navigation system. Once he had an idea of where he was taking her, he turned the volume down. "He's a lot older than you."

"Twenty years."

"How long were you together? If you don't mind me asking."

"We started seeing each other when I was twenty-three."

"And how long since you've dated him?"

"We broke up less than a year ago."

"So you were together for almost a dozen years?"

Impressed he'd figured it out so quickly, she nodded. "Give or take." Although they spent years apart, her heart had never moved on.

"That's a long time." The GPS told him to turn and gave a few other instructions about mileage for the upcoming exit. "That makes you what, thirty-five?"

"Thirty-six." She thought about the young boy on the television. "How old are you, Parker?"

"Twenty-six." He was silent for a moment. "Does that bother you?"

It bothered her that age played such a great role in dictating her life, stifling her happiness in the name of propriety, deeming something beautiful as inappropriate until it almost seemed shameful when it never was. "No. Age is just a number."

"I agree."

He didn't seem to have any more questions, but she had the urge to keep talking. He'd been very open with her after the confrontation with her brother and she didn't want secrets between them, even if this was the last time she'd ever see him.

"No one knew—about Sawyer and me. We never told anyone."

He glanced at her in the darkness then returned his focus to the road. "No one? For over a decade?"

"We weren't together the whole time. I went to school. He did his thing." She shook her head. "At first, we kept it a secret because of our age difference and his association with my father, but then... Those things stop mattering once you reach a certain age."

"But you still kept it a secret?"

She nodded. "Some days I liked that it was ours, something that belonged to us that no one could take away, because they didn't know it existed." But in the end it was Sawyer who stole it from her. "Other times I resented feeling like a shameful secret."

"Why didn't you just tell people?"

"My father would have reacted badly, possibly threatened his position with the company. My brother was a close friend to Sawyer's son."

"Slade?"

Again, she was startled by how familiar he was with the players in her life. "Yes. There was a falling out of sorts between Slade and Lucian, so the timing never seemed right to tell my family about Sawyer." She gave a small, humorless laugh. "It doesn't matter now."

"Do you still love him?"

If she didn't, she'd be perfectly fine now, but she wasn't. "Part of me will always love him, but he doesn't love me."

"Are you sure? The way he looked at you..."

"He doesn't love me." Maybe if she kept saying it out loud it wouldn't hurt so much over time.

The rest of the ride to her house was quiet. Parker seemed to be in deep thought. When he pulled into her driveway, she hesitated, unsure if she'd ever talk to him again.

"Isadora, I have to tell you something and it might make you angry."

Her stomach clenched. She couldn't handle any more surprises tonight. "What is it?"

"The falling out between Slade Bishop and your brother... I had something to do with it."

"*What?*"

He shook his head. "It's a long story, but ... your brother hated me and when Slade offered me a job he was furious."

She scoffed, somewhat relieved by his explanation. "Despite what he might believe, Lucian doesn't control the universe. He can't forbid people from hiring who they want."

It had been that sort of attitude that ruined their relationship with the Bishops.

"If one of my friends betrayed me the way Slade betrayed Lucian, I'd have been just as angry. It was wrong and I knew it the moment I accepted the position. I just didn't care at the time."

"Did you take the job to purposely hurt my brother?"

He didn't hesitate to give her the truth. "Yes."

This was all very worrisome. Not only was he wrapped up in some old rivalry with her brother, he was remotely tied to the Bishops. She pressed a hand to her forehead where it started to ache.

"I understand if this is too much for you."

"It's a lot," she sighed, overwhelmed. "I'm

still trying to process all the ways you know the people in my life and, to be honest, none of them seem to be singing your praises."

Well, except for Evelyn. She seemed fine around him.

"I'd like to say it's just a case of being the new kid on the block, but I have to take some accountability for my actions. I'm not proud of the things I did during that time of my life. If I could take back some of my choices I would, but sometimes our mistakes lead us to the right place."

When he said things like that, sounding so genuine and open, she found it hard to believe he hid a mean streak. "Your history doesn't match the person I met tonight."

"People change. I'm proud of the man I am today. It took a lot for me to get to a point where I can say that and mean it. A lot can change in two years, Isadora. I'm not that guy anymore."

She shut her eyes, exhausted. "What guy are you, Parker?" He openly admitted to showing people what they wanted to see and hiding behind a façade.

"I'm still trying to figure that out. But I know when a shoe doesn't fit, and I've tried on enough in my life to know not to toss away something that feels ... right."

Was he talking about her? Was she a *shoe*? "I need time to think."

He nodded. "Take as much as you need. I'm not going anywhere."

A light flashed on and she suspected Toni had spotted them. "Thank you for driving me home."

"My pleasure. I'm really sorry for knocking you down and..."

She smiled. "I forgive you." But she didn't know if the rest of his character could be redeemed.

He waited until she made it inside the house before pulling away. She'd barely stepped out of her shoes when her sister's voice echoed down the steps.

"*Ooooh*, Lucian is *mad* at you. He was *steaming* the entire way home."

And so it began.

"I think you are wrong to want a heart,
It makes most people unhappy.
If you only knew it, you are in luck not to
have a heart."

L. Frank Baum
The Wonderful Wizard of Oz

THE FOLLOWING morning Isadora ignored several calls from Lucian. She was tired of thinking, so she tried reading, but her brain wouldn't shut off. Around eleven, a door slammed, followed by heavy footsteps.

Operation Avoidance was over.

She shut her book and took a calming breath, waiting for the accusations to fly.

"You don't know how to answer a phone?" Lucian barked the second he stepped into the den.

"Good morning, Lucian."

He scowled. "I called you over a dozen times."

"I know. I was busy."

"When did you get home?"

She stood and put her book on the table. After righting the pillows, she walked past him toward the kitchen. It was almost lunch and she was in the mood for a salad.

"Isadora."

"Yes?" she called, making her way to the fridge.

"Are you going to tell me what happened?"

She pulled out some lettuce, tomatoes, tuna, and—*ooh, peppers.* "No."

Setting the cutting board on the granite countertop, she withdrew the serrated knife from the butcher block. Lucian continued to scowl.

"I'm sorry, did you want some?" She gestured to the food with the knife.

"I didn't come here to eat."

"I know. You came here to badger me for

information. Unfortunately, all I can offer is tuna salad. The details of my personal life are off limits."

"You're making a mistake."

"Am I? Hmm, I wonder what that's like." She shrugged. "I'm pretty sure I'm due."

"What the hell has gotten into you? This isn't you. You're the sensible one."

She shrugged, scooping the chopped tomatoes into the bowl. "People change, Lucian."

He scoffed. "You don't."

She put down the knife and stared at him —insulted. "Why can't I change? I've always done everything everyone expected of me and I've never asked for anything in return. You and Toni got everything you wanted and now you're both out of this house, living the lives you've chosen, and I'm stuck here wondering where my place is. Something has to change, Lucian, because I can't go on living like this. I'm not satisfied that this is as good as it gets. I want more."

"I'm not saying you can't have a life, Isa. I want you to be happy. But Parker Hughes is a manipulative little—"

"Hey!" She pointed the knife at him. "I understand he's not your favorite person, I can even sympathize with some of your reasoning

—though I don't know all the details—but he's someone I'm still trying to figure out. Respect me enough to let me draw my own conclusions."

"Whatever he told you, I'm almost positive it's all bullshit. The kid's a liar."

"First, he's not a kid. Second, what he told me did him no favors, so I wouldn't be so sure he's lying."

"You wouldn't trust him if you knew who he really was." He followed her to the table.

"Really? Is he not the man who tried to steal Evelyn away from you? The same man who took a job at Leningrad, causing a huge fight between you and Slade, which in turn ruined our lifelong friendship with the Bishops?"

He blinked at her for a solid ten seconds. *"And knowing all that you still want to associate with him?"*

"People make mistakes, Lucian."

"Jesus Christ, Isadora, *why* are you being so stubborn about this?"

"Because!" She paused, then admitted, "I like him." Saying it out loud felt really good.

"God help me..."

"Look, I'm not saying I'll see him again. I may not even talk to him again, but last night... Something terrible happened to me.

Then I ran into Parker and he ... helped me. He was an absolute gentleman until you showed up."

He frowned. "What happened last night?"

"Nothing you need to worry about." She wiped her mouth. "I'm just saying—"

"What the hell happened to your face?" His eyes darkened and he growled, "Is that a bruise?"

She rolled her eyes. "I bumped into something and fell over. I'm fine."

"Were you drunk?"

"No, I wasn't drunk! I wasn't looking where I was going. But I will say the moment I fell Parker was there, insisting he get me some ice and that I sit down for a minute."

"I think he knew who you were. I don't believe for a second he was surprised by your name last night. I won't let him use you in some vendetta."

"Sorry to disappoint you, Lucian, but I think he's over you. But thanks for implying the only reason a man would be nice to me is to get close to my brother. Always what a woman wants to hear."

"Not a man. A snake."

"Look," she snapped, done justifying herself. "I appreciate your concern, but I'm not going into this with my eyes shut. I'm a big girl."

His jaw ticked. "I don't want to see you get hurt."

"Sometimes that's part of life. I've been hurt before and I'm still here."

He threw his hands up in frustration and slammed them on the table, causing her to jump. "Goddamn it, Isa, he's in love with Evelyn!"

She countered his rage with calmness. "No, Lucian. He *was* in love with a kid named Scout. Evelyn's your devoted wife. And people accidentally fall in love with the wrong people all the time. I wouldn't expect a man his age to have never loved before."

"This is ridiculous. Doesn't it bother you that his father was Dad's nemesis?"

She laughed, *really* laughed. "I'm sorry. Are you referring to the father you hated for most of your life? The one who walked out on us when I was fifteen? Or the man who forgets my birthday every year? Which father, Lucian? Or maybe it's the one who never once—not in his *entire life*—thanked me for raising his children. Which one am I supposed to be loyal to?"

"All right, you've made your point. I just

don't understand why you can't like someone else. Why *him*?"

"I haven't even decided if I'm going to call him! You're the one treating this like a betrothal."

The doorbell rang and she stood. "I have to get that."

She went to the door and a deliveryman dressed in brown greeted her. "Isadora Patras?"

"Yes."

"Sign here, please."

She scribbled her signature on the electronic scanner.

"Here you go."

She took the flat package. "Thank you."

Turning around, she saw Lucian had followed her from the kitchen. "What's that?"

"I don't know." She peeled open the envelope and laughed as the sleek, stiff cover of a book peeked past the seal. She pulled it out and smiled at the sketch of a Grinch sneering back at her.

Lucian frowned as he watched her. "Is that a children's book?"

"Mm-hm," she answered, still smiling. "It's *How the Grinch Stole Christmas*."

"It's March."

"I know." She opened it to the title page and was deeply pleased to find a note.

"The most likely reason of all... may have been a heart two sizes too small."

So glad we met. I think my heart grew three whole sizes yesterday—the biggest yet.

Thinking of you...
~Parker

"Who sent that?"

She snapped the book shut and held it protectively to her chest. "You're nosier than an old lady at a stitch and bitch. Don't you have a million other things you should be doing?"

"*He* sent it, didn't he?"

She rolled her eyes, groaning as she walked away, returning to her lunch. "Goodbye, Lucian."

"He's after something!" her brother yelled.

"I hope it's me," she murmured under her breath, snickering.

"I never want to hurt you."
Sawyer

AS IT TURNED OUT, Isadora did have a date that night, just not the date anyone expected. Walking into the familiar restaurant on the first floor of the Patras Hotel, she showed herself to the restaurant in the back. Evelyn waved the moment she spotted her.

"Sorry I'm late," Isadora apologized, settling her napkin on her lap.

"Thanks for meeting me." Her sister-in-law grinned.

"No problem. It's been a long time since

we had one of our lunches, although this is technically dinner."

A waiter came by and took their drink orders as they perused the selection. Once Isadora decided, she closed the menu and placed it aside.

"So, is this a social thing or a follow-up to Lucian's visit this afternoon?" There was no point beating around the bush.

"A little of the first, nothing of the second, and a bit of my own concern."

One thing she appreciated about Evelyn was her ability to be direct.

"Well, let's get the concerns out of the way so we can move onto the fun stuff."

"Deal." Evelyn nodded, folding her hands on the edge of the table. "What are your intentions with Parker?"

She laughed. Maybe direct was an understatement. "I don't have any intentions yet. Is there something you want to tell me?"

Evelyn smiled and sipped her water. "He's a good guy, Isa. I'm not going to warn you away from him."

"Good to know and I appreciate that."

"So you *are* interested."

"I didn't say that. But it's nice not to have another person in my life telling me what I should or shouldn't do. Just out of curiosity, what would Lucian say if he knew you felt that way?"

Evelyn laughed. "Oh, he knows. I don't hold anything against Parker. Yes, he did some underhanded things and no, they were not his proudest moments, but deep down, he's a good guy and he's always looked out for me, even when I didn't need his protection."

"I, um... I'm still trying to process the fact that he lived at the shelter."

Evelyn shrugged. "All kinds of people live in shelters. It doesn't matter if they were always poor or once rich. A catastrophe can ruin any sort of person."

"Well, like you, he seems to have found success."

"He could have left the shelter years ago. He's always been really smart. I think he waited so long because he kept pace with me. Part of me feels guilty about that, but another part of me is grateful. He made life ... better."

"He worked at Leningrad." She still couldn't get over that.

"Don't assume he's completely to blame for the falling out between Slade and Lucian a few years ago. There's a lot more to that story than people realize."

Her brows lifted. "Such as?"

Evelyn's full lips twisted. "Sorry. It's not my place to tell. And I know Parker's position didn't help matters. The point is, there were problems there long before he came into the picture."

Isadora sat back and digested that bit of information. Slade and Lucian had always been so close. What could have possibly interfered with that if not Parker? "Lucian and Slade seem better now."

Evelyn smiled. "They're working through their issues. I was never Slade's biggest fan, but he loves your brother. Lucian loves him, too— like a brother. It makes me happy to see them talking again."

If that was the case they should all let sleeping dogs lie. "Tell me more about Parker."

Her crystal eyes lit with affection. "He has a gift when it comes to business, but if you asked him, he'd call it a curse. His success far out-shines mine. Which reminds me." She reached into her bag and withdrew a little gift box. "I made you something."

Isadora smiled. Two presents in one day? She untied the ribbon and lifted the lid. A small bracelet rested on a cotton pillow.

"Oh, Evelyn, it's beautiful. Thank you."

"You're welcome. The stones are called tiger's eye. It supposed to help with decision making and deciphering emotion, if you believe in that sort of thing."

Isadora slipped it onto her wrist, admiring the swirls that cut through each bead. "I love it."

"So," Evelyn said, getting back on topic. "Lucian seemed pretty frazzled after he got home from your house." She snickered. "You didn't tell him anything, did you?"

"Nope. Sometimes he needs to be reminded he's only human, not a god."

"True story." She laughed again. "He's going to nag me all night for details when I get home."

Isadora regretted hearing that, as she could really use some advice. "Will you tell him?"

"Not if you tell me not to. You can trust me."

She relaxed. "Thank you." Letting out a long breath, she confessed, "To be honest, I don't know what I should do. Part of me thinks Lucian is making this too much about himself. It's my life and I should be able to talk to whomever I want."

"Absolutely."

"But then I worry I'm putting stress on our

family, which we certainly don't need. We have enough drama."

"You talking to Park shouldn't cause stress. I just wouldn't expect your brother to trust him. I'm not sure he ever will. But for what it's worth, I do."

Isadora glanced at the table, her voice softening. "Did you love him?"

"Well, if you asked me that a few years ago I would have said no. But my understanding of love's evolved since then. Now?" Her pale eyes gazed upward as she smiled. "Yes, I loved him. I still do. I probably always will."

Isadora was relieved by her honesty, but troubled by her words. "A romantic love?"

"No, not even close. At one point I wished I could feel that way for him, but he was too much of a friend."

"I can't imagine what it must have been like for you two."

Evelyn's gazed turned contemplative. "When I first met him I thought he was trying to steal my shoes. He was actually trying to give me his. I think I called him an idiot. His shoes were the nicest I'd ever seen—rich people shoes. No one ever gave stuff like that away. He had other things, too. But having fancy shoes and good clothes made it hard for him to fit in."

"Because he came from wealth?" Isadora asked, trying to piece the puzzle of Parker Hughes together.

Evelyn laughed. "He showed up with *luggage.* That first winter he sold a lot of the stuff he came with, but he always bought me things with his money, a warmer coat, food, little packets of soup mix. He was always looking out for me and Momma."

It was difficult to imagine children living in such terrible conditions, but she was starting to understand the strong bond they shared. "Thank you for telling me that. I know you don't often talk about your life before Lucian, but it helps me make a little more sense of things."

Evelyn expression sobered and something flashed in her pale eyes. "Just ... don't hurt him, okay?"

Startled by the request, her eyes widened. "I won't. I promise." But then she thought about Sawyer and his broken promises. "I promise I'll always be honest with him."

"Thank you." Satisfied, Evelyn folded her hands on the table. "Now, let's talk about names."

"Names?"

"Yup. I like Evan for a boy and Lucinda for a girl."

Isadora's mouth gaped. "Are you...?"

Her sister-in-law laughed, her face beaming. "I am!"

Isadora squealed, disrupting many of the patrons' meals as she jumped out of her chair and hugged Evelyn. Tears of joy sprang to her eyes. "Oh, my God! A baby? Does Lucian know?"

"Of course."

"Why didn't he tell me?"

"We were going to tell you last night, but you took off. Toni knows."

"That little witch! We talked for an hour when I got home and she never said a word."

Evelyn laughed. "I think she's put out about not being the baby anymore."

"Oh, this is fabulous! I can't believe it! A little baby in the family again."

They chatted ceaselessly through dinner, eating only between words and letting most of their meal go cold. When she left the hotel, she was on cloud nine.

Her mind raced with ideas for a baby shower and little itty-bitty outfits and soft blankets. Oh, she was going to spoil that kid rotten!

As she pulled onto the highway her phone rang. Since she was driving, she didn't look at the caller ID.

"Hello?"

"Bella?"

Her smile faltered. "S—Sawyer?"

"How are you?"

"I'm ... okay." Why was he calling? "Is something wrong?" He hadn't called her in months and now, after running into him just last night, he was talking to her again?

She caught her breath. Last night she'd fallen right to sleep, without sparing Sawyer a single thought. Considering what had happened... The realization shocked her.

"I wanted to speak to you—in person. Are you free tonight?"

She frowned, her stomach pinching with uncertainty. She couldn't see him. Seeing him led to tears and she didn't need to cry anymore.

Make up an excuse! "I'm in the city, well, just leaving it anyway."

"I can wait."

Her gut instinct was to say no. "I don't know, Sawyer—"

"Please, bella. I need to see you."

Her voice was small, weak. "Okay."

She hated that he still had the power to

make her change her mind. But what if he'd changed *his* mind?

Her breath turned labored as she questioned what this might mean, if she wanted it to mean anything. Part of her hoped it was nothing, but... God, she was weak. She'd see what he wanted and if this was some trick she'd get out of there fast.

"I'll be there in about twenty minutes."

"I'll be waiting. Drive safe."

She ended the call and stared blindly at the road. Her car found its way to his house as if by heart. When she parked in his driveway, she shut off the engine and waited, unable to bring herself to open the door.

She should have been thrilled to hear from him. But dread filled her chest, too many layers of hurt and distrust. He'd broken her heart so many times she never knew if she should brace for pain or nurture the last flicker of hope. Her trust in him was beyond fractured.

What did this mean? What about the other woman?

She sucked in a breath as he appeared on the patio and approached her door. He pulled the handle and the interior lights came on, illuminating his smile.

"Thanks for coming."

He looked good. The same. But nothing was the same and part of her feared whatever this was would confuse her all the more.

She was paralyzed, unsure how to protect herself and afraid to get out of the car. "Is something wrong, Sawyer?"

"Come inside."

That would be a mistake. Or maybe she was just overthinking. He took her hand, his fingers lacing with hers and fitting as familiar as an old leather glove that would always be the perfect size.

Following him inside, she walked slowly to the living room. "You got a new couch."

He poured himself a drink at the kitchen counter. "The old one was shot. Wine?"

His question startled her. He acted like she'd been there yesterday. "No, thank you." She continued to stare at the couch, wondering who else had sat there.

He lowered himself to a cushion and gestured for her to have a seat beside him. "You look great."

"Thank you. So do you." Her body rested on the very edge of the cushion, her spine stiff.

"Did you enjoy the party last night?"

She had a difficult time looking at him,

afraid of what she might see in his eyes. "I was only there for a little while."

"Oh, I assumed you would have come for Lucian's speech."

"I did. Then I left."

His hand caught a strip of her hair, turning it in his fingers and sending a shiver down her back. Her lip trembled. She couldn't handle this.

"But I saw you after midnight—with Parker Hughes."

Her brow puckered as she tried to figure out what exactly his angle was. "And I saw you—with Cassandra whatever her last name was."

He released her hair, his motions now tentative. Her nerves prickled at his nearness. She fought the urge to lean into him the way she always had, old habits now far from appropriate. At the same time she fought the instinct to run screaming.

"Are you and Hughes an item?"

She scrutinized him. Was this his way of checking up on her, seeing if she'd moved on? "No. We just met."

"So, it isn't serious?"

Balancing their dialogue around an unvoiced issue drained her. She was tired of secrets and surprises. "Sawyer, what do you want?"

"You."

Her heart stilled as her stomach flipped. That had not been what she expected him to say. Chills raced up her spine, too many various responses taking place at one time. Excitement, fear, longing, anger...

Her stare jerked to the carpet as she croaked, "But..."

He scooted closer, brushing her hair over her shoulder and pressing his lips to the side of her throat as he whispered, "I need you, bella."

Her nipples hardened and her eyes started to close.

No!

She sprung off the couch the second she felt the touch of his tongue. "Whoa! What is this?"

He seemed taken aback by her response. "If it's not serious between you and Hughes—"

"What, you thought you could call me after not contacting me for months and I'd show up, strip, and roll over?" *What does Parker Hughes have to do with any of this?* "I'm not a fucking dog, Sawyer!"

"Of course not!" He seemed genuinely offended by her words.

"Then what *is* this? Last night you were on a *date*."

He waved her words away. "She was a plus one—"

"No," she sneered, her eyes narrowing. "I saw you. You... You kissed her."

He frowned. "When did you see me?"

"Right after Lucian's speech. You were in the hall by an alcove outside of a balcony. She was laughing and touching you and you..." Her stomach revolted, but she held it together. "You liked it. I could tell. Then you kissed her back."

His gaze lowered. "If I'd known anyone was watching... I'm sorry. That couldn't have been easy for you to see."

She wished she could fuck someone right there on his carpet and make *him* watch. "That's why you're sorry? Because I *saw* you?"

"Of course I'm sorry."

"What about not dating? No relationships? What about the pills you refused to take?"

He flushed. "I'm not in a relationship. And as far as the pills... They don't seem to bother me anymore."

She was going to be sick. The only way he'd know the pills didn't bother him was if he'd wanted something—*someone*—enough to take them. *Oh, God...*

"You had sex," she wheezed, a sharp stab of inadequacy lodging in her chest and making her weak.

"Isadora, we never made any promises to each other after you left. I know there have been other men, but I certainly don't need a report card from you."

Her jaw locked. She didn't leave! He *dumped* her.

And there had been no other men. She'd been celibate for far too long and it was making her crazy. She was busying herself with functions and garden shows and falling right into spinsterdom. *While he was fucking all of Folsom!*

She could have sex with him right now. All it would take was a green light from her and a tiny blue pill for him.

Her thoughts were chaotic, jerking her from all angles. But within the tornado of wildly spinning ideas storming through her brain was a slender shred of dignity standing tall.

She would *not* give him the satisfaction.

Anger, sadness, it all muddled together. Over a decade of this on-again, off-again superficial security. Him being the hand on a yo-yo that jerked her life this way and that. She was fucking tired of being treated like a worthless pawn meant only to serve other people's needs.

Her heart was bruised and battered, but her wounds were so deep, no one could see her pain. She just lived with it, day in and day out, feeling like the only woman alive who no one would ever love.

She'd fallen for Sawyer at a vulnerable point in her life, loved him to distraction over the years. It wasn't about being weak or strong, but about what love dictated. She might never be as tough as she hoped to be, but she was a hell of a lot smarter then she was at twenty-three.

Shaking her head, drawing in an unsteady breath, she stared at him. "You broke my heart and you don't even care."

"I care, Isadora. I'll always care."

"But you'll do it again. I'll give myself to you, heart and soul, and you'll enjoy me for a time, but then you'll send me away, claiming to know what's best for us, acting like you know me more than I know myself."

The satisfaction of being with him now paled in comparison to the pain of losing him.

She'd never survive him pushing her away again.

"I can't let you do that to me anymore, Sawyer. I'd rather be alone than in a relationship where I have no stability, no say whether it lives or dies."

"Isadora... You know I care deeply for you."

"*Love!*" she shouted. "*It's supposed to be love!* I have enough people in my life that *care* about me. I need someone to *love* me. I needed *you* to love me!"

She withdrew her keys from her purse, hands clumsy and shaking.

Sawyer stood. "Please don't leave like this. You're upset. I'll worry about you. I didn't mean to upset you."

She laughed coldly. "I've been *upset* a lot longer than just tonight. No need to start worrying now." She pivoted and stormed to the door.

"Isadora!"

She couldn't turn around, couldn't bring herself to look at him. "What?"

"I..."

Her eyes closed as she waited for him to finish the statement, tell her he loved her and finally cut the string from this yo-yo so that they could fall. Together.

If he could just confess his true feelings she'd forgive him for all the years he made her wait. But after an embarrassingly long silence, she blinked through her blurring vision and turned the knob, not even sparing him a goodbye or a single tear.

*"But since of diff'rent dishes we should
taste;
Upon an ancient work my hands I've
placed;
Where full a hundred narratives are told,
And various characters we may behold..."*

Jean de La Fontaine
The Servant Girl Justified

ISADORA WAITED five days to call
Parker.

She'd wanted to call him sooner, but she
needed time to calm down after her fight with

Sawyer. She couldn't get over him inviting her to his house like that. He'd never made her feel like a whore until that moment and his doing so disjointed parts of her heart, damaging them like pieces of a worn out puzzle she couldn't solve.

What they shared was perhaps the most precious thing she'd ever owned, but his recent behavior summed up their time together as a cheap and tawdry affair. How dare he taint her beautiful life and all she valued, summarizing years of affection with the shabby necessity of lust?

He had no right, and she'd likely be angry with him for a long time, longer than she wanted to spare. Putting her hurt feelings aside, she covered her pain with little distractions, buying baby clothes for the next Patras, weeding out her gardens, and making the executive decision to dismiss everyone else's opinions of Parker and give him a chance to show her the man he actually was.

She'd let the probability of her family's objections dictate the last decade of her love life. No more. They all knew about Parker and whether they approved or not, she needed to see how things went for herself.

Mind made up, she'd picked up the phone

and called him. For once doing what she felt was right for her and not worrying about how it might upset or disappoint others.

Parker was gracious and sweet when she spoke to him. "Can I take you out?"

Her life, up to that moment, seemed so commonplace, so tepid and uneventful, she tried to think of the last time someone had asked her on a date.

Tyrian had taken her out to movies and dinners. Looking back, the whole ritual of serenading a woman with food and meaningless traditions seemed pathetic. But what else did people do?

"Sure," she agreed, thinking the same redundant prelude would be the conclusion to nothing spectacular.

She'd become so jaded.

"What day do you have free this week?"

All of them. "How about Friday?"

"Friday's perfect. Why don't I pick you up around eleven and we'll go from there?"

A lunch date? That seemed even less romantic than dinner. "Okay."

"Oh, and dress warm."

"O—okay."

Friday morning, unsure where they were going, she opted for a pair of jeans and a cream blouse. Recalling his suggestion that she dress warm, she switched out her pumps for a pair of boots and grabbed a cable knit cardigan. Maybe they were going to the theater, which could get drafty sometimes.

Parker's Jaguar arrived at precisely eleven o'clock. He climbed out and she met him halfway, liking the sight of him in worn jeans, a dark gingham button down nearly hidden by a thick sweater and duffle coat. His hair looked windblown and his jaw wore a thicker layer of scruff than it had the night they met.

He smiled as he held open the passenger door. "Your chariot awaits, m'lady."

She slid onto the sleek leather upholstery, finding the interior of the car pleasantly warm. Once he was seated behind the wheel, he expertly backed out of her driveway.

"I meant to thank you for the book. I love it."

He smiled, his gaze focused on the road. "I debated between that and *Lord of the Flies*. Seuss seemed more appropriate."

She was glad he chose the children's book. "Where are we going?"

"It's a surprise. You're free for the rest of the day, right?"

She didn't have plans, but the idea of

spending that much time with someone she hardly knew was daunting. "Yes, but…"

He glanced at her, those sharp eyes taking a quick assessment. "If you have to be back by a certain time, that's fine. I just want to know what time frame we're dealing with. The place I'm taking you is an hour away."

That was a long time in a car with a semi-stranger. "I don't have any other plans."

He nodded. "How was your week?"

Her week had been… It was hard to say.

She'd kicked it off with a fight, but once she cooled down she hadn't cried or anything. She simply pushed the Sawyer stuff to the back of her mind and moved on. She'd ordered some new perennials for the garden and made a list of things that needed to be done in preparation for spring.

"My week was typical." Sort of. There seemed a difference she couldn't quite put her finger on.

"What did you do?"

He sure was curious. "I picked up a few gardening books."

"Do you like gardening?"

"Yes."

"What do you grow?"

"Mostly flowers. I have a small herb garden, but I'm terrible with larger vegetables."

He smiled. They were heading east toward the coast. "Do you like English gardens or more of a colonial revival garden?"

Impressed that his question revealed a bit of knowledge on the subject, she relaxed, comfortable with the topic. "I prefer Spanish gardens, actually. I love climbing plants and water."

"Do you have a pergola?"

She grinned. "I do. It's my favorite place to read. In the summer the wisteria takes over. I know a lot of people find it to be a bully of a vine, but if you take care of the buds and train the shoots, it can be really beautiful. I've tamed mine into a lush awning. It makes a beautiful canopy."

"Sometimes, when things take a little work, the reward's that much sweeter."

"Yes."

He turned onto the highway and she tried to imagine where they could possibly be going. There wasn't much out this way, a small naval base, a few hotels, and the coast, but nothing would be open this early in the year.

Trying to pass the time, she admitted, "I'm thinking about making a labyrinth garden. I started sketching one out, but I'm still looking into which hedges are best for that sort of thing. I order a lot of my plants online, because the colors are usually listed."

His brow lifted. "Like a big labyrinth? The kind someone could get lost in?"

The idea came to her when she'd been thinking of a little Patras running around. How darling would it be to have a permanent maze for little ones to play? She wanted to hide flowers and secret gardens inside.

Her smile trembled. She wanted to chase her own children through something like that, could almost hear the echoes of unborn laughter. She shook off the fantasy.

"Yes, a large one. We have several acres that aren't being used."

"Something like that would take years to cultivate."

What else did she have to do? "I know."

"I think that sounds like a great idea. Really interesting and fun to plan. Things like that last for generations."

"If I ever actually plant it."

"You will. So what do you like to do when you're not gardening?"

She was adjusting to his attention, unable to recall the last time someone took such personal interest in *her*. "I like to read. I attend social functions for the family business from time to time. I take night classes and this summer I'll have my masters. I volunteer at St. Christopher's and The Women's House. That's a place for—"

"Women escaping domestic abuse."

"Yes. Do you know it?"

"For the past year I've volunteered there once a month."

She rarely saw men at the facility. "You have? Doing what?"

"They have a program that prepares women to enter the workforce. Some of them never worked before. I walk them through mock interviews and help them with their resumes. The job placements are slow, and sometimes they need more skills, but eventually, they find something."

Maybe she should have him look at her resume. "How is it you know how to do that?"

According to everything she'd heard, he'd just started his career. Though going by his car, his clothing, and his attendance at the opera house fundraisers, he'd clearly found immediate success.

He shrugged. "You only have to know the right question to ask. When women are forbidden to work they sometimes struggle to identify what they're passionate about. There are countless jobs out there. Sometimes it's just a matter of admitting what they want to do with their life, realizing they have the right to choose. Choice is a powerful thing."

Yes, it was. Asserting her autonomy had been a lifelong struggle. At thirty-six she was still trying to find her calling—and her voice.

Though she'd managed a house, raised two children, and mingled with the visionaries of tomorrow, she often felt guilty when it came to deciding what was best for her. Her life was a constant loop of reassuring herself that she was entitled to decide her future, but she never managed to get very far from where she started.

"And what about you, Parker Hughes? What do you do?"

A dimple appeared in his cheek as he smiled. "I like helping others. Charity can be more rewarding than any paycheck, but there has to be some sort of income. I invest and try to keep a secure cushion, but the idea of wasting away behind a desk is terrifying to me. I think I'll always be a little more comfortable in a community center than an executive office."

She frowned. "But you're one of them."

Parker not only worked at Leningrad but also climbed quickly to the top. He had an unnatural gift when it came to the stock market, according to what she found out from Evelyn.

He laughed. "I'm accepted as one, but only because they don't know how to read me. They see money and that's what they want. I'm just a tool that adds to their wealth. I play the market because I'm good at it. It's a hobby."

"How good?"

He gave her a sidelong glance. "Good enough to guess if you put fifty thousand on Sidewize Inc. today, you could have a million dollars by the end of the week."

"Seriously?"

"It's not a science. I have the instinct, but that doesn't mean I abuse it. I earn enough to buy my freedom, but I'll never be indebted to my own greed."

"You're saying you didn't buy that stock, even though you believe it'll turn that much?"

"Nah. I avoid it when I can. It's an addicting rush."

She reached into her purse. "Let's see if you're right."

He glanced at her as she texted her brother. "What are you doing?"

"Lucian controls my shares. I'm telling him to buy a thousand dollars worth."

His brow creased. "What if you lose?"

She laughed. "Now you're unsure? You just sounded so certain."

"There's no such thing as certainty in the stock market. That's the one valuable lesson I learned from my father."

"Well, it's money I earned from whatever Lucian does with the shares I inherited. I never touch it. I just let him move it around however he sees fit. If you're wrong, I lose a thousand dollars. If you're right, I make a pretty penny for my savings. I'll take my risks."

He continued to frown.

"What's wrong?"

"Nothing," he answered, mouth tight. "I just ... didn't expect you to trust my word."

"Why wouldn't I?"

"Because of my past, my father's record, and the bad blood between your brother and me."

"That's between you and Lucian. You've never done anything wrong to me." He still looked concerned. "Plus, I spoke to Evelyn and she assures me you're a good man."

"She said that?"

"Yes." She'd said other things too, but Isadora didn't want to divulge too much.

She was happy he didn't ask for more details since she preferred to be the most interesting female during a date and would have felt slighted if he asked more about the woman he once—maybe still—loved.

"So where are we going?"

He chuckled. "We're almost there. If you look in the back there are some clues."

Glancing to the backseat, she saw a folded tartan wool blanket, and a shovel. "Are you planning on burying me alive?"

He laughed. "No, I'll need your help, so we'll have to keep you above ground."

They drove for another twenty minutes and the roads turned to open paths that wove through scrubby marshlands. The salt of the air had her cracking a window and breathing deeply, recalling a time when they were young and visited the coast for the summer months.

Her mother had been healthy then, and she would walk them down to the beach, lather them up with sunblock, and let them play until the sun set. That was before Toni was born. Isadora couldn't quite recall her father's presence in those days either.

As he drove over a bridge they were deposited into a small shore town. Kite shops and Victorian style houses stood like still life. No one seemed to be present this time of year, but cars were parked randomly here and there.

Parker turned away from the bay in the direction of the ocean and pulled into a vacant lot where parking meters stood like pickets. "We're here."

"The beach?"

"It's the best time of year. Warm enough to play in the sand, cold enough to have it all to yourself. Shall we?"

She wasn't quite sure what they were doing there. He left the car and came around to open her door.

"You'll want your sweater. It's windy."

Standing, she stretched her legs and donned her cardigan. The blustery breeze was briny and warm, the gusts cutting through her blouse and chilling her skin. Her hair whipped about and she gave up any thoughts of having good date hair.

Parker retrieved the shovel and blanket from the backseat and then popped the trunk. "Can you carry the blanket? I'll get the rest of our supplies."

A large duffle bag sat in the trunk, zipped shut so she couldn't see what it held inside.

"Why do we need supplies?" And what sort of supplies?

They walked to the cement barricade coated in a cracked layer of tar. He helped her step onto the path cutting through the dunes.

"We're building a sand castle."

She laughed. Of all the things she expected to do today, playing in the sand had never crossed her mind. "For what?"

He glanced over his shoulder and winked. "For the fun of it."

Her boots trudged through the fine, loose sand making it difficult to walk. Parker slung the duffle over his right shoulder and grasped her free hand.

As their fingers entwined a steady pulse built in her veins. The sun was high above them, countering the breeze coming off the ocean, but her insides were warmer than she'd expect for a day reaching only the high sixties.

"This looks like a good spot." He stopped midway between the ocean and the dunes. The sand was packed tight where he dropped the supplies.

There were no signs of life for miles, aside from the few gulls she spotted in the distance. Only their footprints marred the pristine surface of the shore.

"I don't think I've ever seen a beach so empty."

"It's nice," he said, unzipping the bag. "Quiet, with just the rushing waves and an endless view."

He removed various tools, setting them out on the beach. They weren't typical sand toys. He had a funnel, a putty knife, a paintbrush, and various cylindrical containers.

"Why don't you spread out the blanket and we'll have lunch first?"

Unfolding the blanket, she flattened out the wrinkles as he proceeded to produce more odd items she'd never think to bring to a beach. He had a melon baller, an ice cream scooper, and two spades. Last, he withdrew a large paper bag.

They sat on the blanket and he paused. Staring at her face, he chuckled. "You look nervous."

"I haven't played in the sand in thirty years."

"Does it bring back bad memories?"

"No, I used to love the shore. I just... Sandcastles are child's play."

He quirked a brow, his hand buried in the brown bag, eyes studying her. "We'll see. Adults forget that they can play, too. And I don't think a child could make what we're going to build today." He withdrew a bottle of wine. "I wasn't sure what you liked, so I went with the basics—wine, cheese, fruit, and peanut butter and jelly sandwiches."

She grinned at his choices—another surprise. "How romantic." Although, she *did* love all of those things.

He smirked and uncorked the bottle with a pop. "I try."

Once he poured wine into the plastic cups, they unwrapped their sandwiches. The grapes and cheese sat between them in absolutely basic Tupperware.

He seemed to have thought of everything for a perfect picnic, but didn't waste time on the superficial frills. It didn't strike her as a lack of effort. On the contrary, he raised the actual date experience to a higher standard, no cheating with distracting bells and whistles.

He kept her on her toes and took away the sense that she needed to make a certain impression. She couldn't explain why she felt so comfortable around him, no pressure at all to be anything other than present. Their lunch date was already overshadowing the fancier dinner dates she had in the past.

"So what exactly are we building?" she asked, nibbling the corner of her sandwich.

"That depends. Every sandcastle's different. It really comes down to how well we work together."

She wondered if this was some sort of test to see if they would make a good team. "Do you do this a lot?"

"No. I always liked the beach and for years I couldn't get here. Let's call it making up for lost time. It's no fun building a sandcastle by yourself. No one's around to appreciate it. Today I have you."

Today I have you...

She liked the way he put that, as if having her company meant more than castles in the sand. Her lips twitched, as she realized how often he filled her with the urge to smile.

She sliced off a piece of brie and popped it in her mouth, chewing slowly and chasing the sharp flavor down with a swallow of wine. Parker untied his shoes—simple, broken-in Chucks—and kicked them off, stuffing his socks inside.

As he rolled the cuffs of his jeans his feet fascinated her. They were manly feet, ordinary, she supposed. But there was something about seeing them on a first date. Something basic and forthcoming that told her he really was comfortable in his own skin.

She turned her attention to the expansive ocean, the tide ebbing and flowing with subdued strength. Her gaze lifted to the sky. White clouds swathed patches of blue in fleecy smears.

"It turned out to be a nice day," she commented, as a few gulls squawked in the distance. One dove to the surface of the water and caught something in its beak. "Did you see that?"

"Probably caught a crab." His eyes squinted against the sun as he carelessly brushed his hair back with his palm. "Look." He pointed. "Something's out there."

A sleek creature leaped from the waves, diving smoothly back underwater. She gasped. "Was that a dolphin?"

"Looked like it. There will probably be more. Watch."

Her smile widened as two more jumped, and then a third, chasing along the horizon in a swift glide of agility and grace.

"Amazing. I've never seen them so close to the shore."

"There's no one here to bother them."

They watched the horizon silently for several minutes and when she finished her sandwich she tossed the foil into the paper bag. "So how exactly do we do this?"

"You might want to take off your boots. We've got a lot of digging to do."

She unzipped her boots and placed them on the corner of the blanket with her socks. She was due for a pedicure, but that didn't bother her like it usually would.

Parker stood and retrieved the shovel, walking several paces away. He carved a large circle where the ocean had receded.

As she stood, the cool earth soothed the soles of her feet. She grabbed a bucket and met him at the circle.

"We need to dig out a moat and make a large pile in the center. I'll start down here and you can use the bucket to carve out the moat."

He proceeded to dig, the scrape of the shovel cutting into the packed sand familiar and comforting. Dropping to her knees, she lodged the bucket into the ground and dumped the sand into the circle.

There was no music, only the sound of their tools working, mingled with the gentle sloshing of the ocean and birds cawing in the distance. They did this for several minutes, the beating of the waves against the shore and the splicing cut of their tools plowing through the earth playing in concert.

"Let's pack the bottom layer with wet sand so we start with a firm foundation."

He removed his jacket. Rolling up the sleeves of his sweater, he reached his arms into the bucket of cold water and pulled out two handfuls of muddy sand and packed it into the ground.

She sat back and watched as he used one of the smaller cups to trim the edges.

"Where did you learn how to do this?"

He shrugged. "Practice, I guess. I don't have any siblings, so when I was young I'd nag my parents to come in the water. They only went up to their knees, so I pretty much stuck to the sand. It's relaxing to build something out of nothing for the sheer pleasure of creativity, even if it might be gone tomorrow."

She'd never thought to do something like that, for the simple pleasure of the experience, knowing nothing lasting would come from her efforts. Perhaps that was her problem in life. Even with Sawyer, she'd always assumed—despite the constant reminders to the contrary—that they'd eventually be a couple, a *real* couple who could outwardly display affection on holidays and plan a future together. She often got disappointed in things that wouldn't last.

Using her hands, she shaped the sand, finding it cool in the shadows of the moat and enjoying the way the little granules stuck to the beds of her fingernails.

They worked in silence, only talking here and there, but there came a way of communicating that didn't require words. Before she could reach for a certain tool, he was there, handing it to her, as if he anticipated her need.

As the minutes passed, the bond they shared seemed to grow, their mutual interest in this silly castle the only thing occupying their minds.

Once they had a pile of sand roughly two feet high and five feet wide, she sat back to admire their work, taking a moment to sip her wine.

Parker joined her for a moment, brushing the sand off his jeans and stealing a grape. "Now comes the fun part."

She shaped a parapet walk while he used the funnel to set the corner towers. With the spade and paintbrush, she dredged a smooth bailey out of the center.

The sun warmed her back through her clothes as she paid great attention to the finer details. She was so engrossed in their sculpture she hardly noticed when wet sand seeped through her blouse.

Parker used his palms to thin out a rampart wall and she went in search of a shell for the perfect drawbridge. They smiled proudly as each detail came together.

Grit dusted her hairline, but she didn't care. Brushing off her palms, she stood, her legs tired in a satisfying way. She took in their work of art and smiled.

"I think that's the nicest sand castle I've ever seen."

"Now we wait." He rinsed his palms in a bucket of clean ocean water and dropped to the blanket, easing back in a relaxed pose.

"Wait?"

"For the tide to come in."

"Oh." Her smile faltered. "I don't think I can bear to watch all our work get washed away."

"It won't. We've built a strong fortress. The water will fill the moat long before the tide gets high enough to wash her away. She's beautiful but tough."

She rinsed her hands and joined him on the blanket, watching the waves creep closer with each lap at the shore. She stared at the sky, marking the distance the sun had traveled. "What time is it?"

"Just after four," he said, not looking at a watch.

She arched a brow. "How do you know that?"

"I can tell by where the sun is in comparison to the horizon." He reached into his pocket and pulled out his phone, holding it so she could see. The screen read 4:11.

"You cheated." She laughed.

"I swear to God I didn't." He pocketed his phone and lounged back, folding his arms behind his head.

She admired the play of muscles in his exposed forearms.

"Come lie with me. We have some time before the tide reaches the moat."

With the sun no longer directly overhead, she reached for her sweater and drew it over her shoulders, hesitating a moment before leaning back beside him. They hardly knew each other, yet she wanted nothing more than to lie beside him as if they were a timeworn couple.

She searched her mind, debating if she was somehow building him up to overshadow other parts of her life, but she honestly didn't believe that was the case. There was just something special about him that had nothing to do with anyone else, and she liked that very much.

She eased her body onto the blanket and scooted close to his side. He wrapped his arm around her shoulders, pulling her alongside his chest so her face rested in the crook of his arm.

Her body tingled with uncertainty. Was it normal to be so comfortable with someone on the first date? She already thought of him as a friend, but there was something more going on here.

She breathed him in, his scent mixing with the briny air. The soft material of his sweater smelled like baked-in sunshine.

She smiled. He smelled like playing outside, like childhood and happiness, and things she hadn't thought about in years. For a moment she lost herself in that incredible fragrance, finding it calming and as addicting as it was nostalgic. She shut her eyes, fighting the urge to burrow closer.

His fingers flexed over her shoulder. "You're fidgety," he teased.

Her heartbeat thrummed in her chest, tight and rhythmic, making her all the more aware of the things she wanted. She relaxed, pushing those urges aside.

This was nice. She shouldn't rush anything.

His hold on her shoulder remained firm and secure, but casual.

Her belly tightened as her legs became restless. It was an effort to remain still with him so close. He turned his nose toward her and she held her breath as he pressed his face to the top of her head and drew in a long breath.

"I like the way your hair smells."

A fleet of butterflies fluttered through her belly and her breasts suddenly felt heavy. That little comment seemed the greatest thing she'd heard in a long time.

Her body sagged into the wool blanket as her desire to feel more of him crept through her like a fever that wouldn't wane.

She glanced up at him, noting the way his jaw relaxed and his lashes rested against his cheeks. Slowly, his gaze lifted and he peeked at her with those fascinating eyes.

"What color are your eyes?" she whispered.

"Green."

Had she never seen green eyes that close before? They were so exotic, flecked and speckled. There was a depth to them she didn't usually see in other eyes. Blue eyes were somewhat striped, and brown eyes appeared rather flat, but green... She loved looking into his eyes.

"They're really pretty."

"Thanks." He held her stare for a moment, the fever inside of her growing hotter.

Her breath caught, as she willed him to move, inwardly begging that he kiss her. Seconds ticked by and he simply stared until finally, he eased closer, turning to his side, still looking into her eyes.

"Staring contest?" he whispered.

Her mouth twitched into a smile, as he drew even closer.

Her lips parted, her anticipation running wild, but he didn't close the distance. "Parker..."

She wanted to ask if he felt everything she was feeling. She wanted to tell him she was scared, but in the best way.

She said nothing, just waited to see what he'd do.

"Can I kiss you?" he whispered and her face heated, her heart pounding faster.

Finally! "Yes."

His full lips pulled to one side, a dimple forming in his cheek as he smiled.

"The thing with first kisses," he said softly. "Is that they're the prelude to every other first. They set the stage, lead to certain expectations. So they have to be perfect."

Her lips parted, her mind now determined

to see what a first kiss from Parker might feel like. She angled her face closer and he pressed his forehead to hers, his eyes teasing.

"Let it build," he whispered, tipping his face as if their mouths were touching, but holding the distance and keeping his eyes on hers.

She'd never wanted someone to kiss her so much in her life, but the unexpected intimacy of waiting as each slow second ticked by had her body tightening more than any kiss could. The anticipation climbed and climbed.

She could just lean forward, close the distance and steal a kiss, but she waited for him, waited for that perfect moment when a first kiss became a permanent memory, distinct enough to carry forever.

Her heart pounded as if she were at the start of a race—a blink and it sped up as if she were already at the end. She was out of breath and he hadn't even touched her. At any moment she might burst with anticipation.

"Not yet," he rasped, his warm breath teasing her lips. "Let it build a little more until it absolutely *has* to happen."

Dear God, she'd never been more excited to be kissed in her life. It was intoxicating.

She could play this game too. "Almost," she whispered and his eyes creased with smile lines.

"Scared?"

Her heart thundered wildly, her body starting to slightly tremble with eagerness. "A little." Not as much as she was a minute ago.

"I won't hurt you, Isadora."

"I've heard that before."

"I know. You're gonna have to trust me."

She believed he wouldn't hurt her on purpose, but what if *she* hurt herself?

Sawyer seemed the only part of her life that worked, yet they were so broken. What if the same pain she felt when she slept with Tyrian came back?

Parker might not want to hurt her, but some things hurt anyway, simply because they broke the mold and took her outside of her comfort zone.

"Still scared?"

Her fear ebbed and flowed, always changing, never completely receding. "I don't know how to do this with someone else," she softly confessed.

"It'll be different. But that's how you'll know it's me."

She loved how he told her things even when they weren't necessarily easy to hear. And yet, those difficult truths always seemed to work in his favor, because he seemed like such an open book. Honest.

His gaze burned into hers. "Are you ready?"

She swallowed, her eyes pleading as she stared at him. So close. "I think so."

The first brush of his mouth had her toes curling into the blanket as her knees drew up and her hand settled onto his side. Chills chased over her arms as every slight caress of his mouth and hands carried the intensity of making love. She moaned softly as he deepened the kiss, teasing and slowly stroking his tongue past her lips.

The fever climbed like brush fire, sweeping through her with impassioned need. Her fingers tightened in his sweater, pulling him more on top of her.

His hands cupped her face, the tips of his fingers sliding into her tangled hair. It was the perfect pace, the perfect pressure, the perfect first kiss. And as far as preludes went, if he took his time with everything the way he was taking his time with this, she'd have no choice but to lose herself in each moment.

He slowly pulled back and smiled. "I wanted to do that since the minute I met you."

She laughed quietly, her face warming. "That was a great first kiss."

"Wait. I wanna do it again."

His lips slid over hers and her hips reflexively lifted into his. Her other hand swept through his hair, pulling, as her mouth greedily took what he offered. The slightest caress fed her craving for more.

"Hey, easy," he whispered, drawing back.

Startled by how strongly her body reacted to him, she loosened her hold of his clothes and blushed. She was practically panting beneath him, her body tight and needy.

Embarrassed she'd come at him so desperately, she turned her face away and blinked at the fading horizon.

"Isadora, it's okay. I just don't want to rush anything," he whispered.

She shut her eyes and swallowed, not used to acting aggressive. "Sorry. It's been a while."

"How long?" His voice was gentle.

"Close to a year." God, why was she telling him that? "Sorry."

"You don't have to apologize. It's been a while for me, too. I just don't want to rush things."

She nodded, doing her best to quell the pent up need raging inside of her.

His fingers gently cupped her jaw, angling her face so she faced him again. Slowly, he bent and brushed his lips against hers, cautiously, as if he didn't want to get swept away.

Her body shook as she struggled to slow her impulses, not expecting this level of attraction. His hand dragged from her sleeve to her wrist and his fingers loosely entwined with hers.

He eased over her, raising her arm and pressing it into the blanket. Her breasts lifted, the tips hardening beneath her clothing, shamelessly begging for attention.

"Slow," he whispered, dragging his lips over hers.

He kissed her jaw, her throat, her mouth, never letting his pace turn greedy, but rather, savoring her, learning her quiet responses. She became a quivering mess of anticipation but tried her best to let him set the pace.

The press of his warm palm burned through the material of her blouse as his fingers curled around her ribs where her cardigan had shifted away. She arched as he kissed down the side of her throat, her legs tangling with his.

The moment he lowered his weight fully over her she moaned, pressing her breasts into his firm chest and gripping his side.

He chuckled, moving that curious hand to rest with the other one above her head on the blanket. "Easy," he said again. "Slow."

She blinked at him, unable to recall a time when she'd been the antagonist. His nose teased the hair tangled by her ear until it fell behind her shoulder. He nudged her jaw with his chin, softly scraping her skin with stubble, as his lips traveled to her collarbone.

Her legs twisted, finding their way outside of his only to have him trap them between his knees again. He pressed into her, the bulge of his arousal abrading the central point where her thighs clamped tight.

Her breath quickened as she realized he had her completely pinned. She was at his mercy and knowing that made her want him all the more.

"Please, Parker..."

His mouth curved against her collarbone where her blouse had loosened. He dragged his body over hers, a slow implication of what he wanted. "Please, what?"

Never in her life had she asked a man to lay his hands on her. Yet something inside of her demanded she beg him.

"Touch me."

Easing back, he stared at her, dragging a

knuckle over her shirt, down the shallow valley of her breasts to her belly. She sucked in and angled her hips toward the earth, lifting her chest.

His fingers slowly tugged the tie of her blouse and humid air met her heated skin. Her nipples pebbled beneath the lace of her bra.

Straddling her hips, he brushed a tender finger down her cheek. "You're so beautiful." He stared at her body, lines of tension forming around his eyes. "We should wait, Isadora. We don't have to rush anything."

She shook her head. "You're not rushing me."

His touch never left her body. It trailed over her shoulder, straying closer and closer to the slope of her breasts and the scalloped lace of her bra. The back of his fingernails tripped over the material, and she sighed with need as he teased her skin.

"I want to put my mouth on every inch of you." He dragged his thumb over the tip of her nipple.

Please do...

She was utterly spellbound. Every look, caress, and breath made her want him more than she had only seconds ago.

Sliding lower, he bent and slowly licked

along the edging of her bra and she gasped. He spread little kisses on her warm flesh, and his lips closed over her taut, lace-covered nipple, pulling softly.

She couldn't take anymore.

Pulling her hands from the space above her head, she sifted her fingers through his hair and held him there. His fingers tugged at the strap of her bra, pulling it with her blouse to her elbows, exposing her bare breasts.

He captured the tip of her nipple in his hot mouth and sucked hard. Her toes pointed as her hips rocked into the blanket, his body grinding heavily against hers. He released her breast and moved to the other—hard, almost greedily groping her tender flesh—sliding his arm beneath her back and lifting her closer to his mouth.

Her fingers gathered the bulk of his sweater, pulling until she felt the burn of his skin beneath her fingertips. Her nails scraped up his back and he groaned, releasing her nipple and taking her mouth in a deep kiss.

His tongue dueled with hers as they rolled to their sides. Her legs now free, she hooked her knee over his hip and pressed her body to his. His strong hand cupped her backside as he pressed against her, holding her to him.

The fingers of his other hand teased the waist of her jeans until the button came undone. Wedging his hand behind the silk of her panties, his fingers traced her wet folds, sending shivers up her spine as he grazed her slit.

He released his hold on her backside, rolling her to the blanket so she was once again beneath him. He tugged at her fitted jeans, his mouth falling onto her breasts as his fingers found their way past the seam of her sex.

She could barely part her thighs with the denim bunched around her knees. He seemed content to simply pet her there, hardly penetrating.

There was something considerably erotic about his gentle touch, the steady brush of his masculine fingers over feminine softness. The longer he teased her, the more she wanted to feel him inside of her.

The broad tip of his finger grazed her clit and she moaned with need. Frantic with wanting, she slid her hand into the back of his pants and gripped his hip. He groaned and finally slid his finger deep inside of her.

She gasped, arching, as he slowly pumped. Her hand withdrew from the back of his jeans and searched anxiously for his zipper, finding the button already undone as his arousal pressed hard against the constricting waist of his pants.

She fed her hand into the cramped space and closed her fingers around his thick flesh and he froze.

His finger remained buried deep inside of her, hers wrapped tightly around his arousal. He blinked, his pupils larger than usual. They seemed to be on the verge of something significant.

"We should stop," he rasped.

"What if I don't want to?" Would he become another man deciding for her?

"I wouldn't be upset if you wanted to stop, Isa. It would suck, but if we slowed down I'd understand. It's up to you."

He'd never know how much she appreciated hearing him say it was her choice. But at the same time, she suffered such uncertainty she had no clue how to decide for them.

This was their first date. She'd waited for something like twenty dates with Tyrian. Maybe they *should* stop. But she didn't want to stop. Everything they were doing felt incredible and she wanted more.

Recklessly, she whispered, "Do you have a condom?"

His lips tightened for a moment. "I don't know how to answer that."

"What do you mean?"

His gaze shifted away. "I want to be with you, but not because we have everything we need. I'd rather it be because it's something we both want. Don't rest your decision on the availability of a condom."

Here she was trying to have sex and he was being all logical about everything—and ridiculously sweet. "The closest store's only about ten minutes from here. It's probably open."

He laughed. "You're a determined little thing."

She smiled. "I'm not usually like this. It must be you."

His nostrils flared, his eyes—back on her—darkened and he kissed her hard. His finger pumped and she moaned into his mouth, her hand stroking purposefully.

Sliding another finger deep, he stretched her, more than she was used to, but she liked it, didn't want him to stop.

It had been so long since anyone touched her. Her body seemed ultra-sensitive. The strum of his thumb over her clit had her gasping, rolling toward a fast finish with little effort.

He scooted lower, freeing her hold on him

as he kissed her hip and pushed her jeans to her ankles. She kicked them away and he opened her thighs, his mouth lowering. Using both hands he parted her folds, spreading her wide as his tongue speared into her.

"*Ah*, yes!"

He kissed and licked her tender flesh, pressing a finger deep with forceful thrusts, as his mouth closed over her clit. Her knees lifted as she moaned, her cries lost in the wind racing over the vacant beach.

Her feet pressed into the blanket, lifting her body to him. Her hands burrowed in his soft hair as she greedily took the pleasure he expertly gave.

Faster, his fingers pumped, the damp slide of his touch an erotic tempo that egged her on. His mouth tightened as he doubled his efforts, crooked his fingers, and then—*bliss*.

Her hearing buffeted, deafened by the beat of her heart, the crash of the ocean, and her sobs of pleasure. Her vision winked against the hazy sky as her entire body quaked in a release so strong it shook her to the core.

Tiny aftershocks trembled through her as she caught her breath. Parker's soft hair teased her belly as he pressed his cheek to her stomach and panted.

"Isadora," he whispered after a few minutes of recovering.

"Hmm?" Her voice was hoarse and her throat dry. Granules of sand clung to her damp skin.

"I have a condom, but I think we should wait. I don't want to spoil whatever this is."

Now that the burning fever had somewhat broken, she was thinking a little clearer. Perhaps sleeping together on their first date wasn't the wisest choice. They should know each other better.

She was grateful he had the honor to remind her several times that there was no rush and it was her choice. She wasn't sure what was right and what was wrong when it came to healthy relationships, so she decided to wait—at least until their second date.

"That's probably a good idea."

He kissed her belly and drew the edges of her blouse together. Reaching for her jeans, he untangled them, separating the silk from the denim and slid her panties up her still unsteady legs.

His cheeks were flushed as he smiled at her, his hair windblown and wildly sexy. Leaning forward, he pressed a kiss over the silk at her apex and stood.

"I'm going to walk down to the water for a minute to cool off."

She glanced at him, feeling like the most selfish lover in the world. "Are you sure you're fine with waiting?"

He bent and brushed a kiss to her lips then laughed. "The right choice is usually the most difficult. So, yeah, I'm sure. Just give me a couple minutes."

She watched as he walked to the wet sand, pausing where the water rushed at his feet. The tide had risen and was nearing their moat.

She stood and brushed off the sand that had transferred from the blanket to her legs then stepped into her jeans. Righting her blouse and sweater, she watched him as he stared out at the fading horizon.

His unkempt brown hair and broad shoulders formed a perfect silhouette against the skyline. His jeans were worn and wrinkled and the hem of his shirt stuck out beneath his sweater. She definitely preferred *this* Parker to the one in a tuxedo.

More than the interesting conversations they shared or the fact that he'd planned a perfect date, there was something undeniably unique about him. Special. Every moment she spent with him seemed to prove that again and again.

With Tyrian, there had been an ease that didn't come with Sawyer—the convenience of acceptability. He fit appropriately into her life, so much so that even when she no longer wanted him there she felt like the bad guy for breaking up with him. No one understood why she'd prefer to be alone than with a merely adequate partner.

Then there was Sawyer. Sawyer was everything taboo and hungry inside of her, all the things others never suspected she felt. But he was also her secret—just as she was his. And over the years that secret changed to a dirty one, tarnished and bent where it had once been beautifully flawless. They rarely went on dates and, on the few occasions they did venture out, it was always to some obscure place off the grid.

She felt herself frown. Her thoughts of Sawyer seemed altered, like a treasured keepsake suddenly tarnished beyond repair.

Since meeting Parker, the idea of Sawyer and her relationship with him seemed tainted. Was that because of Parker or simply timing?

Parker wasn't like Tyrian or Sawyer. He wasn't going to be easily accepted, but she didn't care—neither did he.

He seemed genuinely interested in her as a person, like she was her own entity, already interesting enough. He had the ease and the hunger, all in one. But he was also clever and sweet, and somehow sturdier than what she was used to.

Last week, when her brother threatened him, he'd been about to back off, but then decided against it, implying she was worth pursuing, opposition be damned. And Lucian was no minor threat to brave.

The fleeting thought drifted through her head that this might all be to spite her brother, but she shoved it away, feeling ridiculous for even considering such a notion. Her brother was an obstacle, not a provocation.

Parker saw something in her worth going after, even if it meant confronting the indomitable Lucian Patras. And *that* was probably the first time a man ever made her feel truly worthwhile. In a way, it was sad he was the first to do it.

Parker slowly walked back to the blanket, inspecting how their castle was holding up along the way. He grinned when their gazes snagged. Wearing a pleasant smile, he strolled closer.

"Better?" she asked, sitting up on the blanket and finishing the last of the wine.

He looked so adorably casual, like a candid picture that perfectly captured his easy demeanor. "Better."

"I had a really great day with you, Parker."

"I had a great day with *you*. I'd like to take you out again. Soon."

"Please do."

He stole another grape and they bagged up the remainder of food. Strolling down to the bank, they rinsed all the sand tools and packed them away.

On their last trip back to the blanket, they stilled as a large wave smacked against the shore and rushed up the beach. She grinned widely as water funneled into their moat and traveled rapidly along the path they'd carved, filling the trench.

"We should take a picture before it washes away."

He reached into his pocket and withdrew his phone. Finding the perfect angle, he snapped several shots, catching the fading sky in the backdrop.

"The pictures do it no justice."

She crowded close as he thumbed through

the images, showing her each one. "Will you send them to me?"

"Of course, but we need a selfie to go with them. A memento of our first date."

"I hate pictures of myself."

"Why? You're gorgeous."

Her cheeks heated. "That's sweet, but I'm plain."

"No, you're not. Here." He held out his phone and snapped a picture of her, but she wasn't ready. "Look at you." He turned the screen toward her so she could see.

She hadn't had enough time to smile. Her eyes were cast upward and her lips were slightly parted. Her hair was a straggly, windblown mess and her nose and cheeks wore a splotch of new freckles from the sun.

"You're breathtaking," he whispered, placing a kiss on her temple. "I'm keeping that one for myself."

Her chest warmed again as he draped his arm over her shoulder and pulled her closer, this time standing beside her when the flash shuttered.

But she wasn't looking at the camera that time either. No. She was staring up at the man who made her feel things she couldn't recall ever feeling before.

PARKER DIDN'T GIVE her time to wonder if he was interested. He showed her in every gesture, every call, and every kind word.

They didn't meet on a specific day of the week or even put much thought into the routine of their plans. He contacted her often, inviting her with him to run an errand or grab something to eat, but she was more than just filler in his free time. She was a spontaneous part of his days, an ever-present thought in his mind, just as he was in hers.

They often did things she wasn't sure typical adults did. They walked the zoo, fed the ducks in the park, and randomly visited pet stores to play with orphaned puppies. She loved being with him, unsure if she'd ever felt so alive and free with anyone else.

With Parker, things never went as expected and that was, for once, a good thing. The most endearing quality he had was his playful side.

He loved to tease her, something she wasn't used to but grew quite fond of. Every day with Parker was full of laughter and the nights... The nights were always riddled with wanting, making every date a lesson in anticipation.

"I will have the filet, medium rare, and the lady will have a lemon."

Isadora paused from perusing her menu and glanced from Parker to the confused waiter. *Did he just order me a lemon?*

"A lemon, sir."

"Yes, one lemon—as a matter of fact, make it three."

The waiter blinked at him with evident misunderstanding. "Will there be anything *with* the lemons?"

"Just the steak and lemons for now."

It was amazing that he could keep a straight face. Isadora wasn't as gifted at holding her composure so she covered her mouth with her fist, trying not to laugh.

When the waiter stepped away, she snorted. "Seriously?"

Parker's face split with a grin. "Watch, they'll actually bring you lemons."

She shook her head and laughed. "Well, you ordered them. Is that all I'm having for dinner?"

"Of course not. We'll get you some croutons or something." He found great amusement in the silly things wealth could garner, and he made a game of appearing as eccentric as money could buy.

The waiter returned with a basket of breadsticks and hesitated. "Sir, would you like the lemons with your meal or before?"

"With, of course. And could you please bring us two walnuts *in* the shell."

The man glanced around, likely looking for a hidden camera. His gaze turned to her, as she did her best to remain straight-faced and as stoic as her date.

With a sigh, the waiter nodded. "Yes, sir."

Isadora shook her head. "You're going to give him a panic attack."

Parker took two breadsticks from the basket and stuck them in his mouth like walrus tusks. "Okay, fine. I'll cancel the lemons and order you a meal if you show me some good breadstick teeth."

Her eyes widened. "This is a *nice* restaurant."

"I know," he mumbled, his words muddled from the breadsticks. "Do you think they'll throw *uth* out?"

Her brow twitched as she tried to decide if that might be his goal. The restaurant staff was perfectly aware they had a Patras and a Hughes sitting in their elegant dining room, but...

Screw it. She reached into the basket and took out two sticks, positioning them behind her upper lip against her gums.

Parker snorted. "*Yer duh thexietht walruth* I ever *thaw.*"

She laughed—hard. "Is your mouth getting a little dry?"

"*Jutht* a little."

The waiter returned, spotting her first. His eyes widened as he tried to mask his shock at finding a woman in his station wearing breadstick fangs, but it was too late.

Parker discreetly removed his breadsticks, but she wasn't as stealthy. A hot flush climbed up her neck as she plucked them from her mouth, feeling quite ridiculous and sheepish.

The server turned to Parker, who sat, hands folded and posture straight, appearing as well-mannered as any upper-class patron.

"Your walnuts, sir."

"Thank you." Parker glanced at her and back to the server. "This is her first time to a restaurant. I apologize."

Stammering for a reply, the waiter turned and walked away.

She scoffed and kicked him under the table. "Parker!"

His laughter burst out in a frenzied show of good fun. "You should have seen the look on your face, gawking up at him with fangs askew."

As embarrassed as she was, she couldn't help but laugh. So what if she wore bread tusks at a celebrated restaurant? And she was pretty sure the man sitting a few tables away was an associate of her brother's. She'd never laughed so hard during a meal.

His smile froze and his gaze steadied on her, quelling her laughter. "There it is," he whispered.

Still smiling, she tipped her head, unsure what he was referring to. "What?"

"Your kiss. Tucked away like a charm in the corner of your mouth, hidden from all the un-magical things of adult life. But when you laugh, it comes out to play."

Her fingers lifted to her cheek, grazing the divot where a dimple sometimes showed. He had such an incredible memory when it came to literary references. "That's from *Peter Pan*, isn't it?"

His eyes creased, his smile telling her she was correct. Parker's stare seemed to reach across the table, unraveling between them like a soft caress, and holding her in its grip.

Gaze soft and hypnotic, he whispered, *"He got all of her ... except for her kiss."*

Any sense of silliness vanished as her smile trembled on her lips. It was such an accurate and flattering assessment. He wasn't just telling her he thought she was beautiful but also recognizing that she was fragile. And he was telling her she was resilient.

Sawyer took a lot of things from her. He owned a lot of her firsts, but after all the happiness and heartache, she could still smile without him. He hadn't stolen her kiss.

Parker's fingers closed around hers on the table. "I'm glad you didn't give your kiss away, m'lady. It's the prettiest part of your smile."

Her lips pursed as another burst of butterflies took flight in her belly, tickling even the breath in her lungs. "You're making me blush."

He raised his brow. "Another favorite part."

She used to read *Peter Pan* to Toni. There was another part where Peter forgets what a kiss is, so he gives Wendy Darling an acorn button. Isadora didn't have an acorn button, but she had two walnuts.

As silly as it was, she kept those nuts, right beside her most valuable jewels in a chest in her room. She never wanted to forget how he described her kiss, and when she was old and wrinkled, she'd come across that walnut and be reminded that she was most beautiful when she was happy.

Parker made her happy.

Their relationship was a collection of odd inside jokes and unpredicted moments that made her laugh long after the days were over. She adored his sense of humor, cracked up at his sarcasm, and found it fascinating how he could transition from teasing and playful to serious and intense.

In a lot of ways, Parker was his own Peter Pan. Yes, he was a grown man who knew how to take care of himself and manage just fine, but hidden below the surface was a lost boy, an orphaned child who faced too many challenges to find time to play.

The irony was, she also hid a lost girl. For as different as their adolescence was, the abandonment, the difficult decisions placed on a set of small shoulders, that part was the same.

Perhaps she needed someone in her life to teach her the world didn't always have to be a serious place. Parker seemed the perfect man for the job.

It was far too early to think of four letter words, but being with him felt like falling. It was fast, thrilling, and something she couldn't stop once it started.

It took only one glance from those watchful eyes to set her insides burning. One kiss and she was pulling at his clothes as he prudently slowed her hands. Some days it was excruciating, waiting for him to touch her, but when he finally did, the waiting made his attention all the more potent.

She'd been ready to sleep with him since that day at the beach, but something held her back, told her to savor every moment and not worry about what might come tomorrow. It was temperance, unlike anything she'd ever known. Perhaps a part of her was terrified sex might spoil their chemistry the way it had with Tyrian. She hoped not.

He'd said he wanted her, fantasized about her, and even called her late at night confessing he'd missed her. But when it came to their time together he always fell back on that unbreakable restraint, reeling in her wanton need until it was needle sharp and barely tolerable. And she *always* wanted him.

When the spring weather finally broke, Isadora invited Parker to the house to see her gardens. She'd spent years cultivating various blooms and no one ever seemed to appreciate her love for her backyard, but Parker had specifically asked if he could see it.

"I want to see what puts that passionate spark in your eyes," he'd explained.

Her terrace represented pieces of past lives, moments when she was unsure or scared and had to think through changes that came whether she wanted her world to change or not. Maybe he understood that, saw her plants as a wordless story of all she'd overcome.

"I planted these when Toni was learning to drive. That was a really stressful time. Every evening after we'd practice driving I'd come out here. Gardening's very cathartic for me."

Parker laughed. "I only got my license last year. I still get nervous driving in the city."

She loved when he shared little vulnerable truths like that. "Well, you're a much better driver than my sister. Lucian had to finish Toni's lessons. My nerves aren't quite as resilient as his."

Whenever she mentioned her brother, he made no comment about their past, which she appreciated, but it also made her a touch anxious.

The more time they spent together, the more frequently she wished Parker and Lucian might someday make amends. But normal had always been a long shot in her love life.

Giving him a tour of the yard was more satisfying than she'd expected. He took great interest in every bed, smiled at each little anecdote, and admired every flower.

"May I?" he asked, bending to sniff a spray of roses climbing up a trellis.

She nodded and he snapped a bloom from the vine, pinching off the thorns.

"For you, m'lady."

Grinning, she took the stem and pressed the fragrant petals to her nose. "Thank you."

"Can you see the color?"

"I see an orangy-pink."

He smirked and she knew she had it wrong, but he didn't correct her.

"Is it pink?"

He wrapped his fingers around hers. "I think, it's whatever you see. Just like how no two people ever read the same book, maybe two people never see the same rose."

"Maybe you're right, but what do you see?" They turned down a stone path leading to the pergola.

Slanting her a sideways glance, he pulled their entwined fingers to his lips and pressed a kiss to her knuckles. "It's yellow."

She snorted. "I was way off."

Slowing his steps, he moved to face her, lifting the rose between them. "Actually, there are a lot of colors in it. Here, in the center of the petals, it's vibrant, like the feathers of a canary. Down here, in the shadows of the bud, it's darker like an egg yolk. But toward the tips it gets paler, almost white, like the rind between a lemon and its peel. In the veins, these tiny little ventricles tapering to the edges, there's the slightest hint of pink. So you really weren't that off."

"You describe it so prettily," she said softly, envious of his vision. She stared at the rose, wishing she could see all the various hues, never realizing there were so many variations of the color yellow.

He lifted the flower and brushed the petals along her cheek. "If you hold it here, close to your skin, it gives you a yellow blush. *That's* pretty."

When he looked at her like that, a delicate chill came over her and she wanted him so deeply she could feel it in the tempo of her heart, sense it in the tremble of her bones.

"I wish I saw what you saw."

His gaze held hers. "I see something so beautiful, I wonder how it's possible others haven't noticed."

Her chest warmed. She decided when she got inside she'd press that rose in the pages of a book and put it with the other amassing keepsakes he'd given her.

Drawing in a deep breath, she smiled and shifted his acute attention back to the beds.

"Show me more."

"I have lilies here." She pointed. "I love the stargazer ones. They have the best fragrance."

"Stargazer lilies," he repeated, as if taking note of the things she liked.

He kept her hand back in his and gave a squeeze. They strolled in silence for a few minutes until they reached an open portion of land.

"This is where I'd like to put the labyrinth."

He grinned, admiring the open meadow. "You have a lot of space available." A rumble of thunder groaned in the distance and they both looked up.

"We should head back."

He nodded and they turned toward the house. The first drops of rain were hardly a nuisance, but then came another crash of thunder and the skies opened, pelting them with fat beads of water.

Parker gripped her hand as they raced toward shelter. Their feet slipped over the wet stone, her shoes sloshing through fast forming puddles.

"Get under here," he shouted, pulling her to the pergola where the wisteria vines formed a porous canopy.

She caught her breath and laughed at what a mess they'd become in a matter of seconds. "We're drenched!"

She shivered, her clothes wet and heavy from only a few minutes in the downpour. Waterspouts rushed with sloshing currents as the spattering raindrops pelted the cobblestone and plants.

The soft splashing formed a quiet roar around them, cocooning them in a steady purr and trickle of rushing water.

"We should wait here until it slows up." She wrung out the front of her shirt, trying to pull the wet material away from her skin. Brushing a hank of hair from her face she looked up and froze.

His gaze locked with hers, raindrops clinging to his jaw and cheeks. His spiked lashes lowered as he pulled her close.

"Come here."

Their slicked clothes clung to their bodies, and her skin chilled as her insides warmed. He tucked the damp tangle of hair behind her ear and smiled, his mouth a mere breath from hers.

"You're so beautiful."

She rose on her toes, pressing her lips to his. His hand skidded over her damp curves and gripped her backside, pulling her hips closer. She hungrily kissed him, the feel of his hardening body bringing hers to life.

"More," she whispered, her smile curving against his.

His touch crawled greedily over her sopping shirt, pulling and tugging. The fabric glued to her body.

Her back leaned into a thick wooden beam and he lifted her off the ground, wrapping her legs around his hips.

"Jesus, Isadora."

Yanking her shirt above her wet breasts, his mouth closed over her nipple. Her head fell back, her lower body desperately pressing into his. The sharp nudge of his arousal digging into her sex caused them both to moan.

"Fuck," he ripped his mouth from her breast and pressed her more into the beam. "Why do you feel so incredible?"

She wanted him inside of her, filling her, thrusting so hard she'd feel him there for days. "I want you," she demanded, reaching for his belt buckle.

"We should go inside."

His belt loosened and he frantically worked the button of her jeans. *Yes! Finally!*

It was perfect and spontaneous and finally going to happen. Hot flesh met her fingertips and—

"Isadora?"

They froze.

Parker's warm breath beat against her neck,

their bodies entwined in a knot of lust and need. "Is that your brother's voice?"

"No, no, no, no, no," she whined, dropping her face into his shoulder. But yes, it was Lucian. "Damn it."

"Can he see us?"

She considered the distance to the house and the angle they were facing. "No." But, damn it! She wasn't in the mood for company. She was in the mood for Parker sex and a world of other things that should not include her brother. "He'll see my car and know I'm home."

"Why is he here?"

"I don't know."

"Shit." He lowered her feet to the ground and buckled his pants. "You should go see what he wants. The rain's slowing down."

Disgruntled, she adjusted her clothes, internally grumbling that her brother rarely visited and now was not the time for him to change his habits.

"What will you do?"

"I don't think now's the time for us to come face to face. I know you want that meeting to go smoothly, and it will, when the time's right. I'll wait here for a few minutes. Try to get him to leave."

She nodded but, again, hoped this dislike between him and her brother would eventually fade. "Okay. He's probably just dropping something off. He usually doesn't stay long."

She turned to go to the house and he snatched her wrist, spinning her back to him and kissing her passionately. When he pulled away she was in a dizzy haze.

"Don't take too long."

She blinked, her body not wanting to leave. "'Kay."

She navigated the wet garden and entered the house through the kitchen, her soggy shoes making a mess on the tile floor.

Yanking her sneakers and socks off with a slurping sound, she dropped them by the door and wrung out her hair.

"Where the hell were you?" Lucian asked, walking into the kitchen.

"I was in the garden when it started to rain."

"You're soaked."

"I'm aware."

"Well, dry off. I have something for you."

"I need a minute."

She slipped into the laundry room and squeezed out of the clothes suctioned to her body. Shivering, she grabbed the first thing she found, an old sundress of Toni's that showed more skin than Isadora preferred.

She returned to the kitchen to find Lucian staring out the window. "You said you had something for me." It was probably just some paperwork he needed her to sign.

"Someone's in the garden."

"I know."

He faced her and scowled. "Who?"

She debated for only half a second. "Parker."

His demeanor darkened. "Why is he at our house?"

"You own half of Folsom, Lucian, but I own this property, so I'm afraid you don't get a say in who I invite over."

They faced off for a silent second, her brother clearly not liking the irrefutable truth in her words, but she silently dared him to challenge her.

He released the curtain. "Let him wait in the rain like a coward."

She scoffed. "He's not afraid of you."

"He should be."

Her eyes narrowed. "Why? You wouldn't do anything to him."

"Wanna bet? I already kicked his ass once."

"I like him, Lucian, and I know you

wouldn't cross that line. For God's sake, let it go."

His lips pressed tight. "You shouldn't trust him, Isa."

"I know what I'm doing."

He arched a dark brow. "Do you?"

She didn't have great judgment with men, but that had nothing to do with Parker's character and everything to do with her. Parker had never given her a reason to doubt his honesty. His past with Lucian was in the past.

"Why are you here?"

Putting aside his open dislike for the company she kept, he reached into the breast pocket of his suit. "To show you this." He dropped a small black and white photo onto the counter.

She crept closer and gasped. "Is that..."

"She had the ultrasound this morning."

Her hands carefully lifted the sonogram and she sucked in an astonished breath. "Oh, my... Is it a boy or a girl?"

"We didn't want to find out."

Her face pulled with a smile, her belly fluttering in awe. "I think it's a boy."

"So does Evelyn. I think it's a girl."

She looked up at him as his voice cracked and her vision blurred. Lucian *never* showed emotion. Even when Monique died, she hadn't seen him cry. But now, he looked like he was holding on by a thread.

"You're going to be a daddy," she whispered and vulnerability flashed in his dark eyes.

His smile tightened, tension showing around his mouth. "Do you think I'll do a better job than him?"

It needed no clarification that he was speaking of their father.

"I think you'll do a perfect job, Lucian."

He carefully took the sonogram and lovingly tucked it back into his suit jacket over his heart. "I don't want him to ever question my love."

"He won't. Or she, if it's a girl."

He drew in a deep breath and chuckled. "God help me if I have a daughter. I'll never let her out of my sight."

She laughed. "Worried about karma?"

"Don't joke about stuff like that."

"I fear for any man that loves her."

"Jesus, Isa. I can't think about that shit yet. I'm barely able to imagine her first steps. What if something goes wrong with the pregnancy? What if Evelyn—"

She tsked and patted his cheek. "You'll be

an excellent father and Evelyn will be a wonderful mother. Nothing's going to go wrong."

He took a calming breath. "Thank you. I don't like situations where I have no control."

She laughed again. "You don't say."

Just then the kitchen door opened and Lucian's expression shuttered. Her gaze shifted to Parker who was dripping wet.

"It started raining again."

"I should go," her brother said, his voice devoid of emotion.

She looked up at him, trying to express that he didn't have to hide in front of Parker, but she recognized refusal in his hard eyes. Maybe in time.

"Okay."

"I'll call you later."

She nodded and he left the kitchen without sparing Parker a word or glance.

When she heard the front door close she gave him an apologetic smile. "At least he didn't threaten you?"

Parker rolled his eyes. "He wouldn't do that here. He cares about you too much."

Impressed that he could infer that about her brother, she smiled. She went to the drawer and pulled out a thick dishtowel.

"How is it you know that about him, but you two were never friends?"

"He knows me just as well. It's what you do when you don't trust someone."

"But you trust him with Scout and you trust that he won't upset me."

"Because I know he loves both of you. He's obscenely loyal to those he loves."

"That he is." Brushing the damp spikes of hair off his brow, she gazed into his eyes. "Do you want to put these clothes in the dryer?"

He debated for only a second then stepped back. "I think I should go."

Caught off guard by his decision, her posture shrank.

"You can stay." She'd hoped he would, hoped they could continue what they started out back.

His head tipped, pressing his brow to hers. "It's not that I don't want to stay, Isa. I do. But it's been a pretty perfect day and it's getting late. It'll keep."

"You could spend the night." The invitation fell from her lips so easily.

He gave her a chaste kiss and stepped back. "Soon."

Everything inside of her wanted to hold

him there, but she wouldn't beg another man to love her. She needed him to do it on his own.

He buffed the rain out of his hair and set the towel on the counter, leaving her uncertain and warring with doubt.

Once he was as dry as he would get, he turned and smiled. "I'll call you."

She nodded, questioning if anyone would ever want her again. "Drive safe."

> *"Hair, bosom, hips, bend of legs,*
> *Negligent falling hands all diffused,*
> *mine too diffused,*
> *Ebb stung by the flow and flow stung by*
> *the ebb,*
> *Love-flesh swelling and*
> *deliciously ...aching..."*

Walt Whitman
I Sing the Body Electric

ISADORA WAS DETERMINED to get Parker into her bed. It shocked her how much emphasis she put on getting him naked. Her desire to have him built into such potent need, she'd hardly been able to hold a non-sexual thought for days.

Everything about him turned her on. The way the stubble on his jaw always started to show early in the evenings. The way his eyes creased with laughter. The amount of focus he placed on a simple task, be it tying his shoes or reading an article. But most of all, the way he looked at her as if he were memorizing her every feature and listening to her every word. All of that gave her the confidence to push toward the next stage.

She wanted to know how a man like Parker made love, hoping that he put as much focus into the act as he did everything else. But not only did she want to experience his tenderness and affection, she also wanted to unleash the intensity she sometimes glimpsed.

Maybe her obsession with sleeping with him was some belated rite of sexual passage she'd skipped. On the verge of thirty-seven, it seemed utterly pathetic that she just now had the urge to ... well, fuck like an animal.

It was the only way she could put it, though she'd never admit such a thing out loud. But silently admitting it to herself filled her with urges too intoxicating to curb.

She didn't want it to just be sex between them, but she also wasn't looking for manners. She was after something darker, something intense, something no one but Parker made her crave.

She wanted it hot, sweaty, raunchy, and unrefined. Pure. Animal. Lust. He'd driven her to this point of near lunacy and she was going to scream if they didn't do it soon.

The dirty thoughts and dark fantasies were definitely a problem. So anxious to have him, she feared she might lunge at him like some sex-deprived maniac and send him running in the opposite direction, because, despite their smoldering chemistry, something always held him back.

It was if he was purposely torturing them. But why?

She was finished trying to figure out why he was so insistent on waiting. It was wonderful that he had gentlemanly traits, but enough already! She wanted him and tonight she was determined to have him.

As she dressed for their date, she fantasized how the night would play out. They'd have dinner, maybe a few drinks, kiss their way through the front door, and fall into bed. They were finally going to cross that line they'd been tiptoeing around for weeks.

Dear god, her panties were wet from just picturing Parker's strong body over hers.

The doorbell rang and her heart tripped into a wild beat. Sliding her feet into sandals, she took the steps two at a time and practically skipped to the front door.

Smiling, she flung it open and her heart jerked hard in her chest. Stark blue eyes greeting her.

"Bella."

"S—Sawyer," she stuttered. "What are you doing here?"

His gaze had the power to paralyze, pulling her back to a familiar place her mind didn't want to go.

"I wanted to see you."

The fact that he'd come by without calling triggered a wave of worry. He'd only show up like this if something were wrong.

What if Lucian or Toni had been visiting? Had he considered that? Maybe he had and didn't care, needed to see her so badly he decided to visit anyway.

Shaking her head, she chastised herself for feeling a slight thrill that his need to see her might be motivation enough. It was too late for little improvements and *normal* behavior shouldn't strike her as something special. He didn't get points for doing something another man in her life did without question.

And there was that other man in her life now, so he shouldn't be popping by unannounced like this. "This isn't a good time. I'm leaving in a few minutes."

"Can I come in? I just need to speak to you for a moment."

Startled by his persistence and worried something might actually be wrong, she stepped back and let him in. "Is everything okay?"

Her mind briefly touched on her father, certain Tibet would have contacted them before Sawyer if anything were wrong. The days of Sawyer acting as her father's go-between ended when their partnership dissolved with the buyout of Leningrad.

He paced, hands in his pockets, brow tense. "Can we sit down?"

"Okay, but I only have a few minutes."

He nodded and she followed him into the den where, despite asking for a place to sit, he proceeded to pace. She rested on the arm of a chair and waited for him to voice whatever he'd come there to say.

"I know the last time we spoke you were upset with me."

"I was," she admitted. *Still am.*

"I'm sorry."

Her brow raised, as she doubted he really understood how hurtful his little attempt to get her back into bed actually was. "Are you?"

"Yes. I treated you ... cheaply. I don't know what got into me, but I'm glad you walked out. I deserved that."

"Is that supposed to be an apology?"

He paused from pacing and met her gaze. "I *am* sorry, Isadora."

She nodded her acceptance of his regret. "Is that what you came to say?"

It seemed strange that this was the first time she wasn't consumed by his absence. Actually having him in her house drove that point to the forefront of her consciousness. Did he sense she'd been getting along fine without him for once?

"Bella, I don't know how to not worry about you."

Her brow tightened. It was odd for him to indicate he thought of her when they were apart. Nice sentiment, but not what she needed at the moment.

"Sawyer, I'm okay."

He stilled and gave her an assessing glance. "Are you?"

She smiled at his concern. "Yes. I was upset and hurt, but I honestly haven't thought about it for weeks."

"You don't hate me?"

"Of course not. I could never hate you." Picturing him with that woman still hurt, but she'd tried not to dwell on things outside of her control. "Maybe this time we're *both* ready to move on."

He frowned and shook his head slowly, his gaze on the floor. "I don't know."

Her shaky smile fell. Breath stilled in her chest as a dull throb started in her fragile heart. Brave indifference faded into something heavy that she didn't want to hold, something dangerous, something threatening.

Sliding off the arm of the chair, she took a step back, her arms closing over her chest protectively.

"Why are you here?"

His expression softened and he approached her. "Something's different this time."

"Different *how*?"

"I miss you ... more. Not just in my bed, but in my life. I know I've screwed this up and I don't deserve anything from you, but...

What if we tried again? It would be better this time. I'd ... try my best to..." His brow creased as he struggled to get the words out. "I've changed, bella. I know that doesn't erase my mistakes, but if you could forgive me we might actually get it right this time. I'm done hiding."

She staggered back another step, certain she hadn't heard him correctly. "What are you saying?"

He thrust a hand through his hair, an uncharacteristic show of nervousness she wasn't used to seeing from him. "I'm saying ... we could be together, a couple. Screw everyone else."

Her eyes widened. This had to be some sort of misunderstanding. "Wha—why now?"

"Slade says the issues between him and your brother are smoothing—"

"No, Sawyer. Give me something a little more definitive than your son's place in our personal life and my brother's issues with him."

"But that was a big deal. Family's important."

"I understand that, but most couples find a balance. They co-exist so one half doesn't take precedence over the other."

"Fine." He drew in a breath and released it

slowly. "You're older now. Our age difference doesn't seem as significant as it once did."

"I'm thirty-seven. How is that any different from when you dumped me last year? You know what, forget it. The difference in our age was never important to me. You were the one who constantly worried about it."

She needed something more from him. Something substantial. Something he'd never given her before.

"What else? Something made you get in the car and drive here tonight."

His jaw clenched as he stared at her, his lips tight as if he forbade certain words to cross his tongue. It was amazing how much his silence could still injure her self-worth.

Shutting her eyes, she silently counted to ten. She'd told him he couldn't keep doing this. She promised herself she wouldn't allow him hurt her anymore. He needed to go.

"You have to leave."

Startled by her words, his eyes widened. "Why?"

"Because I'm with someone, Sawyer."

"Hughes?"

"Yes, and it's not fair for you to come here making promises you should have made years ago."

"But you said it wasn't serious."

She scoffed. "That was two months ago! Time moves on, whether *we're* on sabbatical or not."

"How serious is it?"

"Serious enough that I'll probably talk to him about this."

Panic flashed in his gaze. "He knows about us?"

She saw the moment he processed this as some sort of betrayal and she realized, for all his claims, things hadn't changed. "Yes."

"Then ... tell him you need time. Any gentleman would allow you that without pressuring you to—"

"No," she said quietly, cutting off his request. "I know what it's like to be cast aside, thinking everything's fine only to get blindsided by someone else's uncertainty. I won't do that to him."

Clearly, he hadn't expected such opposition. "Do you love him?"

Her molars locked. He had some nerve, tossing around words he couldn't say.

"I care for him."

"What you two have can't compare to what we've shared, Isadora. We have a history."

"What does that matter in regard to the future? Do you plan to marry me, Sawyer? Will you have children with me? Is that what you're offering?"

"I'm not sure children are possible at this stage."

"Charlie Chaplin would argue that."

"What man wants to be seventy-five when his child's just graduating high school?"

She gave a sad smile. "The irony of our situation is, had you asked me for more ten years ago, we could have had a flourishing family by now. But you never wanted more children or a second marriage. You only assumed I did. To be honest, I had no clue what I wanted at that point—aside from you.

"I was exhausted by my responsibilities, still raising Toni and always worrying about Lucian. I could've been happy just to be with you, but you kept us wrapped in this neat little box. Sometimes I was happy, inside of that box with you, but then..."

The memory of his past rejection stabbed deep. She loved him, would always love him, but he'd hurt her more than anyone else in this world. Perhaps that was always a risk when you trusted someone with your heart.

Collecting her composure, she blinked, only meeting his gaze when her vision cleared.

"There were times I had to sit back and watch you dine with other women, attending the same functions I attended. I let you get away with a lot when I was young, but I want more now. I want someone who's certain they want a life with me. Someone who doesn't see it as any sort of sacrifice. I don't want to negotiate my happiness and you can probably take credit for me finally realizing that."

"I know I've hurt you and I'm sorry," he whispered. "I never wanted things to get this complicated. I was only trying to protect you."

Maybe that was true, but she was never as threatened by others' opinions as he was. She never gave her reputation half the thought he did.

Years of feeling like she had some dirty secret to hide—like *she* was a dirty secret—had filled her with so much unnecessary shame and self-doubt. She couldn't go back to hiding.

Swallowing tightly, she gave him the painful truth. "I spent years being your kept secret out of respect for your insecurities. I'm not sure you ever considered mine. People have assumed I'm everything from frigid to gay, because my life with you has always been the clandestine reality of a paramour. Your wife passed away long ago, and I was nothing more than the mistress to her ghost."

"That's not true. You were always my first priority."

She scoffed. "Unless you count your colleagues, your social status, and your son."

"I was protecting you, bella."

"You were *hiding* me!"

"It wouldn't be like that now. I don't want to hide anymore."

She tilted her head back, trying to imagine how it would be. Would they live together? Would he put some large stone on her finger like a placeholder in a book, buying time without losing his spot? That's how he made her feel, like an unfinished novel, coveted yet cast aside over and over again, never truly loved to the end.

With a sad smile, she shook her head. "I'll always love you, Sawyer. But you were right. I deserve the real thing. I deserve the fairytale. I want a family of my own and I want the undying devotion of a man who relishes the idea of a future with me. I'd never beg that from any man. If it can't be given freely, I'd rather live alone. If anything, you've prepared me for that."

It was the hardest truth she'd ever come to

accept. Sawyer, Parker... It didn't matter. She wanted someone to love her without hesitation, without conditions. Irrevocably. Passionately. And eternally.

Anything less was just an illusion and as much as she despised feeling lonely, she'd rather be alone than give her life and heart to someone who couldn't give her all of theirs in return. She not only wanted but *deserved* the fairytale.

His gaze lowered to the floor, his posture one of dejected hope. "I made a lot of mistakes with us, bella. I didn't realize what I was doing..."

They were both to blame. "That's partly my fault. I was so desperate to have you—any part of you—I kept a lot of my feelings buried inside. But I want to be happy, Sawyer. I want the love of a man who doesn't need to be convinced I'm worth loving."

"And Hughes is willing to give you that?"

"This has nothing to do with him and everything to do with me."

He stepped forward and looked her in the eye. "I want to make you happy, Isadora. Whatever that takes. I believe I can. Give me another chance. At least think about my offer before you toss everything we've shared away."

His offer for a future with him, devoid of

offspring, ripe with recollections of a passionate start that cooled and heated so much over time that her body was growing immune to the burn?

"Sure, I'll think about it." Unfortunately, she wouldn't have a choice.

Years spent trying to forget him had proven he would always be a part of her, a tattoo on her soul, a scar on her heart, a sad smile on a lonely day. Regardless, she wasn't signing over her future to any man that couldn't admit he loved her.

The doorbell rang and she sighed. "You have to go."

He nodded, cupping her shoulders and leaning in to brush a kiss on her cheek. His arms held her in a brief hug. "Promise me you'll consider what I've said."

"I promise." The bell rang again and she pulled away. "Excuse me." She left the den, tucking away her consideration for a rainy day.

As she opened the front door Parker smiled and she struggled to find her earlier excitement. "Hey."

He pressed a kiss to her lips and paused, his body slightly tensing. Drawing back, he frowned. "What's wrong?"

Before she could explain, his gaze lifted

over her shoulder, his eyes narrowing. She turned and found Sawyer standing behind her in the foyer. Deflated, she sighed, pretty sure this night would not end the way she'd hoped.

"I was just leaving," Sawyer announced, stepping past them to get through the door. "I'll talk to you soon, Isa."

Parker silently watched as he walked to the car and drove away. "What was he doing here?"

"He just stopped by to talk."

"Are you okay?"

Uncomfortable with the situation, she moved to the hall table and inspected her purse, not looking for anything in particular. "Mm-hmm."

"Should I be concerned?"

"Nothing happened."

He stepped to her back, his hands gently resting on her shoulders. "Physically, you mean? I know that. I know you wouldn't cross that line without talking to me first. But that's not what I was asking."

Her hands were suddenly shaking. As calm as she'd held herself in Sawyer's presence, now that he was gone and Parker was there she trembled with uncertainty.

"He wanted to talk about us."

"Look at me, Isadora," he said softly, and

she turned. His brow pinched with obvious concern. "You can talk to me about him. I know he's important to you."

She shut her eyes, fighting the urge to cry or throw something. This wasn't how tonight was supposed to go. She didn't want to deal with these confusing feelings anymore.

"Hey." He pulled her into his arms and hugged her, balancing his chin on top of her head as her ear rested over his heartbeat. His lips pressed to her hair and he whispered, "It's okay. I'm not upset with you."

"I'm upset with myself."

"Why?"

"Because I feel like no matter what I do, I have no control over the direction of my life."

He led her to the steps and they sat down. Keeping his concerned gaze on her, he brushed her hair behind her ear.

"Maybe you're not supposed to have control. I'm not an expert, but maybe love isn't something you manage. Maybe it's something that happens *to you* whether you're ready or not. What does your gut tell you?"

She glanced up at him, amazed by how easily he could talk about her history with Sawyer and issues even Sawyer couldn't face.

"My instincts have never been dependable

where love's concerned. All I ever wanted was for someone to love me and now... My life's different. There's you and ... I'm not sure what he's looking for, and he keeps changing everything."

His eyes held a sort of sympathy that hurt more than his anger would have. She didn't want anyone's pity. She wanted to once and for all be in control of her own happiness.

It was wrong to discuss this with him. "I'm sorry—"

"Wait." He caught her hand. "I know you love him, Isadora. I'm not trying to erase that. But maybe the love he can offer isn't the sort of love you need any more."

Her face tipped away. Having never been loved, she wasn't so sure she had the right to be picky. "I don't know enough about love to know how it's supposed to feel."

"But you know what love should be. It should be so passionate, so blatant, there's no room for guessing. Love decides for us, not the other way around. It's everything we are and were and will be, folded into an emotion too powerful to control. You shouldn't have to stop and think *if* you still love someone. You either feel it or you don't."

"It's never been that easy for me. There are

always conditions."

"Then it's not an unconditional love. I think when you find the right person, everything else is proven wrong. True love should be the most real thing you know."

Maybe she didn't love anyone the way she should. It was too early to decide where things stood with Parker and possibly too late to fix things with Sawyer.

"I don't know what I'm doing."

He let out a slow breath. "Isadora, if you need time to figure things out, I can try to give you some space. I'm not sure how long I'll be able to stay away, but I can do my best if that's what you want."

She didn't want to waste any more time. She wanted to shut every complication out of her life and get lost in the present. She wanted to be happy and she had been, up until ten minutes ago.

Aggravated, she snapped, "This would never have happened if we hadn't run into him two months ago."

Parker arched a brow, appearing surprised by her anger. "I think Bishop's threatened. You're moving on and he sees that. He had years to get it right and he's terrified he blew it. I would be too if I were in his shoes."

His words were logical but depressing. She couldn't honestly say after everything Sawyer had put her through that it was over. No matter how much time passed or how many times they stumbled, he always seemed like an unfinished part of her life, an old habit she couldn't quit.

She rubbed her eyes and groaned. Confident women wouldn't put two seconds of thought into a man who broke their heart twice. "What's wrong with me?"

He laughed, not knowing how screwed up her line of thinking was. "Nothing's wrong with you. Someone just came into your home and left a bunch of shit at your door. There's no rule that says you have to do something just because someone else thinks you should."

She laughed without humor.

All of her life that was exactly what she'd done. Other people's choices always influenced her next move. She needed to be responsible for her own mistakes if she wanted to someday be able to take credit for her happiness.

He pulled her into another hug and pressed his lips to her neck. "Do you want me to kick his ass?"

She tsked and shoved him away. "Parker!"

He shamelessly smiled and shrugged. "I'd be entitled."

She hoped he was teasing her. "That's awfully territorial, considering we haven't even slept together, yet."

He chuckled. "Did you want to remedy that?"

She glanced up at him and pursed her lips, still unsure why they hadn't had sex yet. "Do *you?*"

He rolled his eyes. "I'm a guy, Isa. And you're a gorgeous woman. Of course, I *want* you." He dropped his brow to hers and smiled. "Very, *very* much."

He had a gift for making her blush. "You see, I knew that. Sometimes I doubt myself, but you never leave me guessing where we stand."

"Well, let me make it make it perfectly clear for you. I think of you first thing in the morning, you're a distraction I can't escape almost every passing minute of the day, and my last thought just before I fall asleep. I like having you in my life and I want to spend as much time together as possible. I don't care what we're doing so long as I get to be near you. And anyone who tries to get in the way of that is going to have a problem, be it Bishop or your brother or anyone else. I know exactly what I have with you and I'll be damned if *anyone* tries to steal it from me."

Inexperienced with that sort of possessiveness, she wasn't sure how to respond. It was nice to feel coveted, but maybe that was some sort of red flag women were supposed to shy away from.

She'd gone so long, never knowing which feelings to trust, it was a relief to have a man take such a direct approach. "I never had you pegged for a territorial guy."

"Maybe I never liked someone enough to feel that way. I just know I like you and the idea of anyone interfering with that makes me want to let the world know, right now, you're mine."

You're mine...

A shiver chased up her spine, triggering all sorts of warm sensations in her body. His confession didn't make her feel objectified. It made her feel safe and protected, like she could put down her worries and he'd guard her against anything or anyone that tried to cloud her vision.

She leaned into him, comforting herself as his heart beat steadily beneath her ear. "I like being yours."

His fingers tipped her chin so she was

looking at him. "Don't make me share you with someone who couldn't appreciate everything you are when he had the chance. You deserve more than that, Isa. I'm willing to give you more without asking for a single sacrifice in return."

Tightening her arms around his waist, she brushed her lips against his. She wanted more.

His mouth opened and his tongue softly caressed hers. She twisted against him, a needy pull starting low in her belly, and he slowly drew back.

"You're upset. Tonight's probably not a good night to make any big decisions."

Being let down after being lifted up, hurt. Rejection hurt. Upset or not, she wanted him. She didn't know how to make that more clear.

"Is it because he was here?"

"I don't like that he was in your house, but I know you didn't invite him. That doesn't negate the fact that I can smell his cologne on your skin."

She looked away. "I'm sorry."

"Don't apologize. I'm trying to do the right thing. That doesn't mean I don't want to strip you naked and slide my hands over every inch of your body until you smell like no one else but me. But the first time we're together, I don't want another man anywhere near either of our thoughts."

Did he think she could possibly mistake him for Sawyer? They were so different.

"I wouldn't be thinking of him."

"Tonight, but what about tomorrow and the next day? I'm a tolerant man, Isadora, but sleeping together changes things. It makes things a thousand times more personal. If we cross that line and he comes back here, I won't stand idly by. Sleeping together means we both want to move forward and leave the past behind. I don't know if you're ready to leave him behind."

She didn't burst out in disagreement because she wasn't sure either. Parker had been honest with her since the night she met him. She'd promised the same.

"I don't know what tomorrow will bring and I've never been able to control this hold he has over me. But maybe..."

Her damaged heart skipped a beat as she debated sharing her greatest vulnerabilities with him.

"No one's ever made me feel the way you have. I don't know what it's like to make love to someone who openly shares their feelings. It's scary and exciting and I want to know what it's like with you, not to compare, but to simply be with you, Parker."

"I want that too. Believe me, you're not the only one who wants to know what that's like."

It was a true show of the holes in his own past. This was new for both of them.

Sawyer had created a consequence that wasn't there this morning and she resented that. She didn't want to put things on pause with Parker because of ghosts from her past.

"Why can't we shut everything else out and make tonight just about us?"

His gaze bore into hers as his shoulders lifted with a long breath. "That won't erase my concerns. If we sleep together, I'm not sure I'll be able to handle him trying to sell you a different future tomorrow."

Her heart raced. Hearing him say his biggest concern was losing her made her realize just how much she didn't want to ever hurt him.

"He asked me to think about it." Maybe she already had. "This is where I want to be."

His gaze intensified, as he seemed to measure the truth of her words. "Are you sure? It might frighten you to see how territorial I can actually be."

"You won't scare me away, Parker. I'm a lot

tougher than people assume."

He smiled. "I know you're tough. But every guy has a beast inside of him. Trust me, I bite."

Not that she wanted to see him pushed that far, but the idea that losing her might cause some sort of animalistic response triggered a part of her feminine psyche. She nestled her nose to his throat and nipped his chin. "I bite too."

He groaned and drew back. "You make it really hard to do the right thing."

"Show me your beast, Parker." Her tongue made a slow glide over the stubble on his jaw. "And help me find mine."

Although their situations were different, if another woman ever tried to steal him she might truly reach a new level of ballistic.

She'd always preferred monogamy, but over the years her tolerance for even the slightest sense of someone threatening her happiness brought about a rage that she wasn't comfortable displaying or even acknowledging inside herself.

His hand went into her hair, his fingers tightening around a fistful of strands and angling her face toward his. He studied her through his lashes and whispered, "For all of your gentleness, Isa, I know there's a lioness hiding inside. I recognized your strength the second I crashed into you. But do you know what the difference is between a lioness and a woman?"

Breathing jaggedly with her throat exposed and her heart knocking against her ribs, her desire spiked even higher.

"What?"

"A lioness never has to remind others that she's a lion. She owns it, radiates courage, and no one ever doubts her confidence even when she's the most agile and graceful creature in the room."

Unable to take any more, she sealed her mouth to his, greedily taking, desperately wanting to let that part of her free. His hands were everywhere, dragging over her clothes and possessively holding her as close as their bodies would allow.

"Don't be shy with me," he rasped, his teeth pulling at her lips. "I want *all* of you. Every inch, every secret, every part they didn't get. Don't ever hide from me."

Straddling him on the steps, she drove her hands into his hair and showed him how much she wanted him with a kiss so raw, so passionate, his grip tightened to an almost bruising hold. Heat spread through her veins as she felt him harden beneath her.

"You have me," she whispered.

Lust tunneled through her blood like heroin as she hungrily tugged at his clothes, desperate to get to his skin. Enough worrying about consequences. She was through making apologies and fearing what others might think.

Parker wanted all of her. He saw beneath the superficial exterior and recognized parts of her soul no one else registered. He might not love her, but he *saw* her. The real her.

Her hand dragged over the bulge in his pants and he breathed deeply, groaning through their kiss. She slid off his lap into the space between his knees. Eyes on him, she reached for his belt and he caught her wrist.

"Do you want to go upstairs?"

She shook her head. She wanted him *now* and didn't want any more interruptions.

He released her wrist and eased back on the steps, his elbows resting at his sides, giving her free rein over his body. The buckle came undone and she tugged the leather free, tossing it to the floor. Her hands trembled as she unfastened his jeans, not out of nervousness, but excitement.

Warmth crested her cheeks as she reached

into his pants, her fingers curling around his thick erection as she slowly stroked. His breath left in a rush and he widened his knees. She nestled her body between his thighs and traced her lips over the smooth tip of his cock.

"Jesus, Isadora..."

Hunger pulsed through her, tugging low in her belly. This wasn't something she had a lot of experience doing, being that Sawyer rarely asked it of her. But this was Parker and she didn't want this side of their relationship to be some polite interaction between them. She wanted to give him everything she had and say to hell with grace and poise.

"Will you tell me how you like it?"

"You'll know."

Trusting his answer, she closed her eyes and took him deep into her mouth. He sucked in a sharp breath, his hand shifting to the back of her neck.

He grunted as she tried to fit all of him. "Slow. Keep going. You're almost there..."

When she made it to the root of his cock he sighed, his fingers massaging the back of her neck as she slowly pulled back.

She continued to stroke him, her mouth pulling up and down with long, tight motions. Her fingers cupped him and his grip tightened on her neck, pressing her even lower in a silent request for more.

When she fussed to get her hair out of her face, he gathered the strands into his fist. "Don't stop."

His words slithered into her, tightening her body and slicking her sex. She took him to the deeper, now moving faster, each stroke of her tongue a bit more brazen than the last.

His groans escaped in panted breaths as his hold on her hair tightened, tingles skating over her scalp. He shifted, lifting his hips, thrusting to the back of her throat.

He never lost control when they fooled around, but she sensed he was close to losing it now. A trickle of arousal teased her sex and she sucked harder.

"Fuck," he cursed, withdrawing from her mouth and rising to his feet.

Keeping hold of her hair again, he gripped his cock and guided her mouth back to him. Greedily, hungrily, she sucked him. Her fingers dug into his thrusting hips as he drove toward the back of her throat.

A pulse trembled through the thick vein of his cock and she moaned, tasting him on her tongue. He pulled her back, yanking the straps of her camisole down with her bra, exposing her bare breasts. He gripped his flesh, tugging hard and quick, panting with each frenzied pull, and she gasped as heat streaked her chest in a burst of pure, unrefined, carnal lust.

Her eyes widened as she stared down at her breasts drizzled in his release. He caught his weight on the banister and panted.

In the distant corner of her mind, she relished the fact that he'd ruined her camisole in a fit of passion, and luxuriated in his marked desire running down her chest.

His eyes found hers and a slow smile curled his lips. "You have about five seconds to change your mind, because as soon as I can feel my legs again I'm coming after you and tearing every square inch of clothing off your body with my teeth. One..."

Her heart was a throbbing mess. "Do you intend to chase me?"

He chuckled and rubbed his eyes. "Running will only make me want you more. Two..."

Smiling, her excitement doubled. She had three seconds to get to her bed or she had no doubt he'd be fucking her on those cold marble steps.

She shakily stood and he arched a brow, accepting his challenge. "Three."

"Four." He panted.

Edging around him on the steps, she smirked and whispered, "Five."

He growled and caught her so fast she hardly saw him move. His tongue stole into her mouth, demanding and full of dirty intentions. Her back arched against his arm as he leaned into her.

"You're never getting away now."

She nipped at his lips, digging her nails into his shoulders. "Who says I want to?"

He growled, his hand sliding into the back of her pants and grabbing a handful of flesh. "You're so fucking sexy. I'm taking you to bed, woman."

Slipping her hand into his, she gave his arm a tug. "Follow me." She showed him to her room, but felt suddenly shy once they crossed the threshold.

No! Her heart skipped a beat as she feared the same inadequacy she'd battled in the past had returned. But as she glanced at him her worry faded. This was Parker.

He sent her a sidelong glance and stripped off his clothes, placing them on the chair by the fireplace and never taking his smoldering gaze off of her. "You're blushing."

"You're naked." She was nervous, but had

no intention of backing out. She slid off her camisole and met his stare.

His mouth twisted into a full on arrogant, male grin. "And wondering why you're not."

"Maybe I like the thought of you using your teeth."

His eyes darkened and she laughed as he stalked closer, backing her toward the bathroom. His hand snaked out and caught her bra strap, tugging her back to his chest as he bit down on her shoulder.

He gripped her sticky breast, his other hand unfastening her pants. "Get these off."

Shimmying out of her pants and kicking off her sandals, she felt his arousal pressing into her. He unhooked her bra and tossed it to the floor, his fingers shoving into the front of her panties as he corralled her toward the bathroom.

He teased her sex, his mouth pulling at her throat and spreading kisses across her shoulders. Withdrawing his hand, he twisted her to face him and lifted her hips. She gasped as he set her on the cool porcelain surface of the vanity.

Wrenching her knees apart, he jerked her hips forward and dropped to his haunches. His fingers tugged the gusset of her panties aside and his tongue was on her again, flicking her clit as she arched in pleasure.

Her fingers scrabbled for purchase as her body was assaulted with determined lashes of his tongue. He penetrated her with a finger that quickly became two. He wasn't gentle but he seemed to know her limits and pushed her right to the edge.

He teased a sensitive spot deep inside of her. Her cries pitched high as his mouth closed over her clit and pulled, nibbling deliciously as her body throbbed against his tongue.

"I plan to wear you the way you're wearing me."

Her eyes widened, never having been made such a suggestive promise in her life. Without waiting for a response, he buried his fingers inside of her and used his other hand to rub her clit hard and fast.

Her mouth opened on a long moan, driven so high it hardly made a sound. Her body locked and her release broke free. It was beyond her knowledge how he got her to climax like that. Shocked at her body's response she gasped and tried to cover herself.

He grinned, a flash of teeth showing virile satisfaction only a man could own. "No hiding," he growled, dragging her hands away.

She could barely catch her breath. "I've never done that before," she panted, her drenched thighs trembling.

"Well, you're about to do it again."

He hooked his fingers deep and pumped hard. Her objection garbled into a deep moan as another release ripped free, just as forceful as the one before.

How was he doing that? How was *she* doing that?

His palm folded over her sex, gliding over her pulsing clit and up her jittery belly. Rising, his body pressed against hers, his erection dragging hard and heavy over her softer parts, until his mouth sealed to hers in a mind-spinning kiss.

She tasted herself on his tongue and he kissed her so deeply it seemed that was his intention. His hand never left her as his tongue drove her to a point of no return.

"So. Fucking. Sexy."

She couldn't form a response because he'd turned her brain into mush.

His grin twisted as a challenging glint flashed in his eyes.

"Give me another one," he demanded, slipping his fingers back inside of her.

Still recovering, she gasped. "I can't." Her

body slouched against the mirror, her lips trembling as she caught her breath.

Where had he learned to do that? Even his kisses had escalated to a degree of intensity she'd never experienced before.

"You can." He pinched her nipple and her eyes flew open. "You're a *lioness*."

Even here, in this mix of lust and carnality, he lifted her up, told her how strong and sexy she was. This was not a silent refuge for them to escape. Parker, for all of his quiet control and patience, hid a world of sensuality and sin behind his composure.

The seductive way he stared into her eyes was her undoing. Breathing heavily, she widened her knees.

"That's my girl, my fierce little lioness." His head dipped, his tongue swiping across her throat and traveling between her breasts.

She gasped. Every touch was divine and astoundingly skilled, taking her places she'd never gone.

He was relentless, pumping, rubbing, *slapping* her sensitive flesh. His words kept coming. Commands and questions flinging from his lips, lit by a fire in his eyes.

"Let me hear you... Mmm, you want more,

don't you? Tell me how bad you want to come again."

"Please, Parker. Don't stop…"

Acute pleasure spiraled and flowed through her limbs, as another orgasm gushed from her. He licked along her sensitive inner thigh as if she were wearing the nectar of the gods.

His intense stare lifted to her face. "Beautiful."

Gentling his touch, he kissed her tender folds. She jerked at the softest swipe of his tongue, her skin exquisitely sensitive and unable to tolerate any more pleasure.

"Shh." He guided her legs over his shoulders, his fingers delicately curving around her hips. "Just relax now."

His hair tickled her thighs as his eyes closed and he returned to her sex, his touch incredibly soft and sensual, a gentle slide and tease of lips and tongue that eased her back down to earth.

His fingertips coasted over her belly where muscles jumped and danced. Looking down, the vision of him between her thighs, hands petting her… It stole her breath away.

Her nipples ruched and throbbed, dark and needy. Her body looked unfamiliar, wanton, sexy, alive. It was as if he made her blood purr.

Shutting her eyes she moaned, falling into his languid seduction and letting her head loll. Lips kissed from her inner thigh to her knee. She was in some sort of sex trance. Her bones were liquid and her flesh hot.

She watched him through her lashes, certain she'd never seen a man so sexy. Perhaps the most erotic thing about Parker was how innocent he looked on the outside. She'd never see him that way again.

Even here, he liked to play. But here she also got his intense side. Muscle, sinew, lust, desire. All that he was, seeped into his every touch. He possessed her. Owned her.

Easing back, he grinned, eyes brimming with self-satisfied male ego. When he rose to his full height, it was impossible to ignore how hard he was.

Yes, he definitely had *everything*.

Parker chuckled and held out a hand. "Ignore it. Let's shower."

It took her a moment to find her balance. As he adjusted the water she admired his backside. It seemed unnatural for a man to have such a perfectly tight ass. He was so fit and lean, but there was a bulk of muscle hiding beneath the surface.

Her mouth slowly curved into an appreciative smile. *If I'm his, then he's mine.*

She caressed his back and wrapped her arms around his waist, leaning into his strength. *Mine.* Yes, she liked the sound of that very much.

He turned and kissed her slowly. "We're not finished yet."

She gazed up at him through drowsed eyes. "I think you have the nicest ass I've ever seen."

He laughed, his entire face coming alive. "You clearly haven't seen yours." He squeezed her cheek and growled. "*That* is a perfect ass."

Steam filled the bathroom and she shivered. He guided her into the shower and followed. Their bodies were sticky and ripe with the scent of sex.

Dear God, they hadn't even *had* sex yet.

Parker's hands lifted her breasts, stroking her heavy flesh with suds and pressing his front to her back. She smirked, leaning her weight into his strength as she felt his desire physically and emotionally. He certainly didn't tire easily.

Resting her head on his shoulder, she sighed and let him bathe her. Her smile held as she let him take over. It was going to be a long and incredible night.

> *"He is a king, a wild lion who owns every day and all hours of the nights, but his strength makes him the loneliest lion of all. Even the intimidating creatures desire love."*
>
> Shamus Callahan

AS ISADORA RESTED against Parker in the shower, her inhibitions washed away. She sighed as he tended to her body, each stroke of his hand soothing her and pulling her deeper into a state of utter contentment.

"I don't know if I should be intimidated or

excited about the rest of the night," she confessed breathily, as he rinsed her torso.

He chuckled and nibbled the lobe of her ear. "What do you mean?"

She stretched against him. "You're very talented. For someone who claims they've only loved one other person, you sure know your way around a woman's body."

The steady motion of his hands stilled for a beat and he cleared his throat. "Let's not get too detailed about the people from our past. I think it's best to leave them there."

She frowned. Parker was usually so open with her about everything. Maybe he was right and their histories should remain private, but she caught a hint of shame in his voice, which contradicted his typical easy tone.

A terrible thought occurred. "Oh God, was it Evelyn?"

"What? No! God, no. Scout and I shared *maybe* a couple of awkward kisses and that was it."

Her relief was short lived. "Then who?"

His touch fell away as she felt his emotional withdrawal. She turned to face him, the water spraying at her back. It wasn't like him to hold secrets—a positive attribute she didn't want to change.

"Parker, I understand if you'd rather keep our pasts private, but... You're being weird, like you're hiding something."

His mouth tightened and he glanced away. "There was a woman. She wasn't someone I was particularly close to, but she taught me how to do certain things."

Why would that make him appear ashamed? She suspected he'd been with women before. Brushing the topic aside, she nodded and finished washing.

As she rinsed out her hair he soaped up his body, but the mood had shifted. He no longer reached for her or looked at her. As a matter of fact, he seemed to be purposefully looking away.

Shutting off the water, she handed him a towel and frowned when he took it without comment, his focus anywhere but on her. Confused by the sudden change in him, she took a moment to comb the tangles out of her hair and then followed him to the bedroom.

He sat with his back to her on the edge of the bed. The atmosphere chilled considerably and her concern grew.

"Parker?"

"Yeah?" he answered, still not focused.

She moved to the corner of the bed to read

his expression, but he was just staring off into space. "You're being quiet."

Lines of tension bracketed his mouth as his shoulders rose with a deep breath. "Come sit for a minute, Isadora. I need to talk to you."

Despite his request, her feet refused to move. Nothing in his tone told her what he had to say was good. This was it. This was the moment every illusion shattered and she learned—*again*—the dangers of trusting someone with her heart.

Her chest tightened as she prepared for some sort of blow, familiar with how hard an unexpected shift could hurt. "What is it?"

He sighed when he understood she wouldn't sit. His gaze rested on her face and she remained braced for anything.

He drew in a deep breath. "I want you to know I've been with my fair share of women, but I've always used protection. *Always.*"

"Okay."

That wasn't too bad. He obviously had some experience. She took a baby step closer, but still hesitated. Should she tell him she'd never used condoms with Sawyer?

"What if I can't claim the same?"

His gaze held hers, but she didn't sense any judgment. "With Bishop?"

She nodded. "There was only one other person, but he and I only slept together once and we used protection."

He glanced at his lap, his expression one of deep concern that she suspected had nothing to do with her. "I'm not really worried about you. Everyone at Leningrad had a great medical package and I'm pretty sure Bishop wouldn't do anything to put you in harm's way. I'm more concerned about my own past."

"Why?"

He looked to the wall, just past her shoulders. "There were people, some names I can't recall. It's not something I'm proud of, and I hate that we have to have this conversation, but I want to be honest with you."

"Have you been to a doctor?"

He nodded. "Yes. I've had my blood work run several times over the past two years and it always comes back clean. My doctor assures me if I'd contracted anything from when I was younger it would have shown up by now, but it still freaks me out."

Okay, maybe this was just a source of embarrassment from his past. She could deal with that. "Why? If your tests are clean, so are you."

"I don't know how to explain it without repulsing you, so I'm just going to come out and say it. When I was on the streets, every other person was sick with something. I was selective, but there was no way to be sure. Then after I got off the streets, there was the woman I told you about. She wasn't someone I dated. She was someone I ..." His jaw ticked. "Hired."

Her head cocked to the side as she processed his words. "A..." She had a hard time saying the word. She'd lived such a sheltered life she never even saw one.

"Prostitute." He spat, clearly bothered by the term. "Before her, it had always been quick, an itch that needed to be scratched. But I wanted to know what it was like for regular people. I wanted to know how it felt to hold a woman—so one day I could."

"But you did more than just hold her?"

He nodded and she closed the distance between them, sitting beside him on the bed. So he'd never made love to a woman he actually cared about, was that what he was telling her?

"Sometimes sex is more of an emotional need than a physical one, Parker. I think it's understandable that you'd want to know what that's like."

"But it wasn't real. It was a job for her and I knew it all along. It bothers me."

"Why?" She could come up with several

reasons it would, but she was more interested in his explanations.

"Because it's a constant reminder of where I've been." He looked at her, his brows pulling tight. "And then I meet you, and you're this gorgeous woman who has her life together and has never known anything other than a gentle hand. You deserve to be—"

"Wait," she interrupted, not wanting him to join the ranks of others that assumed they had her all figured out. "Before you finish that sentence, let me assure you that I *do not* have my life together and the last thing I need is to be coddled.

"I appreciate you telling me about your past, Parker, but you've done the responsible thing and I don't think your concern's necessary. You're right, I've never really known anything other than a gentle hand, but I'm not as fragile as everyone thinks. I can handle this. It's not going to take away from how I feel about you."

His mouth formed a flat line as his brow creased. "I know you're strong. But you *are* fragile. I *never* want to be the cause of your tears. Part of the reason I waited so long for us to sleep together has a lot to do with my fear that I'm not good enough for you."

Her head tilted as so many things finally made sense.

"Parker," she said softly, turning his chin so she could see his eyes. "I feel like I've been on a pedestal all my life, never taken down, just moved from one tall place to another, be it for my name, or my social status, or the fact that..." Pain tightened her chest and her voice seized. "The fact that my lover saw me as some crime he couldn't help but commit.

"You say I'm beautiful, but it will always mean more when you tell me I'm witty or you laugh at my stupid jokes. I can actually take credit for those things. I like being with you, because you're the first man who sees *me* just the way I am. I'm no better than anyone else and you're the first man who's actually treated me like an equal. Don't change that. Don't doubt who you are or what you deserve. You're an incredible man."

They were silent for a long moment. Slowly, his hand reached for hers and their fingers laced together, his grip closing tightly around hers.

"It's hard sometimes, because I look at you and I'm just ... staggered. You're exquisite, Isadora. It's impossible to ignore. And you're good. You have this gentleness about you that draws me in. I don't want to ruin anything, because I'm pretty certain this relationship is the best thing I've had in a very long time—possibly ever."

His words were too much. "Parker..."

"I know I'm baring my soul here and it's probably freaking you out, but it's the truth. In the last month, I've started seeing you in everything I do. You're always on my mind. Every time I kiss you I feel like I'm part of some trick, unable to make sense of how I got so lucky. I never thought..." He shook his head and swallowed. "When your brother told you about me, I figured that was it. I'm so used to losing what's important. I don't want to lose *you*."

Her heart pounded. Each word burrowed deeper and deeper into parts of her soul she hadn't even realized were empty. Her vision blurred, but she didn't want to cry in front of him. Casually, she turned away and wiped her eyes.

She didn't know how to respond to so many sweet words, unsure how anyone could think that much of her. She was speechless.

Knowing she had to say something, she focused on the simplest thing to process out of everything he'd said. "Lucian and I don't always agree."

"You have no idea how glad I am for that." He took a deep breath. "Just ... please, keep in mind that my past isn't a blank slate as far as relationships go, okay?"

A man was actually sharing his vulnerabilities with her. If he only knew how much that added to his character, how much his honesty meant to her.

"Despite our different upbringings, I think we're both a little bit hardened and fragile and a little bit clueless as far as normal is concerned."

The corners of his mouth turned up with a slow smile. "I guess we are."

"We'll just have to be patient with each other. I trust you, Parker."

He let out a long breath and laughed. "How do you make me feel like the most powerful man in the world *and* the most breakable?"

She understood that more than he probably realized. "You know, I never imagined anything like this. When I bumped into you—well, crashed—I was literally dying inside, silently swearing I was finished with men. Sometimes I wonder if it was fate that you were standing around that corner at that very moment. Not only did you save me that night, you showed me how to laugh again, how to take a chance with my heart again. I'm breakable too, but the way you make me feel... It's unlike anything I've ever felt."

He kissed her, slow and passionately. When he pulled away, his fingers teased through her damp hair. "I think, even if this somehow broke me, I wouldn't be able to let you go. Thanks for not listening to everyone when they warned you away from me."

She pressed her lips to his and smiled. "Not everyone says terrible things about you. Just Lucian."

He chuckled. "Somehow his opinion seems the equivalent of a hundred men."

"Let's both agree to never tell him you said that. His ego's big enough."

"Deal."

Her lust was replaced with something more meaningful. Trust. Friendship. An alliance of two orphaned souls that seemed destined to cross paths.

Leaning into him, she did her best to explain everything he made her feel. "There are a *lot* of attractive qualities in you, Parker. Don't ever doubt that."

He pulled her into a hug and they fell to their sides on the mattress. His gaze stayed on her face as he whispered, "When I was young I had to hide any signs of weakness. Then as I got older I had to hide my past. I don't want to hide from you. Maybe that's foolish, but you make me feel like I can just ... be. I've never had that with anyone before."

She thought about her past with Sawyer and how they ended things after she found out he'd kept a secret from her. But she hadn't always been honest with him either.

So much of their relationship endured for the simple fact that she kept her deepest desires to herself. There were so many things she sacrificed just to be with him and they were never together the way normal couples were.

"You don't have to hide who you are from me," she whispered, her fingers entwining with his. "Hiding only hurts in time. I'll show you who I am if you promise to always show me the real you."

He gave her hand a squeeze. "You have a deal."

As they lay in silence, her mind turned over all the things he'd said to her tonight. Earlier, he'd tapped into some possessive part of her, but now... Now she suffered a different type of possessiveness, the sort that made her want to protect him, shelter him from anyone that came close to hurting him. She wanted to give him things he never had and she hoped every part of their relationship stayed as genuine as it felt right now.

He was nothing like Sawyer and somehow that was a good thing. Parker was open and honest and looking for something significant in a cold world, a place to belong where he only needed to be himself. She wanted the same.

She actually felt sorry for every person who ever met him, because they probably missed how incredible the real Parker was. But *she* saw him.

"Parker?"

"Hmm?" He looked at her, their eyes only a few inches apart.

"Make love to me. I want you to hold me and I want to wake up in your arms."

His expression shifted and she knew he understood what she was asking. She wanted him, emotionally, physically, and romantically. This was not an itch to be scratched. This was a desire to know him the way no one else ever had.

"You'll be my first."

Lifting her hand, she slowly traced a finger along his jaw. She smiled, giving him the same words he told her on their first date.

"Firsts are important. They set a precedence for everything that follows. Let your heart lead. Somewhere in the middle, it'll find mine."

He looked into her eyes as if he could see something far off, something that made him smile and caused his hand to tighten around hers. "I wonder if it already has."

Part Two

Him

"It is a far, far better thing that I do than I have
ever done;
It is a far, far better rest that I go to than I have
ever known."
Charles Dickens
A Tale of Two Cities

SHE WAS soft and gentle and kind and
good. She was everything he never imagined
having, which was probably why he felt like a
thief in the night, taking what he had no right
to touch.

But here she was, staring into his eyes after

he bared the darkest spots of his soul, asking him to make love to her.

He'd hesitated, fearing this moment would mark the end of them. But now he felt like his life was just beginning.

It seemed an ongoing struggle, coming to terms with the direction his life had taken since St. Christopher's. After getting off the streets, his days always struck him as a partial illusion, the surreal never amounting to any level of true satisfaction. Discontent had ridden him hard and, after only a short time, he'd lost interest in the games.

But Isadora was everything real. She satisfied parts of him he assumed would die of starvation. She brought him back to life, brought actual feelings to the surface, and made it impossible to hide. He desperately needed to hold onto whatever this connection was they shared.

There was no quelling the desires she stirred in him. From the first time they met, he was captivated by her beauty and knocked back by her personality. She was—to his way of thinking—perfect.

She was so put together. Mature yet childlike. There was an innocence about her that called to him. He wanted to guard it and nurture it and covet it. He loved that others didn't seem to know that side of her existed.

Equally attractive was her indulgent ambition, the side of her that rose to a challenge like a gentle wind, but built with the energy of a hurricane. She was a force of nature, a woman who redefined beauty and wore sincerity like a second skin. Her intoxicating blend of innocence, boldness, and modesty disarmed him.

He wanted to give her everything, wanted to trust that she wouldn't recoil as he unveiled his deepest secrets. It was a big step, putting his heart in another person's hands.

His background was tarnished, but she never judged him for the things that had been outside of his control or the things that weren't. Her acceptance of him just the way he was, seemed the greatest gift anyone had ever offered. And he wanted to protect that gift, never give her a reason to regret trusting a man who had done nothing to earn her faith.

A carnal fire burned so hotly in his blood, he could do no less than worship her. He wanted no barriers between them, knew in that moment he was crossing into uncharted territory. Maybe they both were and that was why this felt so monumental.

The breath in his lungs left in a rush as he

glimpsed her shy innocence, bolstered by re-fined courage as she reached for him.

He swallowed hard, but couldn't catch his breath as her towel slid open.

She was so goddamn beautiful, so incredibly loving and caring, he couldn't believe she'd made it this far without a ring on her finger. Their gazes tangled in a slow smolder that never waned.

His mind jerked back to the start of their evening, a sudden tension locking in his bones as he recalled the look in her eyes when she confessed everything Bishop had offered her. The threat of another man stealing her away made this moment all the more significant.

"Kiss me," she whispered.

His mind shifted through every overwhelming emotion she stirred in him, reluctance warring with want, as he considered how this would change things, make her impossible to give up.

"You're sure this is what you want?"

"I'm sure." Her fingers traced over his chest where his heart raced wildly.

She was all white lace and purity. He was a hodgepodge of mistakes, tainted by bad choices and thoughtless actions. If he could take it back, he'd erase every smear on his character —for her.

Shadows passed over her delicate features. Her scent crawled into him, luring him in until her warm mouth met his. A hunger flooded his veins as he pulled her closer, his grip tightening for fear she might slip away.

Take it slow. Don't rush her...

Her fingers brushed softly over his as she guided his hand upward to cup her curves. Pulling her beneath him, he pressed his weight into her. The rightness of her warm welcome was his undoing and his body trembled with sharp desire.

She gazed up at him, soft and wanton, her lips trailing across his bare shoulder as he pressed his mouth to her thrumming pulse. Stretching her hands onto the downy pillows, her nipples peaked, scrapping sensually against his chest. Her legs coiled with his, his towel slipping away, as the heat of her body burned through him.

"Isadora," he whispered, wishing he knew how to tell her how much she truly meant to him.

Beautiful, taut nipples beaded tightly, as he trailed his mouth down her throat, breathing in the scent of her hair and delicate skin. His lips grazed her breasts, and she arched into him, her soft, keening breaths building to a staccato call.

Swirling his tongue, his lips closed tightly over the tip. Wet heat dragged hotly over his flesh as her lower body coiled around him, dragging, rocking, tempting...

His kisses traveled lower, skimming down her flat belly, as his body grew heavy, seeking her warmth. He gently nipped her side with his teeth and she giggled, the sound so delicate and feminine his heart nearly buckled in his chest.

The air thickened with the scent of her arousal, driving his senses wild with lust as he pressed a kiss to her hip, brushing his cheek down her thigh and breathing in the fragrance of her there.

He urged himself to take it slow, but everything inside of him wanted her *now*. His tongue slid in a savoring glide over her clit and she drew in an audible breath, opening for him. He teased her folds with careful strokes, his own body hard and ready, pulsing with anxious need to take her, possess her, make her irrevocably his.

Slow...

She stretched and keened, each kiss coaxing a plea from her lips for more.

His desire built and built, urging him on.

His need to possess her was perhaps the most frightening instinct he'd ever known, yet somehow he maintained control.

The yearning to know her heart overshadowed his greedy sense of urgency. He wanted more than just her body. He wanted her soul.

Broken syllables fell from her lips as he stroked her. Her channel tightened around his touch and she came on a breathy sigh, her sex pulsing with soft tremors.

"Parker... Please..."

Sliding up her body, he kissed her long and slow. "Can you feel how much I want you, Isa?"

"Yes."

His hands trembled as he caressed her face, touched her hair, and stared into her eyes.

"So much." The raw truth of that statement knocked something loose in his chest. "Never doubt how much."

Their connection wasn't one-sided, but her feelings weren't as developed as his. She had others, a family and so much love surrounding her. He had only her, but he desired the connectivity of a loving family as much as any human being. And he wanted to find that connection with her. In time.

Reaching to his wallet on the nightstand,

he situated himself with a condom. The pounding of his heart turned to an erratic drumbeat, not from exertion, but from bearing the weight of this moment, its implication inescapable.

This woman had somehow become his every waking thought, his deepest dream, and his compass in a dark and lonely world. He was falling in love with her, and that sense of falling eclipsed every emotion he knew.

Resting over her, their bodies aligned as he framed her face with trembling hands, brushing her dark, chestnut hair back so he could look into her eyes. Everything inside of him wanted to confess his feelings, but he held back.

Everything he dared to love in the past was stolen from him in the blink of an eye. Saying the words out loud seemed a blatant invitation for a cruel fate to snatch away his happiness once more.

He brushed his lips against hers, trying so hard to show her everything she made him feel without tempting fate. "Look at me, Isa."

Her lashes flickered and her dark eyes softened. She brushed a hand down his cheek and pressed her lips to his. "I'm with you, Parker. I trust you."

Knowing trust was the singular, most essential part of love, he let her words settle his nerves. As his fingers curled over her hip, memorizing every slope and curve, his body pressed into her tight heat and his lashes lowered on a deep sigh.

She arched closer as he filled her, a delicate moan crossing her lips as her hands fluttered to his shoulders, nails pressing lightly into his skin.

"You feel so good," she rasped. "So right."

Unable to speak, he kissed her jaw, his mouth tracing her rapid pulse as her body tightened in soul-shattering welcome. His head fell to her shoulder as he breathed through the incredible connection.

"Just give me a second."

Her fingers gently sifted through his hair, holding him. "I'm not going anywhere."

The words weren't spoken as any real guarantee, but they satisfied his deepest longing to never let her go. His cock swelled as possessive intent unleashed inside of him. She was his and no one was taking her away from him.

He drew back and thrust deep. Her head tipped as she gasped, her fingers scraping down his arms as she pressed closer, taking him even deeper.

Mine.

Hungrily stroking in and out, skin slick, they watched each other closely, an unexamined emotion seeming to pass between them. It wasn't about reaching the end. It was about savoring the journey. Marking time and claiming his woman.

He cherished every second, loving her well, caressing every exposed bit of flesh until he lost track of where she ended and he began. Heated cries and gasps of pleasure peppered the air. Her sex contracted, pulling him deeper with every flutter, gripping him as he held her trembling body tight. The sultry space warmed around them, cradling them in a sweltering blanket of unrepentant lust.

Mine!

She became an instrument, a beautiful song that kept time to the beat of his heart. Pleading, sighing, calling his name. She was the sexiest woman to ever walk the face of this earth and she was in his arms, taking him places he'd never gone.

He's never getting her back...

Nerves raw and exposed, muscles quivering, his release left him in the wake of countless shivers. His breath shuddered as their limbs knotted together as one.

It was dangerous to care this much for another person. He'd learned that lesson early on in life. But no matter how he tried, no matter how hard he willed himself to take it slow, he knew there would be no undoing the imprint Isadora left on his soul.

She was an addiction he couldn't resist falling into, a breaking point between his solitary existence and a possible partnership, a beautiful sense of home felt only in her presence. He'd surrender every pleasure to keep her. There would be no letting go of her. His Isadora.

> *"Sometimes I worry our past will follow us like a shadow we can't escape, dark, looming, always a little bigger than we actually are."*

Scout

IN A PEACEFUL SLEEP, Parker's subconscious prickled before his eyes opened. The sense of being watched slithered through him and he only spared a second to take a deep breath before catapulting into self-defense mode.

Bolting upright, he cocked back and took aim. A sharp intake of breath—Isadora's gasp —jerked his brain into the present and his surroundings registered.

The thud of his heart competed with the sharp intake of her panted breaths. Regret seeped through him, washing away the remnants of slumber, and leaving him positioned like a fool with his fist in the air.

Muscles flexed, he focused on uncoiling the tension in his shoulders and forcing his fist to drop. Isadora watched him with large unblinking eyes as she cowered at the edge of the bed, her body twisted into the pose of a frightened child.

His fingers unlocked, and he slowly showed his palms, fingers splayed wide and unthreatening. "I'm sorry."

Her brow twitched, but she made no other move to show she heard his apology. Her body language remained distrustful and rightly so. He'd drawn back ready to kill someone. What the fuck was wrong with him? He stumbled off the mattress, giving her space.

The tense set of her shoulders loosened only after he staggered a good six feet from the bed. More than the startled look in her eyes was the shocked uncertainty of someone who had their trust shaken.

Giving his head a hard shake, he roughly rubbed his face. "I'm sorry. I forgot where I was..." Fuck! It wasn't a nightmare, just more fucked up baggage he'd assumed he'd let go years ago. It wasn't about her.

Keeping a safe distance, he calmly tried to explain. "I'm used to sleeping alone."

He hardly recognized the thready rasp of his voice. Distrust clouded her expression, ripping through his chest with a sharp ache.

"I wouldn't hurt you, Isadora." He hadn't hurt her. He'd snapped out of it in time to realize he was safe. But he didn't feel safe now.

What if he found control two seconds too late? Just enough time to prove she was sharing her bed with a guy from the wrong side of the tracks. Fuck!

He wouldn't blindly swing at her. It was just an old habit—one he thought was dead and buried. He hadn't hurt her.

Fear lingered in her dark eyes, filling him with self-loathing and the all-consuming worry he'd just ruined everything. Mortified, he took a small step forward only to freeze in his tracks as she drew her body back, away from him.

"I didn't mean to scare you."

She had to know that. He would *never* lay a hand on her or purposely frighten her. The idea of hurting her made him sick to his stomach.

But how would she know that? Everything they had was based on blind trust. All he had to do was *show* her Lucian was right and she could bolt.

Breathless with fear, he looked away. Actions always spoke louder than words, but this was an accident. A reflex. "I'd never hurt you, Isa."

She didn't move from the edge of the bed, but tilted her chin toward her chest and whispered, "You were going to *hit* me."

He shook his head adamantly. "I wouldn't hit you. Ever."

Her shoulders remained locked, her hands behind her hips supporting her weight as her knees pressed together in a self-protective pose. "I was just watching you sleep."

His mouth tightened with distaste. Normal guys didn't flip out when their girlfriends watched them. What the hell was wrong with him?

"I know. I'm sorry."

He didn't want to start the day with recollections of his past. He wanted to hold her and enjoy her, yet he couldn't stop corroding normal moments with the filth of his unsavory background.

Last night was supposed to be perfect, and it was until he had to do the right thing and tell her he had the track record of a junkyard dog. Now this?

Eventually, he'd reach her limit and she'd see he wasn't worth her trouble. He just wanted to be normal and have an ordinary fucking life!

He needed a moment to find his bearings, and by the look on her face, so did she. "I'm going to go wash up. Please ... just ... don't go anywhere."

She nodded, but didn't move from the corner of the bed. Her gaze followed him as he stalked to the bathroom.

Shutting himself inside, he braced his palms on the vanity and glared at his reflection. Muscles taut, he clenched his teeth. If anything like that happened again, he couldn't continue to stay the night with her, at least not until he was certain his old demons were out of his system—which he'd stupidly assumed they were.

He was not a violent person, but kick a

kind dog long enough and it would eventually bite. His earlier years quickly taught him to never leave himself vulnerable. There was nothing more vulnerable than a young orphan sleeping in an abandoned mill full of derelicts and thieves and perverts.

In the past, he'd woken up to his possessions gone, strangers rummaging through whatever belongings he'd scavenged the day before, and, worst of all, predators pushing their luck on his defenseless body.

It was literally beaten into him to wake up swinging and ask questions later. But Isadora wasn't a predator or a thief. She was his girlfriend.

Shutting his eyes, his breathing gradually settled. "Jesus."

He cleaned himself up and warily returned to the bedroom. Isadora had moved back to the head of the bed and sat cross-legged with her back to the pillows. As he met her gaze she pulled the sheet defensively higher on her chest. Her eyes reflected misgivings that hadn't been there last night.

Sighing, he paused at the foot of the bed. "I can go."

"I don't want you to go."

"Well..." It was as if she'd put a shield

around herself. "Could you please stop looking at me like that? I forgot where I was and I..." His shoulders drooped. There was no excuse. "I'm gonna go."

"Wait," she leaned forward and paused, worrying her lip. "Does that always happen?"

His dry chuckle was full of self-loathing. How should he know? He hadn't slept beside someone in ages, and he'd never slept beside someone he loved. His thoughts derailed.

Did he love her? A resounding *yes,* echoed through his brain. It made perfect sense he'd realize that the second before she learned how broken he actually was. He needed to fix this.

He understood a person's subconscious could backtrack, but he didn't expect his to spring back to those tendencies now, not after so many years. And he didn't want to keep reminding her where he'd come from, but they had to move forward with eyes wide open.

Sitting on the edge of the bed, keeping his motions slow and passive, he sighed. "It hasn't happened in a long time."

"But it *is* a habit of yours, to wake up swinging?"

He shut his eyes, wishing for a moment that he could be someone else. "Get robbed in your sleep enough, you eventually stop caring who you hurt."

She drew in a sharp breath and worry clouded her features. "But I wasn't touching you."

Yes, but you're someone I value and someone I don't want to lose.

Maybe his instincts were triggered because of that. It had to be the significance he'd tied to her and his underlying fear that everything he loved eventually got ripped away.

His gaze dropped to the carpet. "All I can say is I'm sorry. The moment I saw you and remembered where I was, I realized my mistake."

She scooted closer and he shut his eyes, afraid his heart might snap in two as she cut him loose.

Her hand softly brushed his shoulder and he flinched. Undeterred, her lips pressed to the center of his back and he stopped breathing.

"I think I understand. And I'm sorry that things have happened to you—bad things—for you to react that way, thinking to protect yourself. But I think I get it, Parker. I believe you're sorry and that it was an accident. I forgive you."

But he couldn't forgive himself. He'd come

to terms with his past. He'd moved on, but rummaging through the debris, baring all his old, jagged scars to a woman who had never known more than a gentle touch or a polite glance... Suddenly, their differences announced themselves in a way that screamed incompatible.

Her hand traveled around his ribs and down his belly, but he caught her fingers before they could travel any lower.

"Isadora."

"What?" Her lips teased his spine as she kneeled behind him, clearly trying to replace the tension with something more palatable. Her other hand trailed over his shoulder, giving his nipple a playful flick. "Forget what happened, Parker. Let's have a good morning. Make love to me."

His inner debate was steamrolled the second she pulled her hand from his grip and reached between his legs to caress his hardening cock. He was weak against such temptation, defenseless against her, but certain he hadn't earned this sort of pardon.

"You don't have to do that."

"Shut up, Parker." She eased his shoulders to the bedding and kneeled at his side. Still naked from the night before, she leaned over him, her pert breasts trailing in a hot glide over his heated flesh.

Her mouth took a slow tour of his chest and abs and his body hardened despite the turmoil in his mind. Staring at the ceiling, he battled with his conscience as his lungs filled with the soft scent of her skin.

The tease of her delicate hair trailed along his stomach. He didn't deserve this. Lower and lower, her lips traveled.

His hips arched forward out of sheer reflex. She chuckled, her voice raspy and flirtatious as his eyes snapped shut and her warm mouth closed over him.

"Jesus."

This wasn't right. He should be driving home after that episode. Why would she forgive him so easily?

"Is this okay?"

Peeking through his lashes, his heart skipped a beat. Her dark eyes shined up at him with absolute innocence.

She was more than okay. She was perfect.

Something broke inside of him, his protective affection for her shoving his own bullshit aside to assure she never doubted how much she pleased him.

He gently gathered her hair, pulling it away from her face. "That's perfect, baby."

She hummed and dipped lower. His chest expanded, unable to draw in enough breath as pure satisfaction unfurled in him. Her palm flattened on his tight stomach, fingers splayed wide as her nails pushed into the muscle. Every touch was ecstasy.

His free hand stroked her spine. The soles of his feet tingled as the pleasure climbed. His fingers traced slowly over the curve of her ass, admiring the slope and smooth texture.

She moaned and arched into his touch like a feline begging to be caressed. So pretty. So sexy.

He twisted and slid his fingers between her lush thighs and glided easily, deep, into her wet pussy. She let out a pleasant sound that reverberated down his cock. He teased and pumped his fingers until her hot breath trailed over his wet flesh in an open mouthed gasp.

Losing a bit of her balance and rhythm, she pulled her hips out of his reach. "I can't concentrate when you touch me like that." She laughed softly, returning her focus to him.

Well, he couldn't keep his hands off of her when she touched *him*. He leaned forward and caught her by the waist.

"What are you—"

"Hush. Come here." He adjusted her legs over his shoulders, her belly to his, and put his mouth between her legs.

She lifted her hips. "Wait!"

No way. Gripping her ass cheeks so she couldn't escape, he pulled her back to him. "I want to taste you."

"Then I'll lie down."

"No, I want you to keep doing what you were doing."

"But—"

He ignored her protests and slid his tongue from clit to taint. They could discuss the logistics of the Kama Sutra later.

"*Parker!*"

"Hush." He gave her soft inner thigh a warning bite and went to work.

Her chest collapsed on his lower body, her breasts smashing against his stomach as he feasted.

Sliding his hand up her spine, he fed his fingers through her hair and turned her head, showing her what he wanted.

"Oh." She sucked him hard, her moans muffled as her own pleasure distracted her from the task until the sensations became too much to passively bear and cried out. "Good Lord, you're good at that."

Dragging his tongue deeper, he held her to his mouth, sucking and pulling and licking her into a trembling frenzy. Her body rocked as he coaxed her release, her arms stretching down his legs as her fingernails dug into his calves. When she finally came it was wild and uninhibited and he savored every drop.

Flipping her onto her back, he tore open a condom. She sighed, her mouth hooked in a cockeyed grin, her half-lidded gaze following his every move.

He needed to fuck her—*hard*. He pulled her legs apart, retaining his hold on one ankle as he raised it to his shoulder and aligned their bodies. He slid into her with perfect precision, stabbing deep and holding them locked, pelvis to pelvis.

He loved the moment of penetration when her lips parted on a profound sigh and her eyes darkened from brown to black in time with his first thrust.

Pulling back, he snapped his hips forward and she gasped. Again he drove into her and soon he had both ankles wrapping around him. He pulled her higher, lifting everything but her shoulders off the bed.

She cried out, her fingers clawing at the sheets with every snap of his hips and he came undone. His control frayed as he pinned her body beneath his, possessively holding her hips to him, driving his cock into her tight pussy with a need so desperate he hoped she'd feel him inside of her for days.

Raw, pleading, lusty breaths beat out of them as they greedily took from each other. Her breasts jostled temptingly. Stretching out his legs, he braced his weight on his palms and sucked the sharp tip of her nipple into his mouth. Her fingers twisted in his hair, yanking the strands in a silent plea for more. Oh, he'd give her more.

His teeth grazed the tight tip, his tongue teasing in rapid swipes as he plumped her flesh in a possessive grip. The fist in his hair tightened, urging him on. Biting the point of her nipple, he closed his lips around the puckered pink bud and sucked as hard as he could.

Her chest lifted, feeding him her delicate flesh as he greedily left her nipples wet and swollen. Stunning. He couldn't draw himself away and she wouldn't let him go. The longer he sucked the darker her skin turned. Rosy. Tempting. His.

Every breath that passed her lips was accompanied by a clipped, raspy moan. She lifted her hips to him and let out a satisfied cry just as her sex clamped tight, milking his own climax from deep within his soul.

Every jerking nerve in his body set his balance off kilter. A guttural moan escaped as he let loose and pumped his hips hard.

His release jerked out of him, thick and hot. His shoulders twitched with every pull of ecstasy. She wrung him dry, left him panting. So incredibly satisfied. He collapsed against her, his arms gathering her quivering form to his chest.

Their hearts pounded as one as he shut his eyes and rested his mouth against her shoulder. They wheezed, their bodies slick with sweat, their flesh smudged with scratches and fingerprints.

The pleasure abated in slow throbs and his nerves twitched with each satisfied sigh. Aftershocks and little convulsions sending random shivers down his spine. He hated the idea of leaving her.

"I'm crushing you." Slowly withdrawing, he stilled when her hand pressed to the small of his back.

"Don't go."

How could he resist such a request? He

rested his weight on her a while longer, truly savoring the aftermath of their lust.

Unfortunately, the more comfortable he got the more aware he became of the condom. "I'll be right back."

Sliding off the bed, he removed the condom and walked into the bathroom. After washing up, he returned to the bedroom, clumsily losing his footing and lurching to a stop as his eyes took in the picture she made.

Isadora lay, sprawled on the bed, the pink of her labia swollen, her hair in tangled disarray, and his fingerprints marring her skin. The marks were already darkening from deep rose to purple. Her nipples were overwrought, engorged and turgid, surrounded by whisker burn from his unshaven jaw.

Son of a bitch. He stepped back and turned away, unsure what to do.

Thinking quickly, he went to the bathroom and turned the faucet to warm. Plush white hand towels rested in a basket and he grabbed two, drenching them with water.

When he returned to the bedroom, she hadn't moved a muscle. Carefully, he parted her thighs and placed the cloth over her swollen folds. She gasped, but settled quickly.

"Shh, just relax and let me take care of you."

He dragged the warm cloth over the darkest parts of her breasts and her mouth turned in a lopsided grin, but her eyes remained closed.

As he washed her skin the marks didn't fade. He silently berated himself for handling her so roughly. "Next time I'll be gentler."

"I like when you're rough," she whispered, her words coming out slurred. "I like when you're gentle, too. I just like *you*, Parker Hughes."

He frowned and focused on his task. Once he'd done all he could, he pulled the covers over her shivering body and tossed the hand towels toward the hamper. Curling under the blankets, he pulled her to his chest and held her protectively. Her breathing slowed and her weight sank into his side.

As she slept, he pressed his lips to her shoulders and frowned, replaying the last hour, trying to pinpoint the exact moment he'd lost control. Unsure if he ever had control in the first place.

She seduced *him*, but when it was his turn, he'd come at her like a greedy bastard, pounding into her and gripping her so tight his fingers left marks.

What the hell had he been thinking? And on top of the shitty way he started the day scaring her... Next time he'd have to keep his head.

Satisfied to hold her for now, he rested his eyes and pulled her closer. His thoughts slowly faded as his mind took him to a strange place.

A large room, like the hanger of an abandoned factory with ceilings three stories high. Gossamer fabric hung in billowy sheets from the rafters as Isadora's laughter echoed. He was laughing, too, trying to find and catch her, but each shadow he chased left him reaching into thin air.

Her black hair whipped against a white curtain as it fluttered and he jerked the material back, her laughter teasing again.

"Don't lose me, Parker," her playful voice called and his eyes snapped open.

He was alone and less startled by his surroundings this time. His hand brushed her side of the bed, finding it cold. Reaching for his pants, he withdrew his phone to check the time.

Damn. It was after eleven. He couldn't believe he'd slept so soundly.

Something caught his ear and his focus pulled to the cracked bathroom door. Sliding out of bed, he slipped into his jeans and padded toward her whispering voice.

"I know," she said softly.

Parker stepped to the wall, not touching the door, but able to see her reflection in the mirror. She sat on the vanity stool, back to the door, spine hunched, with her cell phone to her ear. Tension tightened her features and he hesitated.

"I just can't. Not right now," she said, keeping her voice hushed.

He didn't like the way she appeared to be hiding, keeping her voice low and cautious. Without hearing Sawyer's name on her lips, he knew exactly who she was speaking to.

The thought of her sharing anything with Bishop tightened his stomach, amplifying every emotion he held for her. There came a physical pain each time he witnessed how much of her still belonged to someone else.

She drew in a slow breath, raising her shoulders and her body seemed to deflate as she exhaled. "You can't keep doing this. You can't decide when I'm appropriate and when I'm not. It's killing me, Sawyer."

His brow tightened as his breathing took

an erratic turn. There was so much conviction in her words, yet they still sounded like a request rather than a demand. He hated the man all the more for not respecting her wishes at the slightest utterance.

"You don't understand. This isn't like before." Her eyes momentarily closed as Parker watched her reflection. "You know I love you."

His jaw locked.

> *"I watch them, the ordinary people doing everyday, ordinary things. I'd give my warmth and my shelter just to know what that feels like for one quick day. But we'll never fit in with them, will we, Parker?"*

> Scout

YOU KNOW I LOVE YOU...

It wasn't a shock. They'd had plenty of conversations about love and its impressive shelf life. But hearing her say such words to another man was like having his flesh flayed off his body.

Isadora was so unique, so different from every other woman he'd ever met. It seemed there was an innate part of her built to love freely and fiercely. How could she not, when she knew exactly what it felt like to be loved so little?

It was as if her heart had stretched to compensate for those who held theirs out of reach —her father, Bishop, perhaps even her brother. But it was her loving nature that drew him in, so he couldn't very well hold that quality against her now.

Glancing away, he quickly assessed his clothes scattered around the room. Maybe he should go. He didn't want to leave her, but this was a lot to stomach and the best thing might be to give her a little time and space. Although that seemed like the absolute worst solution for him.

"There isn't one."

He paused, hating the effort it took for her to restrain her voice when Bishop was clearly pushing her limits. He wanted to march in there, rip the phone out of her hand, and tell Bishop to go fuck himself.

"He has no hold on me, Sawyer. I just like the way he is with me."

Parker stepped back a pace, unsure if he

should keep listening or at least let her know he was awake.

"Sometimes," she whispered, her voice a sad rasp of what it usually was, "you give someone your heart and they take it without condition. I gave you mine ... and you gave it back."

She sniffled, and Parker's heart pinched tight. She shouldn't know that sort of rejection. Ever.

"I have to go."

His gaze jerked to the mirror. She set the phone on the vanity, ending the call.

He should walk away, should hide the fact that he'd been eavesdropping, but he just stood there, unable to move, paralyzed by the sight of a slow tear trickling past her lashes. He should not have to see her cry for another man.

You are not going to wipe away tears spent for him.

His jaw locked and his fists clenched. She reached for a tissue and stilled, her gaze connecting with his in the mirror.

"I didn't realize you were awake."

She swiped a tissue from the box and blotted her eyes as if her tears were as insignificant as downed leaves caught in an autumn wind. There was no attempt on her part to hide the fact that she'd been on the phone. "That was Sawyer."

"I know," he said, voice devoid of censure.

Something warned he should be angry, but he couldn't muster the emotion. Her tears and the way she ignored them unraveled parts of his soul.

Her eyes closed and she exhaled. Her posture wilted as her hands fell lifelessly to her lap where she clenched the crumpled tissues in her fist.

"I'm sorry. He called and I answered the phone without looking at the caller ID because I didn't want the phone to wake you."

That seemed reasonable, considering that he'd almost lunged at her that morning when he'd woken up disoriented. He nodded his understanding.

She lifted her lashes and held his gaze in the mirror. "Can I tell you something, Parker? I mean, honestly?"

Although he hated seeing her cry for another man, he hated her sadness more and would do anything to ease it. He took a cautious step into the bathroom.

"I'd prefer honesty."

"I don't know what I'm doing. These past few weeks have been ... incredible. I love spending time with you and when we're intimate..." Her gaze flashed with something that had him catching his breath. "I've never felt so desired, so ... wanted. *You* make me feel that way and I like it—maybe more than I should."

Before he let her words go to his head he silently admitted Bishop most likely had his own unique claim to her heart and he shouldn't get too cocky. "But?"

"But..." Her expression tightened with regret. "I don't want to hurt you and I don't trust myself very much right now."

"Do you want to go back to him?"

He needed to know the truth before he invested any more emotion into their relationship and before he lost his heart any more than he already had.

Too late.

He wouldn't be able to step aside and let her go, even if that was the right thing to do. Perhaps she'd hate him for that before she ever had time to love him.

She reached for another tissue and dabbed her eyes. "No one's ever asked me what *I* want. All my life I've been told what's best, and dutifully done what was asked of me."

"You're not a little girl anymore, Isadora."

He made the statement only to remind her she had a choice, not to mock her in any way.

Why were those closest to her always deciding for her when she'd been taking on big responsibilities since she was a child? It didn't make sense.

She laughed without humor. "No, I haven't been a little girl in a long time, but sometimes I feel as clueless as one. That must sound so silly to you, having been on your own since you were fourteen."

"Not at all."

He would have killed to have someone else decide for him. That was probably why he always hung around Scout. She had a way of assessing tricky situations and charging forward without hesitation. It was a lot easier to follow her lead than trust his instincts, or lack thereof.

He looked at Isadora, despising the sense of inadequacy he detected. "I don't think you give yourself enough credit. Your father left when you were fifteen. You've been on your own longer than most."

"But there was always someone watching. I never made the big decisions and even when I became an adult ... Sawyer always advised me."

And wasn't it honorable of him to climb into

bed with her at the first chance he got? Fucking prick.

He went to her and dropped to his haunches, gathering her delicate hands in his. "I want you to be happy, Isadora. I'm trying like hell to be enough for you, but..." His jaw locked, stifling his offer as regret gutted him.

The absolute agony of loving someone hadn't changed. He'd been so worried she wasn't ready. He'd tried to wait as long as he could, but he'd rushed forward anyway.

Now they were right where he never wanted to be. If not for Bishop, everything would be perfect.

Parker loved all of her, the beautiful woman, the timid little girl, the imperfect way she defined flawless. He loved every bit of her. It was only the uncertainty of their situation he hated.

He grit his teeth and took a deep breath, forcing the words out. "If it's him you want ... I need to know."

Jesus, he couldn't win for losing and it was his own damn fault. But he wanted her without reservations.

Her brow pinched as she visibly struggled to keep her composure. "I hate what he's doing to us."

Hate seemed too mild of a word. To think he'd once respected the man.

"Then tell him to back off, Isa. Tell him you're happy and you've moved on."

Her eyes shimmered as she looked at him and he saw the truth in her gaze. She'd moved on, but her heart had not.

He released her hands and stood, a sharp, insufferable knife of injustice impaling his heart. "I'll go."

"Parker, wait!"

His chest tightened, bracing against the pain, as he glared at the door. He was allowed to have limits, but... God, did they cost him.

"I'm here, Isadora. I want you. And I don't want any doubts between us. You need to figure out what you want. *You*. Forget everyone else."

Unfortunately, for her to do that, she'd also have to stop worrying about hurting others, including him. He couldn't influence her decision if he wanted her to make it honestly.

"But you're upset. I don't want you to leave," she pleaded. "Forget he called. *This* is what I want."

She was lying to herself as much as she was lying to him.

"If your feelings for him were gone, you

wouldn't be sitting here crying. I don't want a future riddled with uncertainty. How long will you play the what-if game? Will it be a few days? Years? Only when he crops up in your life and does something to turn your world on its back? I want *all* of you, every part, *without regret*, and I'm afraid I'm not built for sharing."

The more he tried to convince her the more he convinced himself this was an inevitable obstacle they'd have to work through—no shortcuts. He couldn't be with someone who always reserved a part of their heart for someone else. No matter how much he loved her.

He turned and faced her. "I think this is something you need to figure out."

"I don't know if I'll ever have the answers. You're the one who said love's uncontrollable and sometimes we love more than one person."

"Not like this. You can love him, but I can't be with someone who's *in love* with someone else. You have to make a choice. Who do you want, me or him?"

"I want you..." There was so much uncertainty in her voice he heard the silent *and him* follow.

Fuck! He forced his voice to remain calm. "You need to figure this out."

He hoped *he* was making the right choice,

hoped she saw he was offering her more. He was prepared to give her a future. Let Bishop have her past.

"Are you saying you want me to go back to him?"

"Fuck no! I'm saying let him take his best shot, call his bluff." He looked her square in the eye, leaning over her and bracing his hands on the wall, caging her in. "But it's going to take more than empty promises on his part. He better be willing to offer you the world on a platter if he expects to knock me out of the game. As it stands, I'm holding on to what's mine."

"What does that mean?"

His lips twisted as he looked down at her, regretting that their morning was ruined. "You tell him I said it's his move, but he better make it a good one, because the game's far from over." He pushed off of the wall, tracing a gentle finger down the side of her face, and forced some space between them. "May the best man win, Isadora."

He had all intentions of capturing the bishop's queen, but she had to stop hiding from the truth.

Part Three

Isadora

"Life is a game of strategy. Time is our enemy,
Every victor looks back and knows they won because their opponent hesitated. Success is about seeing what you want and making the first move to grab it."

Lucian Patras

ISADORA DREW in a breath and knocked, her first instinct to bolt, the second to scream. Her nerves were frayed, her guilt an unmanageable part of her psyche, but she needed to figure this out once and for all. She was tired of having her heart jerked around.

The door opened and her frustration chilled, sliding into a containable place the moment she looked into Sawyer's eyes. Not really the response she'd been expecting.

"Bella."

Be strong. "I came to talk."

Appearing startled by her impromptu visit, he stepped back from the door and waved a hand for her to enter. "Come in. Is everything all right?"

No, nothing was right. Everything had been an absolute mess since Parker left that morning. She wasn't sure if he meant for her to seek Sawyer out or if he just wanted her to think things through. But after six hours of staring into space, her mind circling the same unanswered questions and starting to ache, she'd gotten into her car and come right to the source of her confusion.

He led her to the couch where they both sat down. "Can I get you a drink? You look upset."

Ignoring his offer, she folded her hands on her lap and tried not to fidget. "I *am* upset. How could you come to my house like that yesterday and then call first thing this morning? I told you I was with someone and two months ago you were, too. Why are you doing this —*now* of all times?"

He frowned as if she'd accused him of something heinous. "I'm not quite sure I understand your anger. You're upset that I told you how I feel? Isn't that what we've always fought about, me being unable to openly express my feelings for you? I thought you would want to know."

"I do, but why now? Is it because I'm with Parker?"

Understanding her assumption, he smirked. "Hughes isn't a bad guy, Isadora. But he's not enough for you. He's unpredictable and I'm not even sure if he's found work since I fired him a few years back."

Parker didn't need to work *for* someone. He was independently successful. He proved his instincts the day his stock tip padded her bank account. But that wasn't the point.

"I'm not interested in your opinions of him. I only want to know if this is a genuine attempt on your part or a jealousy thing. If Parker wasn't involved, would you even miss me?"

He laughed without humor. "You're defensive of him."

She waited, not denying she felt a very strong protectiveness toward Parker. He didn't deserve to be toyed with.

"All right," he said, crossing his arms and leaning back. "I've never been anything but genuine with you, Isadora. I'll admit, the thought of you with a man like that bothers me. I'm not sure he's good enough for you. I don't know that he's dependable enough to give you the future you deserve."

"But you suddenly fit the bill?"

"How do I know you're serious and this isn't just another turn to derail my life?"

He arched a brow, clearly not approving of her choice of words. "This isn't some pissing match to unveil the bigger man. I told you I'm serious and I told you I'm prepared to try in ways I never have with anyone since my wife died. I'm not threatened by Parker Hughes."

She measured him carefully, sensing nothing but assured determination in his words. "Maybe you should be."

He scoffed. "You've known him for what, two months? He can't compete with what we have."

Had. "You can't expect me to drop everything for you. It's been over a year, Sawyer. A lot's happened."

"I don't expect that. But I'm offering to try and I can't very well do that without your co-operation."

"So, what, we go on a date where everyone can see?"

"That would be a start."

She sat back and tried to picture that. What if Lucian saw them? She didn't need her brother's approval, but what sort of message would that send? He'd probably be relieved she was with anyone but Parker, but her and Parker weren't over. She didn't know what they were. Jesus, now she wasn't sure if she wanted anyone to know about her and Sawyer—*if* there was anything *to* know.

Out of respect for Parker, she didn't want to grandstand on her hypothetical with Sawyer.

"I'd like to keep this private until I figure out how I feel."

He tipped his head. "Okay, but don't hold that against me if you're the one asking for discretion this time."

Maybe he wanted people to know so he could win their favor. He knew about Parker's history with Lucian. Slade had been wrapped up in that mess, too, so Sawyer likely knew more about what happened than she did.

"I need time to consider my feelings. I don't trust you right now."

He drew back, appearing cut by her sharp words. "And what about Hughes? You trust him?"

She believed Parker was trustworthy, but she was scared. "More than anything, I don't trust myself and I won't hurt him." *I won't let you hurt him.*

"Will you tell him to back off?"

She laughed. "No. You said you're not threatened by him, so what does it matter if I continue to see him."

His eyes narrowed. "Are you sleeping together?"

"That's none of your business."

"I disagree. If you expect me to—"

"I don't expect anything. That's the problem. You blindsided me yesterday with some offer that would have made my dreams come true a year ago. *You* did this, Sawyer. If you want me to come back to you, you're going to have to convince me it's safe."

His jaw ticked. "I see. And I suppose Hughes will be doing his best to convince you what we had meant nothing."

The truth was, Parker never bashed what she shared with Sawyer. That's why this was so complicated. But he'd convinced her that—Sawyer aside—they had something special as well.

He was the one who said he didn't want her doubting her choice. That he never wanted to give her a reason to ask *what if.*

"He doesn't try to influence my feelings about you. He believes this is my decision."

His lip twitched and she sensed he took some form of satisfaction in knowing he could disturb her relationship with Parker and turn his open-mindedness into a downfall.

"If you're willing to give me the opportunity to show you it will be different, I'm not going to turn you down. I want to be with you, bella."

Damn her battered, bleeding heart. That simple statement wheedled its way into some neglected part of her needy soul, and the little girl lost inside of her begged to find out if he was telling the truth.

"Then prove it."

The following day both Parker and Sawyer called her. Entertaining a possible future with each of them didn't sit right and she hated feeling like she was betraying either of them.

"Did you see him?" Parker asked, his voice

traveling through the phone with no detectable emotion.

"I went there last night—just to talk."

"And did you figure anything out?"

Unsure how much she should disclose, she decided honesty was best. "He wants to prove he's serious. He wants to take me out this Friday."

Parker was silent and the longer he said nothing the harder her guilt gnawed at her insides.

"If this is too much I can call it off. I don't—"

"No," he interrupted. "Go out with him. I think you need to do this. Words are one thing, actions are something different."

Her brow tightened as she questioned his sincerity. Maybe he needed to prove something to himself as well.

Even with his permission, she could still say no. "What if I realize something neither of us wants to face?"

He sighed into the phone. "It's better to be realistic. No illusions, Isa."

She didn't want illusions. She wanted real. She wanted simplicity, but everything was suddenly so complicated. "What are you doing tonight? Can I see you?"

"That depends."

"On?" Maybe seeing him would only obscure things more, but she missed him.

"On whether or not you open the door."

Her head cocked in confusion. "Are you…"

She went to the front window and drew back the curtain, a silent gasp leaving her lips when she spotted his car. Rushing to the front door, she pulled it open and smiled widely, phone still to her ear. "You're here!"

"M'lady." He tipped his head in a slight bow. "I thought you might be in the mood for pizza." He lifted the box in his hand and the scent of Italian seasoning wafted to her nose.

She shut off her phone, not wanting any interruptions and pulled him into the house. "Oh, my God, I'm a mess. I wasn't expecting anyone." She shut the door and he placed the pizza box on the foyer table.

"It turns out I can only go about thirty hours without seeing you before I get squirrely."

She put her phone on the table and hugged him. "No one ever surprises me with food." As much as she was excited about the pizza, she was more excited to see him.

"Wait, wait…" He reached into the back pocket of his jeans and something rattled.

"There's more." He withdrew two large boxes of movie theater candy. "I wasn't sure if you were a *Good and Plenty* girl or more of a *Sno Caps* woman."

She snatched the *Sno Caps* out of his hand and laughed. "Definitely *Sno Caps*. I love anything chocolate. You know that."

They went to the kitchen and she pulled out plates as he cut the pizza. Her smile lingered as they ate. She loved that he could do something so simple and surprise her so much.

"What's that look?" he asked, tossing a chunk of crust on his plate.

Her mouth tightened in a shy smile as her fingers nudged his on the table. "I think you're sweet."

He grinned, his thumb rubbing over hers. "I think you're sweet, too."

She wondered how long he planned to stay, hoped he'd spend the night. "Is this a dinner only visit?"

His eyes darkened as he looked at her, dragging out the seconds before he answered. "Do you want it to be?"

Slowly, she shook her head. "No."

"Then, no."

The air thickened as she watched him rise

and carry the plates to the sink. He returned and plucked the *Sno Caps* off the counter.

"Can't forget these." Holding out his hand, he winked. "M'lady."

Her fingers closed around his and he pulled her to her feet. He led her up the stairs, her heart racing a little more with each step.

When they crossed the threshold to her bedroom, he let go of her hand and she faced him, suddenly shy. "What now?"

He stepped closer to her front and tipped up her chin. "Now, you let me kiss you." His lips closed over hers, softly teasing.

She wrapped her arms around his neck as he corralled her toward the bed. When she lost her balance, he caught her weight and fell with her to the mattress, laughing.

"You have too many clothes on," he murmured, unfastening her jeans and yanking them off in one pull.

Her blouse rode high on her torso as she watched him strip out of his shirt. His body always amazed her. Not that she first assumed he was poorly built, but under that casual façade hid a world of muscular dips and curves a woman could spend days tracing with her tongue.

Shoving down his pants, he climbed back

onto the bed and pulled off her shirt. His mouth found hers and they rolled across the covers, kissing like a couple of teenagers in their underwear.

The longer he kissed her the hotter her body burned for more. Every teasing touch along the lace of her panties or the strap of her bra hiked her arousal up another degree. But he never did more than kiss her.

Their legs molded together, grinding and rubbing in all the right places. Their tongues teased and her mind fell into a blissfully erotic place where only she and Parker existed.

He gently took her wrist, placing it in the pillows above her head. He did the same with her other hand. "Be a good girl and stay like that."

She giggled and stretched beneath him as he unclasped the front of her bra, her excitement doubling. His tongue teased her nipples, slowly, hardly making contact until she was arching into him, mutely begging for more.

Sliding his thumbs under the material at her hips, he gradually lowered her panties and took his time working his way back up, kissing parts of her legs that had never been kissed.

When he hovered just above her sex, he

drew in a long breath. "I love the way your scent changes when you're turned on."

Her lips parted. No one had ever made a comment about her scent, let alone *there*. She lay before him completely naked, yet he took his time teasing and discovering the hidden parts of her body.

"I'm going to make a meal out of you." His tongue dragged across her ribs. "First, I'm going to suck on your nipples until they're cherry red." He pinched the tips and she sucked in a needy breath. "Then I'm going to eat your pussy."

Her lashes flared as her heart rate quadrupled.

"Open your legs for me, Isa."

Her thighs slowly parted and he kneeled between her knees, his fingers trailing up her side as goose bumps scattered along her skin.

"You have a little cluster of freckles right here. It looks like sprinkled cinnamon." His head bent low, his soft hair teasing her hungry flesh as his mouth trailed under her breasts, between them, and dangerously close to her nipples. "And these..." His tongue swirled over the tip, making her flesh tighten. "They're like tiny little raspberries. Sweet. Tight." He flashed her a half grin. "Biteable."

Her mouth opened on a deep gasp as he closed his lips around one nipple and sucked it into a sharp point, his large hands cupping her tender skin and plumping it as his lips tightened. He treated the other to the same pleasure, leaving the tips dark and wet. He purposely blew a slow breath over her skin and made her shiver. Eyes on her, he gently caught the tip of one nipple between his teeth and pulled back until it slipped from his bite with a satisfying pinch.

He tuned her so tight her insides were quivering. Her sex pulsed, a slow and steady throb begging for contact. He bent and kissed her, taking his time and pulling back with a slow grin.

"And your mouth... Oh, I could do so much to that mouth."

She wasn't sure if she'd ever been so turned on. The longer he dragged out this slow torture the closer to delirium she fell.

He slid her knees as wide as her body comfortably allowed. Reaching into his briefs, he gripped his length and dragged his engorged flesh slowly over her slick folds, the tip of his cock teasing her wet sex as his eyes rolled back with a groan.

"And this... this is my second favorite part."

Second? She was panting with need, so it was a little hard to concentrate. "What's your first?"

He smiled as though he'd hoped she'd ask. Easing close enough to tease his lips over hers, he whispered, "Your mind."

It was the most flattering thing a guy could say. And as her body lay splayed, naked, beneath him, it was the last thing she expected to hear. She didn't quite understand why her eyes burned with unshed tears, so she reflexively took shelter in his body. Wreathing her arms around his neck she distracted herself from the sensation of being utterly exposed and toppled him to his back.

Straddling his hips and kissing him deeply, she gloried in the slick press of their bodies, her arousal the evidence of what he did to her. He caught her hips, stilling her, but she couldn't wait any longer.

Shoving down his briefs, she reached between them and lifted her body. His cock was so hard, so full of pumping blood, it beat within her grip. She lowered herself onto him, lining up their bodies.

"Isadora, wait."

"I can't."

"We need a condom." He wrapped his

hand around her fingers gripping his cock, stopping her from sliding onto him completely as he reached with his other hand for his jeans.

She watched as he slipped the latex over his length and entertained the idea of not using a condom. That was the first time it actually occurred to her that Parker could get her pregnant if she stopped taking the pill. *We could have babies...*

"Now I'm ready," he said, dropping his back onto the mattress again. "Hey. Where'd you go?"

She blinked at him, wondering in the span of a fleeting second what kind of father he'd be, if he wanted children, and immediately deciding it would be a tragedy for a man like Parker *not* to have kids someday.

"You okay?"

She smiled, a tempting possibility opening her future. "I'm perfect."

He guided her onto him and she sighed, her body fitting to his in a perfect glide of pleasure. She rode him slowly, balancing her weight on his shoulders as he held her hips and watched her with those mesmerizing eyes.

It seemed strange this was only the third time they'd slept together. Everything came so naturally with him, like they'd been lovers for a lifetime.

His eyes closed as his grip tightened. He rhythmically pulled her hips down, speeding up her pace and creating a delicious friction. There was always a sharp moment when he switched gears, lost a bit of himself in the motion and took full control. She loved that moment and gave over to it the second she felt it happening.

His hips rose off the bed and buried himself deep, the tendons of his neck thrown into pure relief as he filled her. He was so beautiful, so uninhibited.

As heat pulsed inside of her, she felt her own release coming. Her hips swayed, using his body to put pressure where she needed it most. Her mouth opened and she cried out, taking her pleasure as he lost himself to his own.

Her muscles gave out and she fell forward, collapsing to his chest and sighing deeply. He cradled her in his arms and kissed her shoulders.

The way he held her... It was not the way someone held a lover they'd only had a few times. There was something sacred in his gentle hold, something meaningful she was afraid to name. Chances were she'd misinterpret his actions far more than intended and land herself in trouble again.

Sliding off of him, she rolled to her back and caught her breath. He held her for a while, but eventually slipped out of bed and disappeared into the bathroom.

When he returned, he jumped onto the mattress, startling her and landing a smacking kiss on her cheek.

She laughed. He could sometimes be so jovial and silly, but he could also be very serious. It was the perfect combination.

The rattle of *Sno Caps* caught her ear and she opened her eyes. Parker sprinkled some into his palm and held the box out to her. "Want some?"

She lifted her hand, but he brushed it away and dropped one tiny morsel between her lips. Sweet chocolate coated in surgery granules melted on her tongue.

"Sex and chocolate. I might have died and gone to heaven."

He fed her another and snuggled under the covers, facing her. "No dying. I just found you."

They rested in bed, eating *Sno Caps* and talking softly. Her curiosity was endless when it came to Parker and she wanted to know everything about him, how he got here, what his life was like before his dad died. After. She found each little detail fascinating.

Though he didn't have much to say about his father—nor did she about hers—he did seem to think fondly of his mother.

"Do you miss her?" she asked, resting on the side of her arm, teasing her fingers through his hair as she looked into his eyes.

"Every day." He shook the empty candy box and placed it on the nightstand. "I try to remember the way she was before everything fell apart. That's when she was just my mom. After that ... she became my greatest worry."

Isadora knew plenty about that. Her mother had once been a very nurturing person, but in the end, she was the source of endless concern, always sad and suffering. As a little girl, it had been very hard to cope with the emotions that followed her mother's death.

Isadora had been heartbroken, but at the same time relieved. Her mother would no longer hurt after she was gone, yet it hurt not to have her there, a constant in her life, gone forever. Parker probably felt the same about his mother.

"Tell me something about her from when you were young."

His eyes shifted and a soft smile crossed his lips. "She wasn't a good cook, but she always did her own holidays. She'd send the servants home to be with their families and do her best in the kitchen. One year she forgot to turn on the oven and we didn't have dinner until after ten o'clock at night." He laughed. "My dad was so aggravated."

She smiled, thinking that sounded like something she would do. "My parents never let any of the employees go home on the holidays. That used to upset me, because a lot of them had children waiting for them on Christmas and other special days. My dad didn't care. He didn't get the importance of family traditions. I don't think either of my parents were necessarily meant to have children."

"I think my mom was, but I don't know about my dad."

She hesitated. "Did you always clash with him?"

"Yes and no. He wasn't impossible to please, but there were always things I'd rather be doing than sitting in his shadow. He used to get irritated when I had my nose buried in a book. He'd rip them out of my hands and throw them across the room, shoving the business section of the paper in my face. He didn't hold an ounce of respect for fiction."

"That's terrible." To each their own, but a parent should never try to stifle a child's curiosity or love for literature—fiction or not.

"Not terrible. Some people have it worse. I hated him after he died. Hated his greed and hated his cowardice. But mostly I hated that my mom couldn't get over what he'd done. It's hard to explain, but before the cops showed up, he was just my dad and I loved him. I guess there are two sides of him and I sometimes forget to remember the one I liked.

"But I got over my hate. Kids are resilient. Adults... They're pretty set in their ways after a certain age."

She rolled to her back and folded her hands over her chest. "I think parenting does that."

He mimicked her pose, but folded his hands behind his head. "She used to tell me to do things that didn't make sense in our situation."

"What do you mean?"

"She had an iron and would get upset if I didn't iron my clothes. She'd make a fuss that we didn't have enough forks when we ate, as if we were still sitting at a formally dressed table and not eating questionable meat out of a can.

I don't know if she had some sort of mental break, or literally felt that those formalities of etiquette were as practical as food and shelter."

She turned her face on the pillow so she could see him. "How did she die?"

"In her sleep. She'd been coughing for a while, like months, and then she started complaining she was always tired. I'd sit with her and she'd sleep. When she woke she'd just stare at nothing. I'd try to read to her, but I could tell she wasn't listening. I wanted to get her help, take her to a free clinic, but she refused to move, claiming she was too tired to walk. One night, she went to sleep and never woke up."

Her heart pinched for the little boy who had lost his mother in such a confusing way. She curled into his side and placed a kiss on his chest. "I'm so sorry."

His hand closed around hers. "She was never like that when my dad was alive. I think, watching a man like him be brought to his knees stole something from her, like her faith in people or maybe heroes. She had no idea he'd been doing anything corrupt. She was so humiliated, she refused to ask her friends for help when we needed it."

Isadora again recalled the day she'd watched his family on the news, remembering the bewildered look in his eyes. But if she thought hard enough, she could almost recall the startled shock in his mother's.

He laughed softly, as though embarrassed. "It's crazy when you think of all the lives I've led."

He'd been a wealthy heir, a vagrant, an orphan, an entrepreneur, and whatever the man was lying next to her now. "You're like a cat."

They stayed like that for several minutes, silently thinking over rarely discussed moments of their pasts. She decided to change the topic when he appeared to have nothing more to say on the subject of parents.

"I've been meaning to thank you."

"For?"

She angled her face so she could see him. "My brother told me my recent hunch in the stock market paid off substantially. According to him, I have a sixth sense." She winked.

He frowned. "Did you tell him I told you about it?"

"No."

His eyes turned guarded, his gaze shifting back to the ceiling. "Why not?"

She shrugged. "I just didn't think to. I rarely discuss you with him."

"That's probably best."

She scooted closer and pressed a kiss to his jaw. "So what new tips do you have for me? I like making him think I'm some sort of Wall Street prodigy." She laughed, then frowned when she saw he didn't like her joke. "I was kidding, Parker. I didn't mean to take the credit."

"It's not that." He adjusted their bodies so they were once again resting with their heads on the pillows, facing each other. "I just don't think I should give you anymore suggestions. People get suspicious."

"Suspicious of what?"

"No one forgets who my father was, Isa. They're all waiting for me to follow in his footsteps."

"You mean insider trading?"

"Yes."

"Well, did you give me that tip because you had non-public information about the company?"

"No, it was just a hunch. But people assume the worst."

She scowled. "I didn't. It hadn't even crossed my mind until you mentioned it."

"I appreciate that, but let's keep my advice between us." He raised a brow, implying he was serious.

"Secrets are a show of shame, Parker. Who cares what people think? You aren't breaking any laws. Your father's crimes can't hurt you."

"With the amount of injustice I've seen in my life, I assure you, the innocent are no safer than the guilty."

She let it go, not seeing the sense in arguing. She didn't care about what his father had done, only that Parker had the moral compass to know he'd done wrong.

12

"With all that softer elegance of mind, By genius heighten'd, and by taste refined. Yet early was she doom'd the child of care, For hapless love subdued th' ill-fated fair."

Hannah More
The Bleeding Rock

"WHAT IS THIS?" Isadora took the slender, gift box from Sawyer, surprised that he'd bought her something. It looked like Tiffany.

"I saw it and thought of you. Open it."

She glanced at the box, trying to recall the

last time he'd surprised her with a present. Once he got her a set of earrings, but they were too heavy so she rarely wore them.

Her fingers tugged the ribbon and it unraveled easily. Sliding the lid off the box, her lips parted as she found a beautiful diamond tennis bracelet inside.

"Sawyer, it's lovely."

"Let me help you put it on." He lifted the chain and closed it around her wrist. "It looks good on you."

She smiled but didn't experience the satisfaction some women might from such a gift, and that made her uneasy. She seldom wore jewelry, other than her mother's pearl earrings. Mostly, she only accessorized when she was attending a formal function.

Turning her wrist, she admired the way the bracelet sparkled, but thought the weight might take some getting used to.

"Thank you."

"I know it's not the diamond you wanted, but it's a start."

She frowned. The diamond she wanted?

Her eyes widened, realizing he was referring to an engagement ring. Thank God he didn't get her one of them. How strange that the idea of something as permanent as marriage with Sawyer scared her after all these years.

"I have something else for you." He moved to the antique secretary in the corner of the room and returned with a long envelope. "I think you'll really like this."

She took the envelope and hesitated, a sense of foreboding coming over her that she couldn't decipher. "Why so many presents?"

"This one's a gift for both of us."

She couldn't imagine what sort of gift could fit inside such a slender envelope. Maybe a gift card for a couple's massage? She drew a blank. Her fingers slid under the lip and pulled out two vouchers.

"Plane tickets?"

"For Capri. You said you and Toni didn't spend enough time there during your last visit to Italy. I booked us a villa for next week. We'll have a private chef and the use of a pontoon boat. Wait until you see it, bella. Our room opens up to the Mediterranean and it's the perfect view of the Amalfi coast."

She loved Capri, but...

Placing the tickets back inside the envelope, she put them on the coffee table. "How long were you planning to go?"

"A week. Slade has everything covered at

work and I think we're both overdue for a vacation."

Worried that he'd massively misinterpreted their situation, she frowned. "Sawyer... I can't go away with you."

"Why not?"

Was he nuts? Parker would flip out if she went to Europe with him—to a romantic villa in Capri—for a *week*. "Because we're not there yet. I haven't made up my mind."

He rolled his eyes. "Or because you think this is unfair to Hughes?"

"Yes. And it's *not* fair. You're moving way too fast."

"I can afford to take you somewhere nice, bella. I shouldn't have to curb my efforts to even the playing field." He swiped the envelope off the table and showed her the tickets again. "I have us flying first class and arriving on—"

She covered the tickets with her hand to get his attention. "You're not listening. I can't go with you. It has nothing to do with Parker's finances."

Parker could afford to take her around the world and back, but that wasn't the point. She didn't need a man to buy her a trip. She could afford one on her own. This was a distraction.

She looked him in the eyes so he would

listen to what she was actually saying. "I'm not ready to go anywhere with you."

"Now you're just being stubborn. It's a gift, Isadora."

"Well, I can't accept it."

Growing frustrated, he took the tickets and walked them back to the desk. "I've already paid for everything."

"Well, you should have *asked* first. What would happen when we got there? Would we sleep in the same bed, staring out at the Mediterranean Sea, pretending everything is normal? Sawyer, it's not."

"I'm trying to make it normal, but you're fighting me every step of the way."

"You're trying to hurt Parker. You want to remove him and taking me to another country is an easy way to do that."

"Do you think I care how he feels, Isadora?" he snapped. "If my plans interfere with his, tough shit. He's interfering with mine."

She stood and shook her head, hurt that he would make this about him.

"What about *my* plans? This whole thing is supposed to be so I can make the right choice. People are already being hurt. I won't make things worse by running off with you and completely shutting him out. I can't do anything until I make a decision."

"Well, when's that going to be? It's been a week. I don't know if you've seen him or not. I have no idea what you're thinking or if I'm wasting my time. Am I even a consideration in your decision? He may be fine with the arrangement as it stands, but I want him gone. It's not fair to *me*, this waiting and guessing where we stand when all you seem to care about is him."

She swallowed tightly. "I see." She didn't know if she should laugh or cry. "It's been one week, Sawyer." She paused to let that sink in so he could gain some perspective. "I waited thirteen *years* for you."

Registering the difference, he took a step back. Something akin to panic flashed in his eyes. "Isadora..."

She held up a hand, not interested in his backpedaling. "This bracelet... Is this what you intended to buy, or did you go to the jeweler with something else in mind and chicken out?"

"I saw it and thought it would look pretty on you. You're reading too much into the gift."

"Am I?"

"Yes! I buy you jewelry and a trip to Italy

and I'm suddenly being interrogated for my efforts?"

Looking down at the carpet she wondered what she was doing, why she was even there.

"I don't need someone to buy me jewelry or vacations. I never have. That was never what was missing in our life."

"Tell me what will make you happy, bella. I'm trying here."

She laughed, but her eyes prickled with un-shed tears. It was so damn simple and he *still* couldn't figure it out. "All I've ever wanted was for you to love me."

"Sometimes actions speak louder than words."

And somehow, after all these years, his actions fell short.

He'd lost touch with the woman she'd become—if he ever knew the real her at all. Maybe it was the idea of her, some innocent, young, pretty thing who could look up to him with inexperienced affection and trust. She was older and wiser now.

He wanted the young girl she used to be, easily swayed by cliché gestures that really meant nothing in the grand scheme of things. She never understood why jewelry and flowers were supposed to be some magic fix in relationships. Romance was nice, but store-bought gifts seemed the easiest shortcut to the heart when the joy of falling in love was hidden in the journey.

She thought of Parker, of eating movie theater candy in bed while trading intimate secrets about their past. Of how he sent her children's books with little notes inside and left novels at her house after he finished reading them, marking his favorite parts so she'd think of him even when her mind was on something else.

She thought of how he had picked her up the first time she'd ever been truly knocked down. He was chivalrous and thoughtful and didn't treat her the way everyone else did. He challenged her and took the time to truly know her, what flowers she liked, what music, books, when her favorite part of the day was. Did Sawyer know any of those things?

Thirteen years and they'd missed so many essentials, so many little details ordinary couples probably took for granted. She never realized just how much they were lacking until she met Parker.

She loved Sawyer, because he'd always been a constant in her life, a dependable pillar she could count on, even when they weren't a couple. But she loved Parker for teaching her that *every* day could be special and—

Oh, my God, I love him.

I love both of them...

She staggered back, the realization hitting her like a ton of bricks. She loved Sawyer, would always love him. But loving Parker... When had that happened?

Did Parker love her? She rolled her eyes. *Does Sawyer love you?*

She looked at Sawyer. He appeared put out by her indecisiveness. It seemed funny, being that she'd always given more of herself than he could reciprocate and yet he still could appear shortchanged.

Had *he* changed? Was he really willing to put himself in a vulnerable place, because love was an uncertainty that ebbed and flowed like a natural current of life? If he was willing to fall, he'd have to let go of all his hang-ups.

"I love you, Sawyer."

The line of his mouth fell. He stared at her as if she'd just announced she was pregnant or dying. She'd never seen a man more incapable of coping with people's emotions. Enough.

"Okay then." This was a mistake. She reached for her purse. "I'm going to assume this night's over."

"You're leaving?"

Her gaze slowly met his, her eyes blinking with amazement. "Yes, Sawyer, I'm leaving."

"What about the rest of the weekend? Do you have plans?"

Throwing the strap of her purse over her shoulder she stared at him, her arms crossing over her chest. "I *love* you, Sawyer. Do you feel anything when you hear those words from me?"

"Of course I feel something."

"*What?* For once in your life have the balls to say what you feel and forget about the consequences."

"I know I want a future with you, Isadora—"

"No!" Her hands flew to her ears. "You don't get the rest of my life if you can't say you love me! You don't get a week in Italy, or even tomorrow! Here and now, *do you love me?*"

Taking several labored breaths, he stared at her.

Silence.

Like a deer caught in headlights, he just stood there.

"I have to go."

He didn't speak or try to stop her.

When she reached her car, she let out a fury

of swear words, her palms slapping against the top of the steering wheel until something caught her eye.

The bracelet. There must be over ten karats on her wrist, but each little stone mocked her. It was a sad substitute for a real commitment. It made a mockery of everything they'd shared and every opportunity she set aside for him. No more. This time *she* was making the decision for them.

Parker was wrong. It wasn't Sawyer's move. It was hers. And she was, once and for all, walking away.

Using her teeth, she unclipped the bracelet. It slithered onto her lap and she tossed it into the cup holder. She was done.

Backing out, she dialed Parker on her Bluetooth.

"M'lady?"

"Hi." Oh, she needed to calm down. Her voice still held that waspish edge. Trying again, she asked, "How's your day going?"

"Okay. You could make it a lot better."

She smiled and navigated her car toward her house. "How can I do that?"

"Just hearing your voice is a step in the right direction."

Her heart melted. "Such a sweet talker. I

had plans but they sort of fell through. Did you have lunch?"

"Nope. Want me to pick you up? We could grab something in the city."

He was so easy, so positive and uplifting. She wondered when she should tell him about Sawyer. More importantly, how long until she told him she loved him?

She never wanted to have those words go unanswered again, so, to be safe, she should probably hold off a little longer. But he needed to know she'd made her choice.

She chose him. "Lunch sounds great."

"I'll pick you up in thirty."

Part Four

Him

Thirteen

"He came into my world like thunder, but became a part of my every day like dawn. I don't know if this is love, but I know each morning is prettier since I've met him."

Scout

PARKER HAD no real plan where they might go for lunch, but Isadora didn't need a plan. She also said she didn't like surprises, but he'd figured out fairly early that was because she had few experiences with *pleasant* surprises.

Whenever he caught her off guard, her eyes lit and her smile was a priceless work of art. She liked surprises, she just hadn't learned to trust them yet.

Today, she beat him to it and surprised *him*. That was progress. That meant she was thinking of him even when he wasn't there, which, considering how iffy things had been since Bishop came out of hiding, proved to be a huge relief. Especially when he thought of her every minute of every day.

The moment she slid into the passenger seat his world seemed to slide back onto its axis. "So, what are you in the mood for? Italian? Or we could do Japanese."

She buckled her seatbelt as he backed out of her driveway. "Hibachi sounds fun. I'm in the mood for something fun."

Hibachi was nice, but it all depended on how adventurous she was feeling. She seemed a little tense. He headed toward the city. "How was your day so far?"

"Beyond frustrating, but I need food in my belly before I can get into all that."

Keeping his expression casual, he chanced a glance at her as he turned the car. Was this about Bishop? Did something happen? He didn't want to push her if she wasn't ready to talk about it.

"How's your day going?" she asked, but she was obviously distracted.

He thought about his day, thought of the highs and told himself to forget the lows.

"My day was good so far. You're here now, so I expect it's about to get even better."

When he glanced at her she wore a soft blush and smiled, but there were lines of tension around her eyes. If that guy gave her one more mind fuck, Parker was going to go ballistic.

He hated seeing her upset for no reason. Okay, she had a reason, but was Bishop really worth it? The man only seemed to make her sad.

"I have an idea." He turned the car off the next exit and followed it down a ways.

She gave him a suspicious smirk. "Not Japanese."

"If you're in the mood for fish, I can do you one better."

They settled in for the drive and he centered the conversation around easy things, hoping to distract her from whatever had upset her earlier. Parking was always a nightmare in the city, but he found a lot a few blocks away from their destination and it was a nice day for a walk.

Once he paid for parking and pocketed his keys, he grabbed her door. "Come on." He took her hand and led her east.

"Where are we going?"

"You said your day sucked. We're gonna fix that." They reached a set of wide cement steps and he paused.

She eyed him curiously. "The aquarium?"

"Why not?"

She laughed and echoed his reasoning. "Why not?"

Being that it was the middle of a weekday, the lobby was clogged with school age children and teachers looking like they'd rather be at happy hour. Parker paid their admission and first took her to the food court, which was as noisy as a middle school cafeteria.

He ordered two hot dogs and a couple sodas then carried them to a simple table in the corner, barely big enough to fit the lunch tray. Isadora smirked as he poured the sodas into paper cups full of ice.

"Not what you had in mind?" he asked.

"Not at all, but somehow better than anything I imagined."

"Wait..."

He leaned over the brick divider where an indoor garden bed grew marigolds and plucked a flower. He popped it into the empty soda can and placed it in the center of the table between their paper plates and dogs.

"Ambiance for m'lady."

Blushing, she bit into her bun. "Are we going to see some exhibits after this?"

"Of course. But I'll expect you to be on your best behavior, Miss Patras, being that we're guests today. No running, inside voices, and there will be a test tomorrow."

"A test? I forgot my notebook."

He tapped his temple. "Then you'd better pay close attention."

They finished their lunch just as one of the nearby classes walked their trays to the trash-cans. A frazzled teacher called for everyone to find their buddy and line up by the ramp leading out of the food court.

She glanced at him. "Will you be my buddy?"

"I thought you'd never ask."

They ditched their trays and trailed behind the class, which seemed made up of nine-year-olds. Though they were stragglers, they remained close enough to hear everything the teacher and the aquarium guide said. They traveled through a tunnel surrounded by sharks, watched stingrays feed, and spent a good five minutes talking like characters from *Finding Nemo* when they visited sea turtle exhibit.

As the class made their way outside they joined another group and gathered around an open tank to watch a live show.

"Who wants to feed the hippos?" a woman asked, her voice echoing over a speaker.

All the children cheered as an aquarium worker searched for a few volunteers, selecting a little boy and a little girl.

"Raise your hand," Parker urged, nudging Isadora.

"No!" She flushed, shrinking into his side.

"Why? Have you fed hippos before?"

"No, but I think she's looking for smaller volunteers."

He scoffed and yelled, "Right here!"

The woman running the show looked their way as Parker pointed at his reluctant buddy.

"Come on down," the lady called and Isadora's blush darkened from soft pink to deep ruby.

Before she could object, he nudged her in the direction of the other volunteers. "Go on. This is going to be on the test."

Isa was adorable with the group of children. The woman in charge muted her microphone and Parker watched, as she enlisted Isadora's help in getting the kids into position. A large watermelon was quartered and they were each given a slice.

"On the count of three, we're going to toss them in. Everyone count with me!"

Parker smiled, watching Isadora and the children turn toward the open tank with their big slices of watermelon. Her nurturing instincts were so evident in that moment, the way she gently placed a hand on one little volunteer's shoulder and pointed to the tank, whispering something into the boy's ear and smiling. She was a natural with children, kind and patient, and he really liked seeing her interact with them.

He counted with the crowd. "One ... two ... *three*!"

It wasn't clear who enjoyed themselves more, the children, the hippos, or the grown woman laughing as water splashed the line of volunteers. He was pretty sure it was the latter.

"You've all been great helpers!"

Isadora came back to the bleachers, laughing and wearing a spot of pink on her damp blouse. "I did it!"

He took her hand and squeezed. "You were awesome!"

"They're a little scary up close," she joked, but he could tell she was glad she volunteered.

"Ready to go see the penguins?"

They blew off the rest of the afternoon, jumping from one class trip to the next. At the end of the day, they sat out front on the big cement steps eating ice cream cones and watching the kids climb onto school buses.

"Thank you."

He cocked his head and smiled at her. "For?"

"This. Everything. Being you."

Leaning close, he pressed his cold lips to her cheek and she turned, meeting his kiss head on. His eyes closed for the briefest moment when everything seemed perfect, but then he reluctantly drew back. "Miss Patras, the children."

She giggled and took a swipe of ice cream with her tongue. "You make me feel like a kid, Parker."

"Is that a bad thing?"

She licked a dribble from the side of her cone. "No. I don't think I've ever really felt like that, even when I was young. You make life fun."

"What else should it be?"

"I guess ... nothing."

He tossed the point of his cone into his mouth and wiped his fingers with the tiny napkin. "I think I'm always trying to have fun because my childhood was cut short. Maybe we're alike in that way. You were only a little older than I was when your dad left. The two of us have a lot of missed opportunities to catch up on."

"Yeah." She nodded, staring off at the children as the last bus loaded. "There's a lot I wanted to do when I was younger, but I never had the chance."

"You still have time." He followed her gaze as the teacher trailed the last student into a yellow bus. He glanced at Isadora, seeing a sort of hidden yearning in her stare. "Do you want kids, Isa?"

She smiled and then, as if not realizing how her expression changed, bit her lip. "Moms have babies in their twenties."

"Not all moms."

She was no longer eating her ice cream. "I raised Lucian and Toni. Asking for more seems greedy."

"It's not greedy. What do you want?" The buses pulled away and the city quieted for a moment.

"I know every family has their issues. Every

marriage has its struggles. And every situation's different. What works for one person isn't necessarily the answer for someone else. I guess I just want to be happy."

He stared at her as she looked straight ahead. Knowing she was thinking of Bishop in that moment, thinking of their past and wondering about her future, he tried to imagine how he was fitting into that future. He wished he had some wise words to say about the missed opportunities of her past, some way of telling her it would be okay.

"Sometimes, life changes in the blink of an eye. Sometimes it's bad, but a lot of times it's good. You just have to keep an eye open for possibilities."

He caught the exact moment she shut away her disappointment and slid on a mask as if she wasn't entitled to hope for such things.

"We should get back," she whispered then laughed and held out her hands. "I'm a sticky mess. We'll need to find a sink before we go."

He hoped she'd eventually get everything she deserved and let all the disappointments go. But he knew that was something she'd have to experience, not something anyone could promise.

"Let's get you cleaned up."

When they returned to her house she seemed her usual self again, but every once in a while he'd catch her frowning, only to have her cover it with a smile that didn't reach her eyes. He waited in the foyer for her as she hung her purse in the hall closet.

They didn't spend much time in the other rooms of her house and there were a lot of areas he hadn't entered. When he visited they usually hung in the den, the kitchen, or her bedroom. Pacing by the stairs, he nudged open a door and found a dark room that smelled musty and unused.

"That's the library."

He turned, not hearing her approach. "You have a library? Why don't you use it?" Isadora loved books.

She shrugged. "It still has a lot of my dad's old stuff in it. You can go in if you want."

He stepped across the threshold and she switched on a light. Dark burgundy walls with ornate mahogany moldings rose over ten feet.

The furniture was medieval and covered with a layer of dust. A gaping fireplace stood at the other end, two winged chairs cozied around a marble table just large enough for the ornate chess set that sat on top. One wall had windows with thick velvet drapes, but the other wall was covered, floor to ceiling, with books.

"You don't like this room?" His fingers traced over the aged spines. A lot of titles written in French and what looked like German.

Isadora stood beside the chairs, looking small and uncomfortable. "I was never allowed in here when I was little. My dad had certain parts of the house he forbade us to enter. His study was another one. I hardly go in there either."

He faced her and frowned. "But you bought the house from him a few years ago?"

She nodded. "It's mine. I had to work for a couple years and bank all of my income to afford it, but I did and I know I can change it. I just..." She shrugged.

It didn't make sense for her to avoid a room as gorgeous as this one. Those walls should hold *her* books. No wonder he always found novels piled in random corners of the house. "It's a beautiful room."

"I know. But it's dark and dreary. Maybe if it was painted a different color, but you know me and colors. I'd have to hire a decorator and—"

"I'll help you paint it. We don't need a decorator."

Her lips parted. "You know how to paint?"

"Anyone can paint." Although... "I mean, I'm no Michelangelo, but I think I could paint a room."

She glanced at the high walls, her gaze slowly moving around the room. "I never considered doing it myself. We always had servants that handled the renovations. I try to fix things here and there, but I usually end up calling a contractor."

Flattening his palm on the wall, he inspected the paneling. "We could totally paint this. What color do you think would look nice?"

"I ... don't know. Something lighter I suppose."

Overlooking the fact that she saw the world in different shades, he moved to the windows and drew back the heavy drapes.

"I can see you sitting here, in the sunlight, reading some ridiculously romantic love story like *Jane Eyre*, on an overstuffed chair. You'll need a table to hold your tissues, because you're a sucker for broken heroes and happy endings."

He moved to the corner where a slightly creepy statue of war figures stood four feet high. "Over here you'd have something ornate, something you found at a rummage sale that was one degree above garbage, but you couldn't bear to see it turn to trash. Maybe a tarnished birdcage or a broken grandfather clock that ticks but never chimes. Whatever it is, you love it, because no one else could and it's secretly your favorite object in the room."

He moved to the desk, drawing back another curtain. "This would go. You'd have a delicate desk, something sturdy, but absolutely feminine, probably with clawed feet."

She stared at him, mouth agape.

"Did I get it all wrong?" he asked, unsure what to make of her expression.

"No," she laughed. "That sounds incredible. How did you..."

Relieved, he smiled. "I know you, Isadora." He knew her by heart.

The center of her throat pulled tight as her breathing accelerated. "What color would the walls be?"

He glanced at the dark tones and scrunched his nose. "I think something cheerful, like a light, buttery yellow."

A slow smile curved her lips as she glanced around the room. "I think that sounds lovely. Will you really help me do it?"

"Of course. Just say when." He moved to the chessboard and bent low, blowing out a gust of air and sending dust motes scattering into the filtered light. "Now this is pretty cool. Do you play?"

"Occasionally. Do you?"

"No. I never learned, but I always wanted to."

She shifted a chair to face the board and sat. "I can teach you."

"Really?"

She laughed at him. "You just offered to paint an enormous room in my house. I think I can handle teaching you chess."

He turned the other chair and sat across from her, his gaze crawling over the intricate pieces. "I'll be the Aristotle to your Plato. I'm ready for my first lesson."

She adjusted the table. All but four pieces were on the board, lined up in neat little rows. "Well, it's all about protecting the king. He's this one and this is his queen."

He listened as she described how each piece moved and what their limits were. "This is the knight. Of all the pieces, he and the queen are my favorites."

"Why?"

Her lips pursed as she stared down at the

board. "She can move as far as she wants in any direction. She's fearless. And the knight... He's unpredictable. He's the only piece that can jump others to get where he wants to go—the usual rules don't apply to him. He's versatile."

As he analyzed all the pieces his brow creased. "And what are these?" He lifted the four that were lying beside the board.

Her lashes hid her eyes. "They're the bishops."

He understood then. When he'd blown off the dust, certain pieces were out of place. The pawns were shifted from the front lines and the queen was moving toward the opposition. All the bishops were knocked out of the game. "Were you the last person who played?"

She nodded and took the pieces from his hand. "The bishops can only move diagonally—"

His hand closed over hers, stilling her from placing the pieces back on the board.

"Why did you knock him out of the game?"

Her face tipped away and her lips trembled. She seemed to struggle to find a decent explanation, but eventually, she whispered, "Because he broke my heart."

Five little words and he was ready to throw

something. His throat tightened as a single tear slid down her cheek. "When, Isa?"

Her head shook and she wiped the tear away. "It doesn't matter."

"It does." He took the pieces from her and set them aside. Sliding the game out of the way, he pulled her chair closer and took her hands in his. "I know you moved those pieces a long time ago, but did something happen today?"

She sniffled. "What happened today has nothing to do with him."

"What happened?"

She looked at him, her eyes glassy and full of innocence. "I realized I'll never go back to him again. It's over."

His heart lifted, seeming to lodge in his throat, but before he got excited, his relief was punctured by her palpable sadness. He needed to understand what happened. "Why?"

She blinked up at him. "Because I'm in love with you."

He stilled. His hands suddenly as numb as his face. "You're..."

"I love you, Parker. I wasn't going to say anything, but I realized I don't need you to say it at the same time. I can be patient and over time maybe—"

He cut off her words, pressing his mouth

to hers. It was a terrible kiss, his mind too hung up on her confession for him to actually focus on what he was doing.

Pulling back, he laughed. "You love me?"

She licked her lips and smiled shyly. "I'm not sure when it happened, but I might have fallen the day you knocked me over—literally and figuratively."

He kissed her again, shocked and amazed and bursting with enough energy to run a marathon. "Say it."

She giggled. "What?"

"Please say it."

She smiled up at him. "I love you, Parker."

His eyes closed as he fell back in his chair, hand on his chest. Peeking through his lashes, he laughed at her expression.

He sat up and took her hands in his. He couldn't leave her wondering. "I love you, too, Isadora."

Her smile fell and her eyes flooded. Her lips trembled and when she blinked, twin tears fell down her face unchecked.

"Why are you crying?"

Shit, he didn't mean to make her cry. He stood and searched the room for tissues, not finding any.

"Damn it, this is why you need a tissue

table in here." He bunched the hem of his T-shirt around his finger and wiped her eyes.

She laughed, which only made her cry more.

"You're like a watering can."

She caught his arm and pulled herself up so they were standing face to face. "I'm crying because I'm *happy*. These are good tears."

His arms dropped to his sides as he stared at her. Really saw her, every perfection and every imperfection that made her the right woman, the most genuine woman he'd ever known. He was never letting her go.

"It's over with Bishop? You're really through with him?"

"I'll always love him on some level, but as far as a relationship... He's too late. Like a knight," she gentle ran her finger over the ornate figure, "you came out of nowhere and stole my heart. It doesn't matter what he offers. He can't give me what I need. You're what I need, what I want."

His lips pulled back in a wide smile. He won. He fucking won! He actually got the girl. Not just any girl—his Isadora.

Jesus, his heart was beating so fast he was going to pass out.

"Fuck." He ran a hand through his hair

and pivoted away, trying to find his bearings, sure he was making an absolute fool of himself. "You have no idea how scared I was. It's only been a *week*. I never expected you to make up your mind so fast and—"

This time she silenced him with a kiss. Laughing against his lips, she whispered, "I'm sorry I put you through that."

It was over. She made up her mind and chose him. "I'd do it all over again if I knew I'd have you in the end."

She was his, without reservations, without any doubts. *His.*

He tightened his arms around her. "I'm never letting you go. Anyone else wants a shot, tough shit. You're mine."

"You're the only man I want."

Every word out of her mouth was a reaffirmation that his heart had led him right where he belonged. He wanted to take her to bed and make love to her for the next month. About to suggest just that, they both stilled as *We Are Family* echoed from the foyer.

She glanced at the door to the library. "That's my sister calling."

"Do you have to get it?"

She hesitated. "She's been having a hard time lately. Her and Shamus... I'm not really sure what's going on with them. They run so hot and cold."

The music stopped and immediately started again. "I better see what she wants." She left the library to find her phone and her voice held a faint echo of concern. "Toni, slow down. What happened?"

Parker edged his way into the foyer to see if there was anything he could do to help, but frowned when he saw the distress on Isa's face.

"No, no. Calm down. I can be there in under an hour."

Accepting that his plans were dashed, he turned his focus to Isadora. Her worry for her sister was evident. He didn't know much about the youngest Patras, but he had no reason to dislike her. To Isadora, she was more than a sister. She was almost like a daughter and sometimes a best friend.

"I'm leaving now. Just stay put." Isadora ended the call and gave him an apologetic glance.

Before she could say a word, he said, "You have to go."

"I'm sorry."

"Don't apologize. Do you want me to drive you—"

Heavy pounding interrupted his offer and

Isadora flinched. The front door rattled as a fist continued to steadily beat against the wood. Whoever was there clearly didn't see the doorbell.

He went to the closet and retrieved her purse, handing it to her. "You get what you need. I'll see who's at the door."

The closer he came, the louder the knocking pounded and he was pretty sure he knew who was on the other side. He pulled open the door and blanked his expression, a mellow sense of victory coming over him as he stared into Sawyer Bishop's icy glare.

"Where's Isadora?"

Parker angled the door, hoping to prevent Isadora from dealing with this right now, but knew it was of little use. "This isn't a good time."

Bishop's cold blue stare narrowed. "Get out of my way."

Parker's grip tightened on the knob as he anchored his weight between Bishop and everything he loved in this world. "Look, I know you want to talk to her, but she's on her way—"

The man shoved him aside and barreled into the house. "Isadora!" He came up short, finding her standing in the foyer.

Parker glared at him, only needing a nod from Isa to throw his ass out the door.

"Sawyer, this isn't a good time."

Bishop eyed her from head to toe. Her face was noticeably tense. Her purse was in her hands. Her keys ready to go. This shouldn't take long.

"I need to talk to you."

Or not.

"I can't talk now. I'm on my way to Toni's—"

"Toni can wait."

Whoa! Parker's jaw locked. Who the fuck did he think he was, giving her orders like that and deciding what was a priority in her life?

"No, Sawyer, she can't!" Isa snapped and Parker's brow lifted.

There was his little lioness. God, he fucking loved her.

Adjusting her bag, she glared at the other man. "I have a family emergency and that takes precedence over you."

Sawyer didn't look happy about being dismissed. Parker was prepared to escort him out, but he moved forward and put his hands on Isadora's shoulders, holding her in place.

A white-hot rage barreled through him as he watched another man—a man she had loved for over a decade—touch what Parker considered his.

"You can't just walk away. You can't quit on everything we have."

Isadora's eyes shimmered as she looked up at him, but she said nothing. Parker didn't know if she was silently agreeing with him or too tired to argue. All of the security he felt minutes ago vanished.

Bishop continued to push. "I made a mistake, buying plane tickets without discussing it with you first. We don't have to go next week."

Go where?

"We can go when you're ready. I'll wait. I won't rush you. I want you in my life, by my side, and I'm not giving up that easily."

Her jaw trembled as she stared at him, Parker's presence apparently forgotten.

Say something. Tell him to get the hell out of your house! Shove him away! Don't let him touch you!

Finally, she stepped back a pace and he released her. "I have to go. My sister needs me."

But what did that mean about everything Bishop just said? Shoving his insecurities aside for a second, he asked, "Do you want me to drive you?"

"No. I'll drive myself."

Both men carefully watched as her gaze traveled from one to the other. The awkwardness was palpable, as she intended to walk out on both of them.

Bishop grabbed her hand and squeezed. "Call me when you're finished." No comment of concern for her sister.

Flustered, Isadora walked to Parker. "I'm sorry."

Sorry about which thing exactly? That she was rushing off or because Bishop's intrusion once again fucked everything up?

He put his own worries aside for his concern for her. He bent his head close to hers and whispered, "She's going to be okay. Go take care of her and we'll talk later."

She nodded, her hand ghosting to his cheek, a thousand unspoken words tucked in her shimmering gaze. "Love you."

Thank God...

The tension in his shoulders unraveled as her words relieved every doubt he'd combatted since Bishop arrived. He kissed her softly on the cheek. "Love you, too."

The three of them exited the house like some twisted triangle of God knows what. He walked her to the garage and helped her into her car while Bishop watched from the driveway.

Good. Let him see them together. Maybe then he'd understand what it looked like to treat her right and take a hint that he wasn't needed.

Parker watched her back out and only when her car turned onto the road did he face his opposition. He glared at Bishop with narrow eyes.

"This is the last time you barge into her life uninvited. Next time she says something, you listen. You don't give her orders."

"Go fuck yourself, Hughes," the older man snapped and climbed into his car, speeding out of the driveway. He stood his ground while Bishop was on the run.

*"...Every gesture, every caress, every touch,
every glance,
Every last bit of the body has its secret,
Which brings happiness to the person who
knows how to wake it."*

Hermann Hesse
Siddhartha

PARKER ARRIVED at Isadora's the following afternoon. He didn't waste time thinking about Bishop or feeling sorry for a man who was obviously out of touch with the woman Isadora had become. He didn't care about what they previously shared. He'd respect it as a fundamental part of her past, but he fully intended to be her future, so he was pulling out all the stops.

She opened the door and her beauty stole his breath. He forgot the gift in his hands when moments ago it was his first priority. That was how deeply she affected him.

His lips brushed hers and the familiar equilibrium he felt in her presence slid back into place. "I have something for you."

"I see that." She stepped back and he handed her the burlap sack.

She examined the roughly wrapped package. It wasn't flowers, that was too cliché.

Flashing him a skeptical smirk, she raised a brow. "What is it?"

"Peek inside." He followed her into the house where she placed the heavy sack on the table.

She carefully untied the ribbon, shooting him curious glances over her shoulder. Pulling back the material, she peered between the folds and laughed. "It's a shrub."

"It's a yew," he clarified, stepping close to her back until the heat of her body burned into his front.

She leaned her weight into him and sighed. "A you?"

"Y-E-W. Yew. It's what they used at Hever Castle in England to build the labyrinth."

She brushed her fingers over a prickle of needles and slowly turned to face him, her expression unreadable and her voice quiet. "You bought a shrub for my labyrinth?"

"I bought you several. They'll be delivered next week so we better get working on that map."

She looked into his eyes, a touch of confusion creasing her brow. Maybe he should have stuck with flowers.

"No one's ever given me a shrub before."

"I..." *Damn.* He thought this would be something she might appreciate, but her expression didn't look flattered. Maybe it was presumptuous to give her something that required work on her part. He was probably overwhelming her with the painting of the library and now this.

He would help, but she looked ... confused. And upset.

Maybe he should leave his other surprise for another day. He had a habit of being a tad too eager once he got an idea into his head.

"If you don't like—"

She flung her arms around him, pressing her lips to his. Catching her by the ribs, too relieved to let her go, he pulled her tight against him and savored her kiss.

"That's the most thoughtful gift anyone's ever given me."

He laughed, relieved. "That, m'lady, is a shame. I think it's time we raise the bar."

Smiling, she rested her cheek on his shoulder, glancing back to admire the yew. "I love it."

"I'm glad." Very glad.

They carried the shrub out back and sat for a while, discussing all the possibilities of her future labyrinth. He loved when she used words like *we* and *us*. He wanted to be a part of her world in every possible way.

"How did it go with Toni last night?"

Her mouth tightened. "She's a mess. I don't know what's going on between her and Shamus. They're very private and sometimes they seem so intense, whether they're arguing or getting along. He's apparently upset because Toni doesn't do everything he tells her to do."

His brow creased. "Well, she's allowed to think for herself. No one should be able to make decisions for someone else."

"That's what I said! But they're ... different.

I can't really explain it because I've never really seen anything like it before, but you pick up little hints here and there. Shamus seems like an easy going guy, but according to Lucian he can be quite *exacting*—Toni describes him as the same."

"Do you think she's in a bad situation with him? In some sort of trouble?"

"Oh, no, nothing like that. They love each other and sometimes Toni can be very high maintenance, but other times she's just sweet little Toni. My sister's always been a little self-indulgent. I think it's difficult for her to cater to a man twenty-four-seven, but that's the sort of relationship Shamus expects, apparently."

"Seems unfair."

Isadora shrugged. "He spoils her rotten, so I guess it's a give and take."

"But she's okay? You were really concerned last night."

"She's okay. I don't know if their relationship is. They can be quite explosive when they fight."

"Volatile."

"Yes. I don't know if that sort of passion is healthy, because when they fight they *really* fight. He'd never get violent with her, but he has a terrible temper, according to my sister.

I've never seen it. Last night he flipped out because she was apparently flirting with some guy. He left her condo and said some pretty nasty things on his way out."

"Did they break up?"

"I don't know. You can never tell with those two. Sometimes she acts like he's her only option, but he's not."

"Why would she think that?"

"Because she's wanted him for so long. I wish she'd date someone else just to try dating someone different for a change, but who am I to talk?"

"Old habits die hard."

She sent him a sidelong glance and smirked. "Well, I finally broke the cycle."

He took her hand and casually asked, "Any echoes from your past today?"

"Is that your way of asking about Sawyer?"

He promised himself he wouldn't, but he wanted to make sure last night hadn't changed anything. "Does he usually burst in like that?"

She laughed. "Not since recently." Shaking her head, she pursed her lips. "I was going to call him and tell him he can't just show up like that anymore, but I don't want to be cruel. I think this is hard for him."

Or maybe she was afraid to say it was truly

over between them. He kept hold of her hands and looked into her eyes. "I'm not going anywhere, Isadora. If he's some sort of safety net for you... You don't need one."

Her gaze darted to the patio and he sensed he was close to the truth. Maybe in time, that would change. He wanted to be the one she counted on.

Her brow pinched as she sent him an apologetic look. "He's always been in the background of my life. I don't want him interfering with us, but imagining him completely gone... It's upsetting. I'll talk to him. I'll make it clear that this is where I want to be and he needs to respect my wishes."

Parker didn't expect Bishop to give up that easily. There had been a sort of desperation in his eyes yesterday, one that told Parker this was far from over.

Glancing at the sky, figuring they had a few hours until sunset, he gave her fingers a squeeze and let go of her hand. "We better get going. I have another surprise for you and I want to give it to you while there's still daylight."

"*Another* surprise? I feel like it's my birthday."

Just wait until that day...

"Come on. We'll go to dinner when we're finished."

He'd made reservations at a small bistro close to his home. He'd always been a bit self-conscious about inviting her to his place, but he wanted her to see *all* of him and didn't want any more mysteries between them.

He wasn't the best decorator and his tastes were rather simplistic, but he knew Isadora didn't put much weight in luxuries. She cared about the more meaningful stuff, which was exactly why he loved her.

They pulled into the parking lot at the *Grounds of Sculpture*, an outdoor museum made up of gardens and natural artwork. The flowers were in bloom and the air was warm and lush, a perfect day to take in the sights.

"Do you smell that?" she asked as he took her hand, leading her through the park gates.

"It's the flowers."

She breathed deeply and smiled.

Parker paid the admission fee and they slowly walked the path. He was nervous and anxious to give her the gift in his shoulder bag, but he wanted to make this perfect, so he took his time leading her to the spot he found earlier that morning.

"Look at that!" She laughed. "It's the Mad Hatter's table."

They walked over to the sculpted hedges resembling a tea party surrounded by the Hatter, the Rabbit, Alice, and even the little mouse coming out of a teakettle. A man-made stream trickled nearby, babbling over rocks and falling over hills. Wildlife chirped and buzzed around them.

Up ahead he spotted a copse of cherry blossoms in full bloom and directed her to the stunning path of pink. "Let's go this way."

"Okay."

He loved how agreeable she was in the face of adventure. The more time they spent together the more daring she seemed, each day pushing past her shyness to try something bold. Yesterday it was feeding the hippos, today she'd step into a whole new world.

His chest got a little tight the closer they came to the trees. Lush lawns sprawled and a path cut through the field ahead, lined by the budding trees. The air sweetened and soon the green carpet of earth was littered with delicate pink petals that had fallen like snow.

He led her to a cement bench. "Let's sit for a minute."

She didn't appear much taken with the path, and he understood she wouldn't be able to see how lovely it truly was. Lowering to the bench, she shut her eyes and breathed in the scents, a smile curving her lips as her chest rose slowly.

"I have something for you, m'lady."

Her eyes opened, creasing at the sides as her smile turned coy. "You're full of surprises to-day. A girl could get spoiled."

"Maybe a girl deserves a little spoiling from time to time. There's a reason I brought you here."

He reached into his bag and withdrew the wrapped box. It was light, about the size of a brick, but nothing heavy inside. However, he hoped this gift carried more weight than any other surprise he'd given her.

He pressed the long gift box into her hands. "Open it."

Smirking, she sent him a sidelong glance and tore back the red wrapping paper. "I do believe you're trying to seduce me with presents, Mr. Hughes. By the way, it's working."

He remained silent as she stuffed the crumpled paper between their thighs and examined the nondescript box. She popped off the lid and her head tilted.

"Sunglasses?" She slid the glasses out of the case and unraveled the protective wrapping.

"Put them on."

She examined the glasses. "They're pretty. You have good taste."

Unfolding the earpieces, she slid them onto her face and he held his breath. She raised her head and her smile fell.

"What do you see?"

Her fingers trembled to her mouth as she gasped. Her entire body vibrated as she slowly rose from the bench.

"Isa?"

He watched as she deliberately turned, her head angling toward the trunks of the trees and grass, her body unsteady as little gasps fell from her lips with every breath.

"Does it look different?"

She sniffed, her face tilting toward to the pink blooms, a sharp breath of laughter escaping as her smile returned, now more radiant than ever.

"Color..." she rasped, cupping a hand over her mouth.

"They work?"

She laughed again, the sound muffled against her fingers, then sniffled, both hands now covering her mouth as she walked closer to the trees where a patch of daffodils bloomed. She lowered to one knee and slowly touched the center tube of the flower.

"This... This is..." She laughed and shook her head. "I don't know what this is."

He stepped closer to the flowers to see what had caught her eye. "Orange. The rest is yellow."

Her shoulders shook as she giggled, her voice a watery rasp of what it usually was. "Oh, my God." She covered her face, fingers slipping under the lenses as she quietly wept.

He dropped to his knee and rubbed her back softly, trying hard to keep his own emotions in check. "It's okay."

She collapsed more onto the ground, sitting cross-legged like a child as she wiped her eyes. "I can see everything."

He smiled, relieved to know the glasses did everything they claimed. "I didn't know if they'd work."

"I've heard about them, but ... I never believed... I didn't want to be let down." Suddenly, she grabbed his face and rose to her knees. "Let me see your eyes."

He looked at her, seeing his reflection in the dark lenses. Her lips parted as her chin quivered. Her fingers smoothed over his brow, her thumb gliding softly over the arch of his cheekbone as if seeing him for the first time.

"Green," she whispered. "Your eyes *are* green. But I see other colors flecked in them, too. And they're *so* white." She held out her hands, looking down at her fingers and gasped. "My nails! Is that red?"

His stomach cramped as if her excitement was filling his soul to a point of near bursting. Seeing her so happy made him happy, more so than most pleasures could.

"Tell me what else you see. Look around."

Her head moved with jerky motion as she continued to laugh in awe. Her cheeks wore tracks of tears, but there was nothing but joy emanating from her. She pushed to her feet and staggered to the trees, her hand touching everything she could reach.

She fidgeted as she meandered down the path, her wrists twitching at her sides as she made a three-sixty. Sliding the glasses down her nose, she'd look at the world, then push them back over her eyes to see it in living color again.

"It's ... overwhelming."

"I'm sure."

"Your shirt!" She rushed over to him, her palms ghosting over his chest and sleeves. "Is that blue?"

He nodded.

"Blue? It's not..." Her brow creased. "*This* is blue?"

"A dark blue, sort of a midnight blue." He could see, in the set of her mouth and the unsteadiness of her motions that so many colors —even the ones she could identify before— were brand new.

She paced to the trees, pausing every few feet as something else caught her eye. But when she stepped out from the canopy and looked up, her breath drew in on an audible inhale as she truly saw the sky for the first time.

He followed her, giving her time to absorb all the beauty. Her attention turned to the grass underfoot and she shook her head.

"This is what you see all the time?"

His throat tightened as her question made him realize how much she'd actually been missing. "Is it that different?"

"I never knew how much..." Her voice broke, heavy with emotion. "It's so ... crisp. Defined. Look at the flowers!"

She rushed over to a low garden bed and brushed her fingers over the purple and pink petals. Her legs collapsed as she sat in the grass, staring at the expansive gardens. She pulled her knees to her chest and wrapped her arms around her shins.

Unsure if this was too overwhelming, he quietly lowered his body next to hers, giving her time to process.

"You okay?"

"It's intense. It's like the world's glowing. I never knew there were so many different shades or that colors could be so bright. This red's different than that one."

"That one's more of a crimson. The other one's a little duller."

She shook her head. "It's like everything has an outline and dimension. It was so flat before. Now, everything pops."

Seeing her so happy, so awed by the world she'd been living in, he felt a fullness he couldn't describe. He kissed her temple and hugged her to his side. "I'm glad you like them."

She looked at him, brow and mouth tight. "It's just so bright. Radiant. I ... didn't know..." She held out her hands. "I'm shaking." Twin tears fell from behind the lenses.

"It's okay. No one's taking them away from you."

She gasped as if it all became too much to bear. "It's so different from what I thought it would be. I've never seen such colors. I didn't know there were so many."

Her head rested on his shoulder and she sniffled. He traced a finger over her arm. "You've got goose bumps."

She examined the hem of her shirt. "What color is this, pink?"

"Sort of like a ... orange. I think the exact name would be coral."

She laughed. "I had no idea. Do my clothes even match?"

He chuckled. "I'm a guy. To me, they match fine."

She sighed and dropped her back to the lawn, a smile permanently stretched across her lips. He rested beside her and stared up at the sky.

"It's so much deeper, all the blues and whites."

His fingers entwined with hers and he squeezed. "They take a few months to come in, but there are a bunch of different styles. If you want to pick out another style I won't be offended."

Her head turned to face him. "When did you order these, Parker?"

His cheeks warmed. "The night you told me you couldn't see *The Wizard of Oz*."

Her mouth opened in a wide smile. "I'll finally be able to see the Emerald City and Oz!" Then her expression shifted, her lower lip pulling between her teeth. "What would you have done if we never saw each other again?"

"I knew where you lived. I would have sent them to you anyway. The world's too beautiful. I didn't want you to miss it."

Her hand tightened in his. "Parker?"

He faced her, the cool blades of grass tickling his cheek.

She grinned as if she had so much to say but lacked the words to get it out.

He could almost hear her love as fully as he could feel it. "I know."

"Do you?"

He nodded. He'd waited a long time to hear her say it, but knew in that moment the words couldn't make it any truer than it already was. She loved him and he loved her. They didn't need the words when it was this palpable.

She sighed. "You know me so well after only a short time. I'm either very transparent or you're the most observant man I've ever met."

"You're not transparent. But you're easy to pay attention to. Watching you has become one of my favorite pastimes."

"I've always wanted a stalker," she teased.

He let out a slow breath, so full of contentment he felt perfectly at ease. *This* was *everything*.

"I think people are like books," he whispered. "Sometimes we rush to get to the end, but the best stories are meant to be savored. You always hear how some couples know each other well enough to finish each other's sentences. I don't want to finish your sentences, Isadora. I care too much about what you have to say. And I'm paying close enough attention to read between the lines."

She leaned close and pressed a kiss to his cheek. "Thank you."

They walked the grounds and enjoyed the most spectacular sunset of his life. Though the sky only had a few streaks of fuchsia and teal, hearing her describe it made it the most breathtaking twilight to ever grace the earth.

She wore the glasses all night, putting them back on throughout dinner and staring her fill at the food, people's clothing, and her surroundings.

"Food's so pretty." She examined a carrot speared on the tines of her fork. "I feel like it tastes better now. Bolder. I know that's silly."

"Not silly."

She smiled at him. "Today's been one of the best days of my life, Parker. You amaze me."

It was she who amazed him. They drove to his home in comfortable silence. When he pulled up to his house she glanced around the property, a delicate smile curving her lips. "Your house is green."

He led her to the door and unlocked it, stepping aside to let her enter first. Though she was holding the glasses in her hand, she often slipped them over her eyes to see something more clearly.

"It's so open."

A polite way to say sparse, he thought. "I'm still deciding which rooms should be used for what." He placed his keys on the hook and led her to the den, which was basically a personal library.

She drew in a long breath as he flipped on the lamp, her lips parting as she surveyed the walls. "You have so many books."

Sliding on the glasses, she grinned at the multiple colored spines.

"Books are my second love," he confessed, as she moved toward the shelves, running her fingers adoringly over the spines.

Many were first editions he'd found online. He considered his collection his one show of selfish indulgence earned from his financial success.

She slid the glasses off her nose and faced him. "What's your first love?"

"I'm looking at her."

She crossed the room and wreathed her arms around his neck. "I wish I met you a thousand yesterdays ago. No one's ever made me feel the things that you do, Parker. You never make me cry from sadness, but you've given me countless tears of joy. The world's brighter when you're near."

Wrapping her in his arms, he kissed her deeply, taking his time and savoring every passing moment. As he pulled away, her smile was like the first ray of light breaking the longest night. She was his new beginning, his endless dawn.

Lifting her into his arms, he carried her up the stairs, stopping several times to kiss her along the way. When they finally made it to his bed, he was desperate to be with her.

Stripping off her clothes, he paused every few seconds to run his lips over her skin, unveiling each little curve like a gift. She laughed and tugged at his shirt, shoving it away in a frantic rush despite his effort to take things slow.

Once they were both naked, she rolled onto him, straddling his hips and kissing him passionately. "I need you inside of me, Parker."

She lifted and took hold of his straining flesh, but he caught her hips. "Wait. Condom."

She smiled and shook her head. Nothing but certainty reflected in her eyes. "You're it, Parker. I trust you."

He hesitated only a moment, but then accepted her decision. Trusted her choice.

Settling into the mattress, he hissed in acute pleasure as she adjusted her body and guided him into her heat. *Home.*

She looked into his eyes and leaned low to kiss him. She rode him slowly, her hair draping over her narrow shoulder as her breasts gently swayed. He caressed her face lovingly. She was so stunning.

"I love you so much, Isadora." He'd never withhold his affection from her.

She pressed her lips to his. "I love you, too."

They made love several times that night, sleeping for increments in between. Sometimes he reached for her and sometimes she reached for him. All that mattered was, every time, the other one was there.

The following morning as they lay in bed,

Isadora rested on his chest and he held her close, trying to recall a time life had ever felt so ... right. A frightening weight seemed to press on his shoulders. It had been so long since he had anything to lose and somehow Isadora eclipsed all he'd ever owned.

Running his fingers through her hair, he made a suggestion he wasn't sure was wise. "Perhaps it's time we did something with your family—dinner or a picnic."

Being in the same vicinity as Lucian was never pleasant, but Scout would be there so the man wouldn't act like a complete lunatic.

Isadora lifted her head and gave him an appraising look. "Really?"

Though he was still debating his suggestion, the look in her eyes told him this pleased her very much.

"Really. If we're going to be a couple, I'd like to mitigate the friction between me and your brother as much as possible."

Her lips pressed to the underside of his jaw. "And that's why I love you. I'll call him today and see what date works for everyone."

His smile was unsure, but this was a step they had to take. Later that day Isadora called her brother and sister. Toni was open to any night, but Lucian was currently out of town with Scout.

Isadora left him a message. "Lucian, I need to speak to you when you get back. Something's come up and I'd like us to get together. Call me as soon as you get this."

Since they had some time before the big family dinner, Parker suggested they go to the hardware store and get the tools and paint they'd need to redo her library.

"I can wear my glasses," Isadora said, excited to select the new colors. "I don't think anyone's ever been this excited to look at paint swatches."

They drove to a chain store outside of the city and he realized something he hadn't known about her once they started shopping for supplies.

"You're cheap," he teased as she debated one roller over the other.

Holding a spongy roller in each hand, she looked up at him. "What? No, I'm not."

He took the better quality tool and dropped it into the cart. "Yes, you are. I think it's cute."

He wasn't interested in her money, but he knew she was sitting on an impressive fortune.

She followed him down the aisle as he pushed the cart toward the drop cloths.

"There's a difference between being economical and cheap. I'm thrifty."

He smirked and threw three tarps into the cart. She was cheap. It was sort of adorable. "Good painting requires good brushes."

Her mouth opened and she paused, her phone ringing from inside her bag. She glanced at the screen and muted it. It was the eighth time Bishop called that day, each call coming closer to the last.

Saving his comments, Parker went to inquire about the type of primer they should use.

On the way back to her house, the car full of renovation materials, she was quiet. Her phone hadn't rung in a while, but she looked at it every few minutes and he suspected she'd set it to silent.

"You can answer," he said when she glanced at the illuminated screen again.

Her eyes watched the road as she folded her arms over the bag on her lap. "No. There's no point. I don't want him to ruin our day."

He respected her decision and didn't bring it up again.

It took several hours to empty out the library and tarp the furniture. It was a shame so many books would be displaced, but Parker took quiet joy in seeing them donated to the public library. This was to be Isadora's room and it only made sense for her to keep the kind of novels she enjoyed.

A shrill ring came from the foyer and they both paused. Taken off guard by the sound of a landline, he frowned.

"You have a house phone?"

Her easygoing mood deflated before his eyes. "Yes. Just ignore it."

The phone rang several times then stopped.

"Sometimes," he said gently, carrying the last box of books to the door. "If you want something to go away, you have to confront it."

"I know. I just don't have anything new to say. Repeating myself will only cause more pain."

For both of them, he assumed.

But the phone calls kept coming and by the time they were mixing paint Parker had lost about all the patience he had with the situation.

"Do you want me to answer?" It was getting ridiculous.

Apparently, his interference was enough to make her confront the situation. She tossed her gloves onto the tarp and marched into the foyer where she yanked the phone off its cradle and snapped, *"What?"*

Parker edged toward the door and watched as her shoulders drooped. Softly mumbled words crossed her lips. "No... You can't keep doing this... Please stop calling..."

When she set the phone back on the receiver, she didn't turn around. He crossed the threshold and waited for her to look at him, but she wouldn't.

"Isadora?"

Her head slowly shook. "Why is he doing this?"

He closed the distance and pulled her into a hug, her back to his front. Resting his lips on her head, he whispered, "Maybe he feels left behind. You're moving on and he can't."

"But he'll never move forward. I used to get so angry when he would talk about my future and act like he was stealing it from me. Now... he's just being selfish. I'm tired of repeating myself. I'm tired of hurting." Her shoulders lowered. "He makes me hurt."

She flinched in his arms as the phone rang again. Having had enough, he went to the wall and jerked the cord out of the socket. The house went silent.

She looked so small, so defeated. There was

something very childlike about her in that instant and he wanted to protect her.

Glancing at the clock, he said, "It's probably getting too late to start painting today. Why don't you take your mind off things? Take a bath or something and I'll run out and get dinner. We can paint tomorrow."

She nodded and turned to the stairs, but made no comment about what she'd like to eat.

He shut out the lights in the library and grabbed his keys. Enough was enough.

"IT MAY...BE *judged indecent in me to come forward on this occasion; but when I see a fellow-creature about to perish through the cowardice of her pretended friends, I wish to be allowed to speak.*"

Mary Wollstonecraft Shelley
Frankenstein

He drove for some time, searching for a place to get takeout. He'd passed several restaurants, but his appetite was fucked. His mind was on Isadora and how defeated she appeared when he'd left her.

This was not okay. It was unacceptable for Bishop to do this to her—again and again. If he cared about her *at all* he would back the fuck off and let her live her life and be happy.

Grinding his teeth, he sped down a country road, waiting for his usual sense of calm to return, but it didn't. No matter how far he went, his concern and anger were inescapable.

Bishop was a threat. They'd never move forward so long as he held her in the past. Parker was confident she'd made her choice, but every time that damn phone rang he saw her certainty waver.

Isadora was a people pleaser and she hated disappointing those she cared about. Unfortunately, that list of people included Sawyer Bishop.

What if he wore her down? He was using her kind nature against her. Every time he called her, her guilt became palpable and that was bullshit because Bishop still wasn't offering her what she needed. The selfish prick was only concerned about himself.

Parker thought about the night he'd barged into her house and told her Toni could wait. What would it take to get him to understand she was through negotiating?

He'd never felt so affronted on someone

else's behalf. It was jarring how deeply her upset crawled into him. It went into his lungs, filled his stomach, and made him angry. But at the same time, her happiness could manage the same. Her pleasure filled him with warmth and a sense of safety like nothing else.

His car veered off the back road and his foot weighed heavily on the gas. He was done pussyfooting around, done with the games. He was tired of moving with everyone else's current.

For the first time in his life, he saw the direction he wanted to go and refused to let obstacles stand in his way. Bishop was a fucking obstacle and if he wasn't going to get out of his path, Parker would move him.

His car navigated through the upscale neighborhood, his memories of visiting this place several years ago making only a sketchy map in his head. He recalled he lived by a country club back when Slade had brought him there to grab some old suits for work. The house had been gray. Hopefully, he'd recognize it even if the color had changed.

Passing the country club, his adrenaline pumped. Maybe Isadora wouldn't want him to interfere. But he'd warned her he would not sit idly by and let someone hurt her.

Bishop crossed a line—several lines—and it was time he understood any mistreatment of Isadora would come with a direct consequence from him.

The house came into view, slightly familiar yet changed. He didn't let off the gas until he was parking in front of the door. With a huff, he climbed out of his Jag and marched up the porch, not thinking past getting out all he needed to say.

His knuckles pounded on the door. Lights were on, but no one answered, so he knocked again—louder.

His heart thundered in his chest as a simmering rage had him questioning his motives. The time for negotiating was over. She was his. People needed to start respecting her limits and that meant respecting his, as well.

"Bishop, open up! It's Hughes. I want to talk to you."

A lock flipped and the door eased open. A flash of concern flickered in the other man's eyes, quickly masked by a blank expression. "What are you doing here?"

"I want to talk to you about Isadora."

"That's none of your business," he snapped, clearly not used to having his indiscretions out in the open.

"No? Well, why don't you tell me what the fuck your intentions are and I'll decide if it's my business or not?"

He scowled, the pigment of his skin darkening. "Why don't you ask Isadora?"

"Because you don't spell anything out for her! That's how you do it, right? Dangle the carrot and make her wait. Meanwhile her life's passing by and you tide her over on crumbs. That's how it's been for years and now you're acting like something's different. But nothing's changed. You're just offering bigger crumbs— like that's some big sacrifice on your part and you should get a fucking award!"

"You don't have a clue what you're talking about. Get off my property before I call the cops." He moved to shut the door and Parker's foot shot out, clogging the opening.

"Not so fast. The closeted life you had her lead ... that was you. She would never have chosen that if you'd given her a choice. Acting like you could openly be a couple now, as though that's some big concession, only makes her feel ashamed. It's not enough and you know it. She's moved on and you're holding her back from the future she deserves."

"Remove your foot and leave."

Parker's eyes narrowed, sensing he'd

struck a nerve. "You can't satisfy her the way I can and you know it. She doesn't need a fucking trip or recognition. She wants the real thing—all of it. I'm willing to give her that. *Are you?*"

"My and Isa's relationship is private—"

"Because that's how you've always wanted it!" Parker sneered. "Any decent man would be proud to have her, but you've always put more emphasis on other people's opinions than *her* feelings, isn't that right? And she let you get away with it up until now. You've gotten away with so much, you don't have a clue how to listen when she says stop."

He sensed himself moving toward a point of no return, and he couldn't prevent his wayward fears from spilling into the open air.

"The calls and visits, this bullshit of harassing her is going to stop right now!" he shouted. "You and I both know you'll only give what you have to. You won't marry her. You won't love her the way she deserves! She doesn't want your paltry crumbs anymore! You feed off her insecurities, swooping in as the doting hero when she's most vulnerable, and giving her just enough attention so she'll willingly fuck you."

"*You son of a bitch!*" The door gave way and

Bishop lunged across the threshold, grabbing him roughly by the shirt.

Pain exploded in Parker's jaw. The amount of force behind the older man's punch rattled his skull. He stumbled back as Bishop barreled into him.

"*Who the fuck do you think you are?* I love that woman! *Love her!* I have since she was a young girl. Don't you *dare* come around here spewing assumptions, defiling what you'll never understand! You're a phase to her, some chance to see how the other side lives. She deserves better and so help me God, I'll do my damnedest to keep her away from you! Get off my property, before I call the police and have you arrested!"

Parker spit, impressed by his impassioned show of emotion, but far from deterred. He might be from the other side of the tracks, but he'd started on the same side as Isadora and he wasn't going backward. Sticks and stones.

His thumb dragged under his lip and he spit again. "Ever tell her that?"

Sawyer stilled, one foot in the house.

Parker's eyes narrowed on the tense set of Bishop's shoulders. "Ever tell her you love her? That's all she's ever wanted to hear. You can put me down and blow off my accusations, but there's a reason you won't tell her and you know it. If you tell her, you give up your hand. There's nothing left to hold out for and she'll eventually see all the hollow holes in your relationship. And that terrifies you.

"You know what you are, Bishop? A fucking coward—nothing without that dangling carrot to lure her back. Whether she deserves better than me or not, you and I both know she can do a hell of a lot better than *you*."

The asshole didn't say a word. His shoulders bunched as he took two tense strides into the house and slammed the door.

Shaking off his wavering vision, Parker cracked his jaw and strode to his car. He was done. He was done with the games, done tiptoeing around manipulative cocksuckers, and done leaving her unprotected from assholes.

She would never question his love. A real man wouldn't hide such a thing. Deep down he believed she was starting to realize that.

Thirty minutes later, Parker carried a bag of takeout into her house. "Isa?"

No answer. She was probably still in the tub.

He went to the kitchen to get plates and stilled when he found her standing on the other side of the island. Her hair was wrapped in a towel and her cell phone to her ear. She did *not* look happy.

Her gaze narrowed on him and she quietly said. "I have to go." Placing the phone on the counter, she glared at him. "I suppose you're pleased with yourself."

The fucker called her? "He can't keep harassing you—"

"I can handle him!"

Startled by the shrillness of her voice, he barked back, "Then do it! All fucking day he's been blowing up your phone. You tell me he makes you *hurt*. I've watched him make you cry. What the hell did you expect me to do, Isa? I love you. I'm not going to stand by while someone fucks with your head!"

"So you go to his house threatening to beat him up?"

"I didn't lay a hand on him!"

"Then why were you there?"

"Because I love you! Do I need another reason?" Shocked he was getting blamed for this, he dropped the bag of takeout on the counter. "And for the record, he's the one who punched me."

"Sawyer wouldn't hit someone without provocation—"

"Stop!" He swung his hand through the air.

"For the love of fuck, stop defending that piece of shit."

"Don't call him that!"

"He's a piece of shit, Isa! He took advantage of a young girl, strung her along *for years!* He's still playing games and you have this obsession with making excuses for him! Why? What has he ever done for you to make him worth all these second chances? You deserve more than that—"

"I know what I deserve!" Her voice broke. "I don't need a man to tell me what I deserve!"

"I'm not telling you—"

The kitchen door crashed open and they both pivoted with a start.

Fan-fucking-tastic. Lucian stood at the threshold, his eyes set on Parker with a dark feral rage. "What the fuck is going on in here?"

"This doesn't—"

"I wasn't talking to you," Lucian snapped. His scowl shifted to his sister. "Isa?"

Her eyes closed and she pinched the bridge of her nose. "Nothing. We're just having a disagreement."

His dark scowl narrowed and moved back to Parker. "Is that how you speak to women?"

"Shut up, Patras!"

Lucian growled, taking a swift step forward and Isadora was suddenly between them.

"*Enough!* I can't take all this fighting! Parker, go home. Lucian, what are you doing here?"

Parker gaped at her, shocked he was being dismissed.

"You called and said you needed to speak to me as soon as I got back. I thought something was wrong. I called but kept getting your voicemail."

He again glared at Parker who rolled his eyes. *Give it a rest.*

Isadora rubbed her temples. "I wanted to ask about dinner. I thought it would be nice for all of us to sit down to a meal together."

Lucian scoffed. "I'm afraid I don't do dinners with—"

"Damn it, Lucian!" she shrilled. "Grow up! The both of you get out! I am sick and tired of people not getting along! I want you both gone."

She shoved toward the kitchen door then paused and pivoted back to the island. Snatching up the bag of takeout, she pointed her chin in the air and left them staring at each other.

Lucian sneered at him. "I ever hear you

shout at my sister like that again, I'll kill you." His gaze dropped on Parker's split lip. "My compliments to whoever did the damage." He strolled out of the kitchen and left Parker standing alone.

This was not how he expected the day to end. Irritated, he shoved through the kitchen door. Fishing his keys out of his pocket, he shut off the foyer light.

"Parker, wait."

He let out a deep breath and silently counted to ten.

Glancing up at the grand staircase, he looked at her, in no mood for more fighting.

Her damp hair hung just past her shoulders. Her face was clean of any makeup, youthful and so naturally beautiful. She wrung her hands at the belt of her robe.

In that moment, he hated himself for upsetting her, exactly why he was so angry with Bishop. He didn't want to fight with her, but... He should have trusted her to handle the situation herself. He should have been more patient.

She stepped onto the first step and placed her hand on the railing. "I..." Regret flashed in her eyes.

His breath caught in his throat. Had he

pushed her too far? No. They could talk this out.

"Isadora—"

"Wait. Let me say what I need to say."

His chest tightened. Apologies danced on his tongue, but he didn't utter a word. He wouldn't lie to her and he honestly wasn't sorry for defending her—even if he knew she didn't need him to fight her battles.

He was, however, regretful that he'd upset her. He anxiously waited for her to say what she needed to say, hoping it wasn't goodbye.

"Some girls are so good at being bold," she whispered, her gaze on the marble steps. "I've never been one of those girls. I'm not the type of woman who fearlessly runs into situations, undaunted by the consequences."

She took another step, inching closer to the bottom of the staircase. "I've never been able to stand up to the men in my life and sometimes I hate that about myself."

She was too hard on herself. Although she had a habit of making do and quietly settling for less than she deserved, she wasn't a waif.

She was a master at finding roundabout ways to go after what she wanted. And she never looked for shortcuts. She was class and grace, but she was also resilient and devoted to her principles.

"No one's ever stood up for me like that," she continued quietly. "When Sawyer called… I don't know what you said to him, but he said he could tell you loved me." She chuckled. "He also said he thinks you're unstable, but… You love me. You don't care who knows it and you make sure I do. I know you went there because you were trying to protect me."

"I did."

She drew in a slow breath. "Sawyer wants something I can't give him. He wants a young girl who doesn't exist anymore. I think he's finally starting to understand that girl's gone. In a way, he made me the woman I am today. I like who I am, Parker. I like the way my life is going and I like waking up in the morning with a smile, because you're either right next to me or the first thought on my mind. I'm not afraid to tell you when I'm angry or upset or happy or anything else, but you can't fight my battles for me. The only way this will work is if you're upfront about your intentions."

He hadn't purposely tried to deceive her. "I should have told you, but I don't know if that would have stopped me, Isa. He was hurting you."

"But I would have been prepared. What happened tonight, that's the sort of surprise I hate."

"I'm sorry. From now on we'll talk. No secrets. No lies. I didn't know I would end up banging on his door. I was trying to cool off and just ended up there."

Her gaze traveled over his face and she sighed. "You were right. I wasn't handling things as much as I could have." She took another step. "You said you'd protect me and fight for me. No one's ever done that. My experience has always been if things get complicated they end—whether I want them to or not. I think I was afraid you'd eventually leave and all of this would disappear—my happiness, my smiles, my hope that I've finally found exactly what I've always wished for. I'm sorry I didn't put more faith into *us*."

His brow pinched, as he understood she was giving him the absolute truth. She was scared.

"I won't abandon you, Isadora."

She nodded tightly. "I believe you."

She'd never trust Bishop not to hurt her again. But she trusted *him*. He didn't want to lose that delicate faith.

"I'll never lie to you either. I'm sorry I went

there without talking to you about it first, but by the time I realized where I was going it was too late. It was killing me to sit back and watch him continuously hurt you."

"I realize why you did it." Her mouth pulled into a tight smile. "Before you walked in I told him the calls, the gifts, the uninvited visits all had to stop."

Relief tunneled through him. "So you did stand up to him."

"I did."

"I know you're afraid of losing him completely and I know what it is to lose someone who's been there your entire life. But sometimes we have to let go of the past to move forward. True friends realize this is necessary and accept it."

Exactly why Scout let go of him and he had to accept that he couldn't follow her through the next chapter of her life. That didn't negate how much he sometimes missed his friend.

Isadora needed to choose, but it didn't have to be all or nothing. Looking up at her, he said, "But in time... You figure out that true friends never really go away. You just learn to live with the space between."

She nodded. "I look forward to the day Sawyer and I accept the space in between. But for now... I'm insisting on distance. I want you, Parker, and I won't let anyone interfere with what we have."

She would never be a woman who rushed into rooms demanding people's attention. She was a quiet presence, but strong all the same.

There was something so compelling about her gentleness, the way a whisper could garner more attention than a shout. And he trusted her. He trusted she wanted this thing between them as much as he did. And while he let his insecurities drive him to drastic measures at times, it was her nature to carefully calculate every move.

She was delicate power, a fragile force that endured many blows, but survived and kept going, wearing each experience, good or bad, like a badge of honor. She wouldn't stop until she reached the end goal. He wanted to be that goal.

He met her on the stairs and took her hands. "I don't like fighting with you."

"I don't like it either."

He gave her a half-grin. "Don't let me screw this up, Isa. I'll fumble, but please don't let me fall."

She leaned into him, her brow pressing to

his as she looked in his eyes. "I think we've already fallen."

God, she was right. He'd fallen fast and hard and there was no pulling back once certain emotions sucked him in. He smiled into her soft gaze.

"Then don't let go. So long as we fall together I won't be scared."

"I won't let go." She tightened her hand around his and led him up to her room.

* * *

The following weeks were quiet, no calls, or unexpected visits. Maybe it was the confrontation at Bishop's or maybe it was what she'd said to him on the phone after the fact.

For whatever reason, Bishop seemed to finally get the message that Isadora had moved on. And that made the both of them very happy.

Parker didn't discuss the other man with Isa, but he thought about him often. Why would anyone deny loving her?

Swallowing that sort of emotion would cause a physical pain Parker would never be able to bear. He might never make sense of Bishop's logic, but he would be eternally grateful the other man couldn't give her what Parker had every intention of providing.

He wanted the fairy tale. The house that was a home, the misbehaving pets, the family, the children... Things he never imagined, actually seemed within reach.

Isadora would have her master's soon and he couldn't wait to see what she did with all that knowledge. He wanted to be a part of her future, even her career—whatever it turned out to be.

They'd lived such different lives, yet their paths crossed at exactly the right time. Both of them trying to solve a puzzle and the more time they spent together the more he felt like she held all his missing pieces. She made him whole.

"Can I see that one, please." He pointed to the velvet tray resting in the glass display case.

Diamonds glittered under the showroom lights and the man behind the counter carefully removed the ring he'd pointed to.

"It's a four karat marquise. The setting's a traditional baguette style reminiscent of the turn of the twentieth century. The band is solid white gold with a total weight of four karats. It's a stunning piece."

He pinched the delicate ring between his

fingers, trying to picture it on Isadora's hand. "Is there a wedding band to go with it?"

"I'm afraid this one would require a custom band, but we could design that for you, sir."

"How long would that take?"

As the jeweler explained the process of matching the ring with a tailored band, Parker became more attached to the piece of jewelry. In his mind, it was already hers.

He paid and left the ring with the jeweler so that the wedding band could be molded in a complementary shape. When he exited the store, he felt another piece of his puzzle slide into place.

*"The knights appear to be focused on one direction,
but are known for making swift,
unpredictable shifts and hijacking the
entire game. He said I should watch out
for you."*

Scout
Breaking Out

IT TOOK NEARLY A MONTH, but eventually, Isadora got her family to agree to dinner. A big issue was Parker's refusal to dine at Patras Hotel. He refused to be the only man outside of his comfort zone and demanded they dine at a restaurant he believed to be neutral territory or dinner wasn't happening.

But they finally all reached an agreement because this was what Isa wanted and neither he nor Lucian could turn her down for long. It was, perhaps, the one thing they had in common—well, second, if you counted their care for Scout.

Thank God Scout would be there. Parker was also grateful for Toni's easygoing presence. At least one of Isadora's siblings seemed to like him.

"I love what you and Isa did with the library," Toni said as they waited at the table for Scout and Lucian to arrive. "Next, you need to tackle the study."

Isadora made no comment. For whatever reason, she never opened the door to the mysterious study so he didn't expect them to be renovating it anytime soon.

He checked his watch. Lucian was fifteen minutes late.

"Should we order?" He wouldn't be surprised if they didn't show.

Isadora fretted and lifted her phone from her purse, glancing at the screen.

"There's Evelyn," Toni announced and waved.

Parker craned his neck and recognized Scout's familiar face practically blanketed by Lucian's surly presence. He acted like he was escorting the pope the way he protectively guided her through the tables like she might break if someone bumped her. Did the guy not remember his wife had won more scuffles than most ordinary men? She was tough, and Lucian's dramatic play at bodyguard seemed overly solicitous.

Rolling his eyes, Parker stood. "Scout."

Her smile emanated genuine fondness as she broke away from Lucian's hold and pulled him into an affectionate hug. *Familiar.*

He wasn't used to her having so much meat on her bones. Even her cheeks appeared fuller. "You look beautiful."

"Thank you."

Once Lucian greeted his sisters, kissing each one on the cheek, he pulled out a chair for Scout. "Sorry we're late."

Isadora smiled and Parker settled into his seat. An awkward silence enveloped the table.

"The waiter should be back soon to take our drink orders," Isadora announced.

Toni wore an expression of intrigue, her

gaze bouncing from her brother to her sister-in-law to Parker.

Isadora had grazed over the details of their temporary truce only so her sister didn't make a scene if anything went wrong. Toni said it was like a soap opera and Parker's instincts told him she was hoping for drama.

When the waiter approached they let out a collective exhale. Lucian instructed their server not to go far and Parker quietly chuckled. Some arrogance never faded.

"So, Park," Scout started, pushing through the tense haze. "Where are you living?"

He wished they didn't have to play catch up, that their friendship hadn't waned. That was his fault. Something he'd likely always regret. But distance had been necessary. He wanted her to be happy.

"I actually bought a house."

"You did?" Her excitement was full on radiance, altering her usual beauty to something enchanting. "That's great!"

His skin flushed as he accepted her praise, knowing she, above all others, would recognize how priceless a home truly was.

"It's far from finished. Right now I just have the necessities. I'm waiting for the day it actually feels like a home." And to see if that was where he and Isa would eventually live. He was pretty certain she'd want to keep her house. It was a nicer home anyway, big enough for a family.

Scout laughed. "By necessities, I bet you mean piles and piles of books." She glanced at Isa. "You finally found someone who loves to read as much as you do."

Isadora blushed. "Parker's been testing my knowledge of the classics. In exchange, I'm forcing him to read my favorites."

He smirked, a touch embarrassed, because some of her novels were sheer torture, but fair was fair. "I'll never understand the appeal of filthy medieval characters taking a bride."

Isadora sighed at the same time as her sister. "I love a raunchy historical," Toni announced. "Nothing better than a domineering man seducing a strong-willed woman."

Isa snorted. "Like you'd ever put up with that in real life."

Lucian's gaze shifted to his younger sister. "How *is* Shamus?"

Toni's expression shuttered. "I don't know. Why don't you ask him? He calls you more than he calls me these days."

Isadora sent her brother a reprimanding look, which Parker appreciated, and the subject was dropped. Her unspoken authority over her brother was impressive.

He pitied the youngest Patras. She clearly was hiding a good deal of feelings regarding her recent breakup.

The waiter returned and they ordered another round of drinks as well as their meals. He blinked in awe as Scout skimmed over the menu and selected her dish. He wanted to comment on how easily she comprehended the words, but he didn't want to embarrass her in front of everyone.

When she returned the menu to the server, her gaze caught his and he smiled. She blushed and he believed she read his thoughts. She'd overcome one of her biggest challenges and was now literate.

If anything, he savored this glimpse of her new life, finding it incredibly reassuring each time she smiled at her husband. She was happy and that brought him an unanticipated level of peace. For her and her alone, this dinner was not a waste. But the idea that two hours might somehow mend wounds between him and Lucian that were years old... Well, that was unrealistic.

Although they sat only two seats apart, they never acknowledged the other's presence.

Parker appreciated that the guy didn't throw a fit when Scout spoke to him.

"Excuse me. I have to powder my nose," Scout announced, and he almost choked on his filet.

It struck him as absurd that this was the same girl who once traded pants with a perfect stranger in broad daylight after winning a bet. The high life had certainly softened her rough edges.

"I'll join you," Isadora announced and stood.

"Me too," Toni said, rising as well.

Ah, fuck.

He and Lucian lifted out of their seats as the women left the table. Hopefully, they wouldn't take too long.

Parker turned his unused fork on the tablecloth as the silence stretched. He thought about the ring he'd picked up that morning. Not that he intended to give it to Isadora anytime soon, but—had this been a normal situation—it would be the perfect time to let her brother know his intentions.

He glanced at Lucian who watched him with calculating dark eyes. Yeah, he wasn't asking his permission for shit.

Another minute passed and there was no sign of the women. "Scout seems happy."

"Does that disappoint you?"

He rolled his eyes. "Is it too much for you to grasp that I see her as just a friend and, as her friend, I want her to be happy? I'm with your sister."

His mouth remained flat, his glare cold. "We'll see how long that lasts."

"You're unbelievable." Dropping the discussion, Parker reached for his drink.

"What's unbelievable is the fact that you've somehow managed to wheedle your way back into my life. It's one thing to interfere with my personal business. Interfering with my family is an entirely different situation. But you've seen what happens to those who upset the people I love. I'd have no problem kicking the shit out of you again."

He placed his glass on the table and gave Lucian his full attention, sitting back, posture straight, challenging gaze daring him to threaten him—One. More. Time. "Do you want some sort of medal because you beat me in a fight, Lucian? Is that what you need to feel vindicated and move on?"

"You couldn't possibly understand my needs, so don't try."

Parker held his glare. "To think there was a time when we got along." It was brief and tentative, but there had been those few minutes.

"If you'll recall, I was unconscious for a large part of that time."

"And if you'll recall, I told her to go to you."

"I don't, nor have I ever, needed your endorsement—"

"We're back," Toni announced, cutting off any further discussion of the past as the women took their seats.

Isadora and Scout passed nervous glances, each wearing an unguarded look of hopeful expectation. He gave his head a quick shake and Isa's mouth turned down in disappointment.

"Should we order dessert?" Toni asked.

"I'm afraid we have to be going," Lucian announced, saving him the trouble of an excuse.

Parker wasted no time removing his napkin from his lap and standing to say his farewells. "It was great catching up with you, Scout."

As they said their goodbyes he kept his focus on the women. It irritated the piss out of Parker that Lucian somehow took care of the check before he had the chance.

"You're being ridiculous," Isa said on the

drive back to his house. "He was being a gentleman."

"The gentlemanly thing to do would be to let me pick up the tab. *We* asked *them* to dinner. I should have handled the bill and he knows it. He likes thinking of me as some sort of charity case."

"No one thinks you're a charity case, Parker. Why would you even say that? I think you're reading too much into Lucian's behavior. He *always* gets the bill."

It amazed him how easily Isa could overlook his past at times. But her brother's memory was long and he'd never forget where Parker came from or the shady things he'd done.

There had been a time that Lucian had actually invited him to the hotel for a meal so that Scout could see him and know he was well. Each luxury flaunted chiseled through a layer of Parker's hard earned pride. It had been intentional then and it was intentional now.

Lucian liked flouting his position over others. And Parker didn't like feeling so exposed in front of Isa's family—in front of her brother.

"Everything he does is somehow manipulating someone or some situation," he grumbled.

"Hey," she snapped. "He's still my brother."

"And you're his sister. Doesn't it irritate you that he's giving us such a hard time?".

She frowned at him. "He might not have been overly cordial tonight, but he wasn't rude, Parker. His manners were fine—considering the history the three of you share."

His mouth formed a firm line. There was no sense in upsetting her by retelling the whole bathroom conversation. He might have missed some etiquette lessons while he was living on the streets, but he was pretty sure threatening dinner guests after the fourth course was frowned upon in all social tiers.

As they pulled into his driveway, she sighed and said, "You know, there isn't a whole lot of difference between you and Evelyn. Lucian loves her and he'd never hold her past against her. He'd be a hypocrite to treat you differently because of your history. Tonight was about starting fresh."

"Well, I certainly don't need his approval."

She unbuckled her seatbelt and reached over the console. "No. And neither do I." Her lashes lowered and her smile softened. Her hand slowly drifted up his thigh. "I know tonight was difficult, but you'll never know how much I appreciate you trying. My family's important to me. And so are you."

His head rested against the leather of the seat as he looked at her through a half-lidded gaze. He'd sit through a thousand uncomfortable dinners for her. "Maybe next time it won't be as tense."

Her fingers ghosted over the zipper of his pants. "Let's not talk about it anymore." The metal catch lifted and the silent car filled with the slow drag of his zipper coming undone.

What was the saying? A lady in the streets and... "Do you want to take this inside?"

She reached into his pants, her warm fingers curling tight around his erection and greeting him with a slow stroke. "Why? Are you afraid someone might see?"

Maybe she didn't need a bed.

He glanced at the neighbor's house. Some lights were on, but the chances of anyone looking into his car were slim.

Her fingers tightened and he stretched back. His hand slid through her hair, turning her face for a slow brush of lips. Her tongue skated over his and he chased it, capturing her mouth and dominating the kiss.

Watching her face as he pulled away, her lips shined full and tempting in the moonlight. He dipped his chin toward his lap. "Do it."

Leaning in for one last kiss, her smile curled against his lips and then her head lowered. The heat of her mouth engulfed him in a haze of ecstasy.

He kept his hand in her hair, guiding her motions, urging her down as low as she could go and letting her up nice and slow. Through his lashes he watched her body move. The pristine clothes, proper pearl earrings, and high-end tights all added to the eroticism, because underneath that well thought out disguise hid a very sexy lioness and he intended to make her purr.

He slid his seat back, giving her more room. His free hand lifted her skirt, his fingers tracing the delicate line of her garters. So utterly fucking feminine. "Do you like doing that to me?"

She hummed agreeably, the reverberation traveling through his cock and vibrating his balls.

His fingers traced the seam of her ass, slipping over the silk of her panties until he found the damp heat of her pussy. "You're wet."

He nudged the fabric aside and teased her folds. She sucked harder, her hand moving in tight pulls with her mouth. He gave one garter a little flick and the clip opened.

Running his fingertips across her thighs, he gradually unclasped each one. "Take your panties off."

She released him, tipping her head to see him. "Here?"

God, she was stunning. Dark eyes flashing like polished onyx, thick black hair falling over her shoulders, a mouth made for sin. He nodded. "Here."

She returned to the space of the passenger seat and slithered out of the silk garment, placing the panties on the floor. Her hands folded over her rumpled skirt, lowering it back to her knees.

"Let me see."

Her gaze met his and he waited. A smile twitched on her lips and slowly her skirt lifted. He reached over the console and hiked it to her waist. Wet, soft lips glistened in the light filtering through the windshield. He was enjoying their little exhibition, but he needed more room for everything he wanted to do to her.

Tucking his cock away. He opened the door.

As soon as the interior light kicked on, her

thighs clamped together and she covered her-self. He rounded the vehicle and opened her door, offering her a hand. They needed to get inside.

Her eyes were full of promise as she glided to her feet and looked up at him with palpable trust. Her skirt fell to her knees, once again hiding any signs of impropriety.

He escorted her in silence and she patiently waited as he unlocked the door. The hall was dark and he didn't bother with the lights. He never let go of her, pressing his front to her back as soon as he shut the door.

"Do you have any idea how sexy you are?"

His fingers teased the hem of her skirt as she leaned her weight into him. Lifting the ma-terial, he cupped her hot little pussy, the heat of her arousal warming his palm. She sighed and sagged into him, her body leaning in between him and the wall.

"I want to fuck you, Isadora. Hard and deep."

Her breath left in a delicate quiver. He moved his hands to her blouse and lifted it over her head, tossing it aside. Her breasts were so perfect, not too big, not too small. He loved seeing them in all that expensive white lace.

He pinched her nipples through the material and she moaned. He thought about their dinner conversations. Not the bullshit with her brother, but the important little hints he learned about her.

"Are you trying to tell me something with all these books you've been making me read?"

Her head lulled to his shoulder, her breath coming faster as he teased her nipples. She didn't answer, so he pinched harder and she moaned.

"Do you want me to take you like one of those men in your stories?" He was starting to see the appeal.

She moaned again and he took that as agreement.

"As you wish, m'lady."

Giving her no chance to object, he twisted and tucked an arm under her hips, hoisting her over his shoulder. She gasped and giggled as he carried her up the stairs. There was no stopping until he dropped her onto his bed.

He grabbed her ankles and yanked her to the edge of the mattress. Pulling her legs apart, he bent close to her sex and breathed her in. His tongue swiped over her clit, quick and enough to get her full attention.

"So fucking sexy."

Stripping off his clothes, he climbed over

her, nudging her slit with the tip of his cock, teasing with a preview of what was to come. His mouth closed over the sheer lace of her bra, his fingers sliding the straps down her arms. Reaching behind her, he unclasped the garment and tossed it away.

Sharp, little nipples beaded tightly and his need grew into a steady throb. "I have to get inside of you."

"Do it," she all but growled, fingers digging into his shoulders as her leg hooked over his hip.

He shoved into her, burying his cock to the root and she gasped, her lips parting as her eyes closed. He didn't go gently and she didn't object. As a matter of fact, his forcefulness was spurred by her pleas that he not stop.

He pumped a few more times, getting his dick nice and wet, then withdrew. Rising, he straddled her waist and teased the valley of her breasts with his glistening cock. "Taste."

Her eyes darkened as her lashes flared. Resting his palm by her head, he gripped himself and leaned over her mouth, tracing the smooth tip of his cock against her full lips. Her tongue snaked out and he pressed in, making a slow glide to the back of her throat.

"Jesus, Isa."

She moaned and gripped his ass, pulling him into her as he slowly stabbed in and out. If she kept at it he'd come before her.

He groaned in pleasure and withdrew, returning to her breasts. "Hold them tight."

"They're not big enough."

"They are." And he was coming to learn how much she liked nipple play, so she'd probably love this.

She cupped her breasts, pressing them together around his length, a satisfied and daring glint in her eye. "Like this?"

"That's it. Good girl." He slid between her flesh, loving the feel of her skin against his. The fit was so tight, so close and a different sort of intimate. Wanting to make it good for her, he found his rhythm and pinched her nipples, pulling just enough to make her gasp.

"Does that hurt?"

"In a good way."

He pulled and fucked, but once again he came close to losing control and he wanted to drag out the pleasure as long as possible. Rising, he dipped back into her mouth and she welcomed him with palpable hunger.

When he returned to her breasts, he was distracted by the dark tips. "Just a taste."

He sucked and bit and nibbled and pulled,

pretty sure he could make her come this way, but not wanting her to climax yet. He wanted it to build until they couldn't handle another second of pleasure. Back to her mouth.

The longer he teased her like that the more frantic she became. Her body twisted and arched beneath his, every inhibition melting away.

Pumping his flesh between her breasts, he reached back and teased her wet sex. His finger shoved deep and she let out a needy moan.

He shimmied down her body and opened her knees, baring her soft pink flesh. His tongue stabbed into her, his fingers rubbing her clit hard as he licked over every delicate fold.

Sitting up on his knees, he slipped two fingers inside of her, stretching until he found that hidden bundle of nerves. He continued to rub her clit with the added pressure of his fingers and she arched off the bed, crying out his name as she came in an unrestrained rush of abandon.

"Again." He pumped his fingers harder, his mouth lowering to pull greedily at her clit.

He nibbled and savored every taste of her pleasure, working another finger into her tight pussy and pressing deep. Her lips parted as she moaned a mixture of broken syllables and gasps.

Her release slicked his fingers and her thighs. Her tired body went limp, sprawled beneath him, satisfied and spent.

Scooping her into his arms, he pulled her over his knees and sat up with her. "Stay with me."

Her lashes fluttered as her arms lazily wrapped around his neck and she straddled him. Face to face, kneeling in the center of the bed, they held each other.

He looked into her eyes, his hands cradling her lithe body to his as she lowered all the way onto him. Buried deep inside of her, his body trembled, emotion tunneling through him with a devastating burn.

His fingers brushed the damp tendrils of hair from her face, his lips pressing to hers, traveling to her cheeks and eyes, her ears and jaw.

"I love you," he rasped, pulling her as close as their bodies allowed.

Her spine arched as she slowly rode him, her motions divine and languid. Situated on the center of the bed, facing each other as they were, he felt his heart shift, all the broken pieces drifting away like dust.

She breathed into his soul. Filled him with

unexpected happiness. She was his everything and he wanted to be hers.

The words left unsaid seemed to pass between them in the silence and something shifted inside of him, something he felt very deeply that hadn't moved in quite some time. Security.

Her fingers combed over the back of his head as she pressed her lips to his. Passion poured from her, breaking down the last of his barriers.

His heart stammered behind his ribs as something choked him. Fear. Happiness. It was the first time in his life he had something so priceless the thought of losing it terrified him to the core. It was the burden of love and, as it settled over him, he accepted he'd wear it like a mantel for the rest of his life.

"You could break my heart so easily," he murmured, his lips tracing the delicate curve of her ear.

Her dark gaze found his as she turned his face to hers. "Your heart's something I'm very protective of, Parker. I never want to break it."

The pressure in his chest tightened, making it difficult to swallow as his breath labored. Her eyes shimmered as she looked at him the way no one else ever had.

"I love you, Isa."

"I love you... I love you... I love you," she whispered, brushing her nose along his cheek until her lips were so close to his ear he could hear her breath tremble past her lips. "You have all of me. There's no hiding. And I'd never let anyone hurt you, including myself."

His hand curled around the back of her neck, his throat constricting as he struggled to breathe. His vision wavered as he kissed her deeply, easing her body onto the bedding.

His lashes clung together as he filled her again, slowly, savoring every upstroke and glide. Her name played inside of him with every downbeat of his heart until the pressure in his chest escaped in a sigh that seemed lodged in his throat for far too many years.

She stripped him bare yet again. All his life he'd been hiding, protecting himself from a cruel world, but she somehow changed that. She saw behind his armor, found every scrape and scar, and loved him anyway.

When the first tear fell he lost a battle he'd fought for as long as he could remember. Her fingertips traced his cheek as she smiled up at him with pure acceptance.

"It's okay," she whispered. "It's okay."

What was happening to him? Where was this coming from?

His face pressed to her throat as he caught his breath. It was a certain kind of surrender. A torturous gift that encompassed more than he could bear. Maybe that was why love took two people, because it was so big, so overwhelming, it needed two hearts to carry all it conveyed.

Her lips pressed to his temple, laying soft kisses as she held him tight. "Do you feel that?"

He didn't know if she felt what he was feeling, but whatever had a hold of him, it was the biggest emotion he'd ever known. It was jagged and beautiful and built out of two broken souls that somehow fixed each other and made one. "I feel it."

"That's us, Parker. Only we feel like that."

Her mouth found his and the last of his walls came tumbling down, all the pressure dissolving into peace. She was his peace. And maybe—just maybe—he could be hers.

"Sometimes Pearl is upset about things I can't feel. But I love her and so I help her. Even when it hurts. That's all I know about love."

Scout

THEY OVERSLEPT the following morning and Parker wasn't sure what time it was when Isa's phone started ringing. At first, she ignored it and they'd fallen back asleep, but later it rang again and again, echoing from her purse downstairs.

"I should get that," she groaned, lazily running a finger over his chest.

"Or you could ignore it."

She giggled, sliding her leg over his, only to growl as the phone rang once more. "No one ever calls me."

That wasn't true. Bishop called her, just not recently. Parker hoped this wasn't the return of a bad habit.

She slid from the bed and he laughed as she pranced naked to his closet and came out in an old cable knit sweater that reached her knees.

Folding his arms behind his head, he admired her long legs, thinking the only thing that would make her a prettier picture would be his ring on her finger. "Aren't you sexy."

"Let me just see who it is. If it's nothing, I'll be right back."

"Take your time."

She left and he stretched, the satisfied man inside of him purring happily until his stomach growled, demanding sustenance. Climbing out of bed, he found a pair of jeans and slid them on. As he took the stairs he collected her shoes, which had fallen off on their way to bed last night.

He kept quiet in case she was on the phone with someone important. She sat on a chair in the den, her back to him, as he crossed the room. His hand lovingly brushed over her shoulders and she stiffened.

Frowning, he turned and looked at her face. She drew the phone away from her ear, her hands shaking as she pressed a button.

"Who was it?"

Her brow pinched as she focused on the phone and tried to dial with unsteady fingers. "My brother. He called six times. Something's wrong." Flustered, she pressed a button on her phone. "*Jesus Christ.* I can't even dial!"

"Shhh... Don't get yourself worked up until you know what he wants. It's probably nothing." He took her phone and pressed Lucian's name. "Here. It's ringing."

She held the device to her ear and stood. "Lucian—" She paced then stilled. "I'm standing. What is it? Is Evelyn okay? The baby?"

Parker's brow shot up. There was a baby?

Why the hell didn't anyone say anything last night? Now it made sense why Scout kept ordering water while the rest of them had cocktails and wine. And her waist had felt thicker when he'd hugged her.

His stomach tightened, as he understood something was clearly wrong. Shit. This wasn't good.

He watched Isadora for any sign of assurance that everyone was safe and nothing had happened to Scout. But as the color fled from her face he felt the blood rushing from his.

"Wh—what?" she choked. Her lips quivered. "I heard you, I just—"

Her lithe body shook fiercely, her fingers white knuckling the phone. Pink shot through the whites of her eyes in an instant and Parker's concern multiplied.

A tear fell, her teeth chattering as if she were suddenly freezing.

A sharp sense of nausea gripped his stomach as he braced for the worst possible scenario. It can't be Scout. Her father? Would she have this sort of response? God, what if something happened to Scout? No.

He wasn't breathing so well. Seeing her so upset and not knowing the cause threw his heart into a rapid tremor.

Was it something with Lucian? Or maybe Toni? Whatever it was it was bad. Fear rocked him to his core, his mind certain it was Scout. Life was never fair. Fuck! *Fuck!*

All the wasted time over the past two years flashed through his mind in an instant. They were so stupid to let her marriage come between their friendship. He couldn't handle anything happening to her—to any of them. *Fuck!*

Isadora's face was white as snow, no expression aside from pure anguish. Whatever it was, he might not be able to fix it.

"Th—thanks for calling me," she wheezed, zero inflection in her voice.

Her hand lowered as the call ended. She stared at him, through him.

"Isa?" He waited, not breathing. He'd never seen her so distraught. "Please talk to me. What happened?"

Her gaze focused, barely, and she shook her head, her jaw trembling.

His voice strained as he asked one of the hardest questions of his life. "Did something happen to Scout?"

She shook her head slowly and sucked in a jagged breath. "Evelyn's ... fine."

Thank God. But something happened to someone.

Her lips tightened as her eyes glazed with another sheet of tears. "It's Sawyer," she rasped.

Parker stilled, his first assumption that this was a family situation shattered. "Bishop?"

Her arms banded around her stomach as she stumbled to a chair, dropping into it and letting the phone fall to the floor. She doubled over and moaned as if in agony.

Panicked, he crouched in front of her, worried whatever happened was more than she could handle. Her brother had no idea how much the man meant to Isadora, he couldn't possibly have known not to embellish whatever the situation was.

"Is he hurt? Was there an accident?"

She gasped and rocked. "He's... Oh, God." She wheezed out a sob. "He's..." A sound came from her as if wrung from the deepest depth of her soul. It was wrought with despair and so broken it managed to jar a part of his heart loose. "He died," she gasped.

Parker rocked back in shock. "What?"

It was unbearable seeing her like this, and horrifying to be on the opposite end of her pain. For as much as he resented Bishop, he'd never wished for this outcome.

He was fucking dead? How?

She choked on a moan as she sucked in a deep breath, her fingers flying to her mouth. "I'm going to be sick."

He snapped out of his daze and flew into action. Rubbing a hand over her back, he tried to soothe her as best he could. "Shh... Breathe, Isa. Deep breaths."

She gasped, hyperventilating, and bolted out of the chair, but didn't make it far. She pivoted, muttered a few whispered words and paced.

Her head shook as she mumbled another incoherent sentence. He didn't know what to do and wanted to call Lucian and blame him for carelessly hurting her, but even he knew this wasn't her brother's fault.

Guilt filled him as he thought about how Bishop looked the other week when he'd confronted him. He hadn't thrown a punch like a man meant to leave this world anytime soon. As a matter of fact, his strength and force had shocked Parker.

"I don't understand. Was there an accident?"

"I don't know. I need to call Lucian back." She searched for her phone, not seeing it right in front of her.

"Here," he said, picking it up off the floor and handing it to her.

She dropped it. "*Goddamn it!*"

Falling to her knees, she gasped and he pulled her to him, taking the phone and holding her tight. "Let me."

She rocked and lost the battle against her sobs. Pressing her face into her palms she leaned into his lap and moaned. The heat of her tears scalded through the denim of his jeans.

He ran his left hand over her back and dialed her brother. "Shh. I'm calling Lucian. We'll find out what happened."

The phone rang for a split second. "Isa?"

"Lucian, it's Parker."

There was a long pause. "What are you doing with my sister's phone?"

"Look, your sister's upset. She asked me to call. Tell me what happened to Sawyer Bishop."

His long sigh echoed over the dead air. "I figured she'd be upset. She always liked Slade's dad."

It was strange hearing Lucian refer to Bishop as only Slade's father. He really was clueless about his sister's private life.

"Apparently, he'd been sick for a while. We're still trying to figure out what's factual and what's hearsay, but Sawyer's always been an extremely private man. Even Slade didn't know he was sick. Vivian Sheffield, a friend of ours, was Sawyer's GP for a few years, but she's only giving us minimal information, something about the right to privacy."

There was another long silence and he realized that was all the information he was going to get. "Thank you."

"I'm sure she'll be fine once she gets over the shock. It was a surprise to all of us. Christ, he's younger than our dad. Tell her if she needs me, to call."

"I will." He ended the call. "Isa?" he said softly.

She lay in a crumpled mess of limbs on the floor, her teary eyes staring at nothing. He suspected Lucian's deep voice carried and she'd heard everything.

She looked so broken, so shattered. He was afraid to move her or touch her in any way, but he couldn't leave her like that. "Let's get you off the floor."

Talking her through each step seemed to be the only way to shove his own shock aside. He swept her into his arms and carried her upstairs to his bed. "I'll take you to bed."

She made no comment when he adjusted the covers over her and hardly seemed to breathe as he asked, "Do you want me to stay?"

He couldn't bear to leave her, but she seemed to be fighting back her sorrow and he wanted her to get it out. "It's okay to cry here."

A jagged sob hiccupped out of her and she

gave into her tears, letting them fall unchecked. She looked so small and fragile, so crushed.

He couldn't leave her to bear such pain alone, even if everything that man represented in her life had threatened his one chance at happiness. Nothing would ever erase the fact that she loved him first. The threat was over now, but maybe this was worse.

Curling next to her, he gently folded his body around hers. This was something personal he was apart from, but she was too upset to be alone. He wouldn't leave her.

There was nothing comparable to the growing sense of powerlessness that took over with each passing minute. A thousand questions raced through his head. But his greatest worry resounded like a gong cracking against his skull.

Did she have regrets?

Painfully, he knew the answer was yes. Maybe this was why Bishop had pushed so hard to get her back. Maybe he knew his time was limited and couldn't bear the thought of her suffering or the thought that she might always have a lingering sense of unfinished business where he was concerned.

He should have told her. If he knew he was

sick he could have prepared her for this—but then she might have gone back to him.

Parker folded his arms around her, protectively pulling her closer. Her grief gutted him, but he stingily couldn't regret the way things played out. He didn't want the man to *die*, but he couldn't imagine a life without her, especially not for someone else's sake.

The horrible truth was, she could have had closure had she chosen differently, but she chose him and now her heartache might never end. Parker wasn't sure how guilty he should feel about that. This morning she was happy, but moments like that now played like tarnished memories in his mind.

A while later, when she'd fallen asleep, he slipped out of bed quietly to find something to eat. She probably didn't have an appetite, but she needed to eat. He returned to the bedroom only to find her staring into space.

"I brought you soup. It's after one o'clock and you haven't eaten anything since dinner last night. I think you should try to get something in your stomach."

"I don't want to eat. I can't."

He placed the bowl on the nightstand and sat beside her. "Isa ... I'm so sorry."

Her shoulders trembled as tears returned to her eyes, sliding slowly into her hair. He swore he'd never brush away the tears she shed for another man, but he couldn't bear to see them fall.

His thumb gently caught a lingering drop and wiped it away only to have another take its place. "I wish I could take this pain from you," he whispered, kissing her cheek.

He silently caught every tear, each one gouging a needle sharp hole in his heart. There were no words, none for him to offer in comfort and none for her to make sense of this news. Just palpable sadness that inflicted every inch of the room, distorting the feelings that were there yesterday.

Last night had been incredible. He'd never been so certain everything was exactly as it was meant to be. This changed everything. It clouded their reality with doubt, stole part of their happiness, and replaced it with sorrow. He didn't know how to help her and he might never be able to when it came to love for another man.

She didn't move from his bed all day. Everything he brought her sat untouched. By nighttime, he was truly worried she was having some sort of episode and he might need to tell someone.

He considered calling her sister but hesitated. He'd wait until morning, not wanting to do anything that would upset her more than she already was.

He awoke to the click of his front door and bolted out of bed. "Isa?"

Looking out the window, he saw a yellow cab pulling away. His jaw locked as his worry mounted. Maybe she just needed time to process and wanted to grieve privately.

Fuck that.

He knew the agony of losing a loved one—had gone through it personally. Had it not been for Scout, the death of his mother would have swallowed him whole. Alone was no way to grieve.

She needed people near her, people close to her to help her through the shock. But even her family, the closest people in her life, wouldn't understand why Sawyer Bishop's death affected her so deeply.

Only he understood and that meant it was his duty to be her rock. No matter how much it cost him, he would not let her face this alone.

"The first thing to know about business, Hughes, is that a pen can be as lethal as a gun when you sign your name to something. Always remember that."

Slade Bishop

HE CALLED Isadora several times only to have quiet conversations over the phone. The passing hours made things worse. She couldn't intrude on the Bishops and ask about arrangements and had to resume the position of a silent secret in the background of someone else's life.

"Maybe you should confess the truth to your family so they understand your grief," Parker suggested during one of their quiet calls.

"No. They'll never understand."

He suspected she was lumping him in with those who could never grasp her pain. "You don't have to go through this alone, Isa. I'm here. Whatever you need."

"I don't know what I need right now." It was disturbing how little her voice sounded compared to the normal confidence it carried. "I have to go."

The call ended and he debated giving her space, but what would that do to help her? She shouldn't have to feel ashamed for loving some-one. That wasn't supposed to be how love worked. But it seemed, even in death, the shame she linked to Sawyer survived.

He drove to her house later that day and found her in wrinkled, mismatched clothes, looking like she had the flu. "You shouldn't be here." She didn't invite him in.

"Why?" he wouldn't argue with her, but he would try to reason with her. "I don't care what did this to you, only that it's happening. Let me at least try to help you, Isa. Please."

Defeated or lacking the energy to convince

him otherwise, she left the door open and walked into the den. Tissues littered the floor and a blanket was tossed on the arm of the sofa.

She curled into a ball on the far end of the couch and he hesitated. Was he making this about him? No. It was definitely about her.

He silently sat beside her. A quiet presence, there if she needed him. But she was so stoic in her pain, she didn't utter a word to help him understand what she might need to make this better. She never once asked for him to hold her. She didn't try to unburden her private thoughts. She simply suffered in silence as if she'd had more practice doing that than anything else in her life.

His inability to help her was infuriating, but he would be patient and promised himself, with a little time, she'd come back to him.

The funeral was set for Wednesday and he, being a former employee of Leningrad, donned a suit and drove to the parlor orchestrating the viewing. Isadora had not answered her phone since he left her that morning, but he knew she'd be among the first to arrive.

He wasn't great with death, having seen too much of it too early in his life. At some point, he sort of started breaking down things into scientific facts. They were there. They were fragile. And when their time was up, it was over.

He wasn't the most comforting person when it came to trying to justify the mysteries of life. Realizing this, made him hope that maybe one of her relatives would step in and say the right words, because for all his love of the English language, he was utterly inept at consoling her to the degree she needed comfort.

The line at the funeral parlor slithered through the colonial entryway at a snail's pace. He stood behind a woman wearing potent perfume and a man who coughed every two minutes. These were the tedious norms he'd never adjusted to when he returned to polite society. His gaze scoured the crowd for any sign of Isadora.

As he made it through the front door, he spotted Lucian walking at a brisk pace, cutting straight to the head of the line. Of course everyone deferred, as he begged pardon and marched right to the front.

Parker frowned and stepped out of line, following his lead. He stilled at the hall to the viewing room as he saw Isadora.

She looked exhausted, as if she hadn't slept

for months. As Lucian took his place beside her she stiffened. Parker noted how much effort it took her to simply remain standing. Taken aback by how much she truly loved Bishop, he numbly drifted into the crowd. Maybe this moment should be hers. He didn't want to intrude on her chance to say goodbye.

It became clear how much Sawyer represented, how wide the gaping void left in his absence would be. Could it ever be filled?

Isadora abruptly pivoted and pushed against the crowd trapping her at the front of the room. Parker's gaze alertly followed her brisk pace as he wondered where she was going.

As the line progressed, the chatter slowed in respect for the mourning family. Her attention appeared riveted on the entrance he occupied, but she looked right past him, her red-rimmed eyes frantic, and she appeared desperate to escape.

As she approached, he tried to catch her attention, but she wasn't looking at him. She reached the hallway and a gasp from her lips drew the attention of onlookers as her hand caught the wall.

"Pardon me," he whispered, rushing to help her as she weaved through the guests.

Though she was barely moving at a staggering pace, there were too many people obscuring his way to catch up to her. He wanted to call out her name, but that would only draw more unwanted attention.

Suddenly, when faced with a mob of mourners clogging the front entrance, she turned again. Parker stilled, silently begging her to see him, but her attention was on the discreet door she'd just passed.

She slid it open and disappeared inside, shutting him and everyone else out. What was behind that door?

The house was old, so he turned the corner, not surprised to find another discreet door leading into the same room. Turning the metal knob, he quietly stepped inside what appeared to be a sitting area and froze at the wretched sound of her whimpered sobs.

She stood by the door, her shoulders quaking as she softly wept, pressing her cheek to the dark wood. He moved deeper into the room, keeping his presence as unobtrusive as possible.

Her whimpers sliced through his chest, each quiet sob knocking his heart. Her eyes were closed, her face pinched tight as she pressed her cheek to the wood and gasped in broken breaths. He placed a gentle hand on her shoulder and she sucked in a startled breath, her hands covering her face to hide.

A floor board creaked as he moved closer. "Isadora," he murmured gently and her body tensed.

Slowly, her hands fell away and she silently turned away from the door to face him. She looked up at him in disbelief, her bloodshot eyes full of anguish, her composure destroyed. Her wet lashes flicked as her lips parted and her chin trembled.

It was unbearable seeing her so distraught. His hand was unsteady as he reached for her face and delicately brushed away a tear. There were too many, and each one was a dagger to his heart. He pulled her into his arms and a piece of his heart broke away as she came to him willingly.

He buried his face in her shoulder, breathing a sigh of relief. "I've got you."

All he'd ever known of love had brought him pain. Until he'd found her. But now, her pain was his, because she was his.

"I'm here. Hold onto me, baby. I'm here."

"Parker…" He heard her fear that this all-consuming pain might never wane and his heart broke.

The man was gone, but he'd taken something from her she'd never have back. "He left knowing you loved him. Do you know what a gift that is?"

Her shoulders shook as she cried, her tears seeping through his clothes and burning his chest. "This hurts..."

"I know." Her pain was his. "Let me take you home," he begged, gently pressing his lips to her hair.

Her shoulders quaked and he tightened his arms. This whole time he'd been focused on getting her over Sawyer when he should have been trying to help her find the closure she deserved.

She drew back and looked up at him with such sadness flooding her eyes. "I'm dying inside."

"No, baby. It only feels like that right now. I know it hurts, but you have to believe it will get better."

"I can't face them. All those people... I couldn't even pay my condolences. I couldn't..."

"Shh." His hand rubbed over her back.

"Don't worry about that. Let's get you out of here."

"I don't want anyone to see me like this," she wept, shaking her head as if he would let anyone see or judge her like this.

He kissed her temple. "They won't."

Much like he'd done the first night they met, he ushered her through the side door and away from the crowd. His body became her shelter as he walked her down a private hall, away from the other guests.

A back entrance led to the side of the house and he kept his arm around her as he slowly escorted her to his car. He buckled her safely inside and focused on getting her away from that place as calmly and quickly as possible. The moment they were off the property there seemed a shift in the atmosphere, like she could breathe again.

Once they were a few miles away her phone rang. She sluggishly pulled it out and placed it against her ear, her voice low. "Lucian."

She waited as her brother spoke. "I had to leave. No, nothing's wrong." Her voice seized. "I'll call you later."

She slipped the phone back into her purse and rested her head on the window, her gaze on the world rushing by as tears trickled down her cheeks.

Once they reached her house, she took a shower and he made lunch, but again she wouldn't eat. She was quiet, but he didn't need her words. He only needed her nearness, however she had to be.

He sat on the couch, as she rested against his side. They didn't speak and she barely moved for over an hour.

Eventually, she broke the silence and whispered, "He never loved me."

Parker turned his body to face her. Voice gentle, he lifted her chin and looked into her eyes. "Isadora, that man *absolutely* loved you."

Her mouth compressed as she struggled to keep her emotions bottled up and failed. "He didn't. He never once told me. For years, I asked him and... Nothing." More tears fell. "And now he's *gone*."

But he did love her. He'd told Parker, only Parker wasn't sure if telling her that would help. It might upset her more that Bishop confessed his feelings to him, but never admitted them to her.

She had nothing more to say after that and he imagined that was because the words she shared were deepest thoughts ricocheting through her mind. A torturous loop she couldn't discredit or silence. She didn't object when he followed her to bed and he was glad she let him hold her in the dark.

The next morning he decided to let her sleep. Maybe she needed some time to decompress alone. Though his gut told him to stay, he needed to give her a fair balance of space and closeness so she could process all that had happened.

His house felt cold and empty. Sitting in the den, he stared at the wall of books, his mind recalling the characters from each story, comparing them to the characters of his life. He wanted to be every hero, but he didn't know how to save his lady now, when her heart was so clearly shattered.

Unsure where to go or what to do, he grabbed his keys and left. He drove for a while, circling familiar city streets and visiting desolate corners he hadn't seen in years.

When his car turned onto a vacant lot, the pavement pockmarked with caved in cement, he shut off the engine. Sitting in the comfort of his luxury car, smooth leather at his back, he looked at a place he used to call home.

The mill was large with gaping windows and a soulless presence that seeped into the air.

Even the clouds overhead seemed dingier than the soft ones in the distance. Abandoned tracks, too rotted for trains to ride, cut through the overgrown field with long rusted rails.

The hole in the chain link fence still was there. A doorway to hell.

As he sat in his car, his mind rolled over all the places he had been and the people who had come and gone from his life. Some were there for only a flash. Some were there too long. The ones he lost that hurt the most... the pain never truly subsided. His mother. Scout.

He refused to lose Isadora. What would be the point of waking if she wasn't a part of his day? So many things needed to change.

This thing with her brother... It had to end. He wouldn't be another sacrifice she had to make. For as much as Lucian got under his skin, he would put all his emotions aside if it made her life better. The man was her brother and Parker wanted to be her husband some day. It was enough. The tension between them had to end.

And Scout... He missed his friend. She was having a child. The thought of not knowing her children—of her maybe not knowing his— drove the issue home. It wasn't right for them to be outside of each other's lives. They'd been a team for too long.

His gaze traveled to the cracked gate on the far side of the mill. Every day he and Scout used to scurry through that narrow opening and find home on the other side.

There had been no security. No guarantees. Very little joy or pleasure. But they had each other and somehow that made the hell they were living in a little more bearable each dreary day.

He sat there for a long time, his mind going over the fundamental moments of his early life and turning to the happier events of the last few months. He had regrets, lots of them. Some scars never healed. The human heart was indeed an irrational thing.

He thought of the regret Isadora might be feeling now. If she didn't find a way through that pain it would fester and grow into something uglier than it was today. Sometimes the mind played tricks to make the heart hurt a little less. But sometimes the mind was the most dangerous villain of all, brutal and relentless in its karmic repetition of repentance. He didn't want Isa to fall into that spiraling pit.

Despite his knowledge that his mother loved him very much, after she died, he'd convinced himself she didn't. It was the only way the young boy in him could justify her leaving this world—leaving him—with hardly a fight.

Anger was a heavy burden to bear, but considerably easier to carry than sadness. It masked a lot for him over the years, but it didn't necessarily help him. Anger took work. Sadness was easy, an effortless surrender that took the reins the moment you gave in. But it all stemmed from resentment.

There was just so much resentment, so much anger, so much sadness he still struggled to understand. That struggle could have been eased with only a few words from his mother, but his earlier life was an accumulation of missed comforts and, deep down, he always believed she'd known she was going to die, leaving him in a terrifying world, alone, with a wide open wound on his heart.

Sawyer could have eased Isa's pain. It would have taken three simple words. He'd never understand why he withheld such a simple gift. Loving her was the easiest thing Parker had ever done.

It was a twisted truth, but Sawyer had been a guiding light in Isadora's life. Her mother had passed and her father had abandoned her. His and Isadora's adolescence were abnormal, but compared to each other, they were the same.

Perhaps Sawyer was the only figure she had to tell her she was doing okay. Right or wrong, the man might have saved her in moments she'd felt utterly alone, just as Scout had occasionally saved him.

Sawyer's passing might have happened sooner than expected, if he had any warning at all, but now Parker truly believed jealousy wasn't the trigger of the man's desperate attempt to reconcile with Isa. Maybe the man wanted to leave this world knowing he'd given the one person who meant anything to him something to remember him by. What if he'd been trying to right a wrong?

Parker absolutely hated that she never got the proof she deserved. She should at least know the man loved her.

Turning the key in the ignition, he backed out of the abandoned lot and left his past where it belonged—behind him. Life was too short to dwell on missed opportunities and the heartache of yesterday. They all needed to look forward to better things. That meant saying proper goodbyes.

When he got home he went straight to the living room and rummaged around for something to write on. He reached into the coffee table drawer and found a tablet. Ripping off his scribbled notes, he crumpled them in his hand and tossed them into the wastepaper basket.

Finding a pen, he sat back and did something he promised her he'd never do, but the only thing he could think of that might make this easier on her. He started a lie.

My Dearest Isadora...

THE NEXT MORNING he was showered and out the door before nine. He'd returned to Isadora's house late last night, but she was as responsive as the day before. It was his day to volunteer at The Women's House, so Isadora expected him not to linger.

As he got on the road, he pointed his car

toward the city. Unsure where he'd find the one person he needed, he dialed Scout.

"Hello?"

"Scout?"

"Parker? Is everything all right?"

"Yes. I need to speak to Lucian."

There was a long pause followed by a skeptical, "Why?"

"I..." God, some things were never easy. "I need his help with something."

"Okay," she said slowly. "He's in the shower. Do you want me to have him call you?"

"I need to see him. Are you in the city or at the estate?"

"We're at the hotel right now."

Not a place he relished visiting. "Could you have him meet me in the lobby in about twenty minutes? Let him know I'm on my way. It's important."

"Sure, but Parker... What's going on?"

"I just ... need..." Fuck. He grit his teeth. "His help with something."

The closer he drove to the city the more he questioned his sanity. As he pulled up in front of the prestigious hotel, a valet met him at his door.

"Good morning, monsieur. Checking in or visiting?"

My, how things could change in the blink of an eye. "Just visiting."

The valet handed him a gold ticket and Parker stepped aside, letting him behind the wheel. He walked up the pristinely swept sidewalk and stilled, his eyes staring at the long red runner with gold fringe. God, he hated this place.

For whatever reason, stepping on that damn rug felt wrong. Every time he'd ever crossed that threshold his world got knocked on its ass.

Rolling his eyes, he marched over the carpet and through the gaping doors. It was a fucking rug.

The scent of citrus furniture polish and coffee welcomed guests, as his gaze drifted over an antique table occupying the center of the lobby, towering almost six feet with Danishes and croissants. He looked for any signs of Scout or Lucian in the crowd of people moving toward the restaurant.

The bay of elevators pinged and he turned and sighed. He was glad to see her first and this time he noted how thick her waist was. "Scout."

She was definitely pregnant. How had he missed that the other night? Not only did she have a bump, she was glowing.

She smiled. "Hey, Park." Offering him a quick hug, she stepped back. "Is everything okay? You were sort of cryptic on the phone."

He smiled, his purpose sidetracked. "You're pregnant. *Really* pregnant."

Her cheeks flushed, those crystal eyes turning shy. "I thought you knew?"

He shook his head. "I thought you looked different, but I guess I wasn't paying enough attention. How do you feel? Are you ... happy?"

She had never wanted children, having had a trying time being one, but he supposed people changed. He at least hoped so because she was definitely going to be a parent in the near future.

"I'm *very* happy." Her hand rested over the bump at her waist and he laughed, she looked so ... normal. Like a mom.

A strange relief filled him, as though a worry he'd carried for years could now be put down. It was a forlorn sort of lightness, but one that wasn't really sad at all. Despite all his doubts and skepticism, he honestly believed her life was right and her heart would always be safe with Lucian.

"Then I'm happy for you."

"Thank you." She turned and glanced at the elevators. "Lucian should be down in a minute."

Of *course*, he wouldn't offer Parker an invitation into their private space. He chuckled. Things seemed so different, yet some things never changed.

"Will you stay?" He wasn't sure if he wanted her to. Some things were better off private.

Her head tilted as she considered his question. Before she could answer the elevator doors opened again.

The sharp, arrogant click of Italian loafers had Parker drawing in a steady breath. Lucian didn't intimidate him. Parker simply loathed asking him a favor.

This isn't about you.

The air thickened, compressed by the weight of the other man's ego and Parker's mouth tightened. "Patras."

"Hughes."

Scout moved to Lucian's side and her husband's expression immediately softened. Rising on her toes, she kissed his cheek. "I'm going to say hi to Patrice and the girls at the salon. Will you order me some French toast?"

"Extra strawberries?"

She smiled, their gazes holding countless secrets as they looked into one another's eyes. "Yes, please."

As she stepped away, she squeezed Parker's arm. "Play nice."

He watched her go, noting how well she fit in with all the luxury, with Lucian Patras. He turned back to the other man. "Congratulations on the baby."

Dark eyes studied him. "Thank you." He glanced at the restaurant. "Shall we?" He strode away, not waiting for Parker's response.

They sat in the back of the restaurant far from other patrons. The service was fluid and flawless, great care taken to meet the owner's needs.

Once the preliminaries were handled, Lucian eyed him suspiciously and got right to business. "Why are you here, Hughes?"

"I need you to give something to your sister."

He arched a brow. "Isadora?"

"Yes."

Parker reached into his pocket and withdrew a long envelope, her name scrolled generically across the front in handwriting nothing like his own. He slid it across the table, but Lucian merely glanced at the envelope with disregard.

"What is it?"

"It's a letter. I need you to give it to her and not say where you got it, only that it was left on your desk."

"You mistake me for a messenger."

"I know exactly who you are, Patras. Hide behind as many power suits as you want, I see the real you."

His black eyes narrowed. "And what is it you think you see?"

"A man who loves his sisters and his wife and will do anything for them. Your sister needs this letter and I can't be the one who gives it to her."

He glanced at the letter. "What's it say?"

"None of your business."

Lucian flicked the envelope back to him. "Give it to her yourself."

Parker gritted his teeth. "I'm telling you she *needs* this. Are you really going to let your arrogance stand in the way of necessity when it comes to those you love? Some things are worth more than pride."

"You trust me not to open it?"

He hesitated. "I'm trusting you now, in this instance, because I'm asking you to trust that I know Isadora—in some ways better than you—and this is something she needs."

There was a long silence and, finally, Lucian picked up the envelope and placed it in his breast pocket. "I'll think about it."

"You'll do what's right. I believe that." Scanning the restaurant for Scout and not seeing her, he finished his coffee and stood. "Enjoy your breakfast."

"Hughes."

He paused, accustomed to men like Lucian always claiming the last word.

"You hurt her and I won't hesitate to destroy you."

"I ever hurt her, you have my full permission to do your worst."

Lucian nodded and Parker left, not drawing in a full breath until he strode through the lobby and his feet crossed the tasseled runner. It was done.

Part Five

Isadora

20

"My secret's long, obscure and unrefined,
Love's quiet whispers between the lines.
You put down your pride to hold me in
your hands,
Swearing tears wouldn't tarnish loves true
plans.
Your sharp edges, they're not so rough,
Endless dredges, and I found love."
Lydia Michaels
My Edgely Boy

ISADORA OPENED THE DOOR, startled to see her brother. "Lucian."

She quickly tried to disguise her disheveled appearance, but it was too late. His perceptive gaze missed nothing.

"What the hell happened to you? Are you sick?"

Tucking her matted hair behind her ear and closing her cardigan over her wrinkled T-shirt, she invited him inside. "I haven't been feeling my best."

"Have you been to a doctor?"

She didn't need a doctor. "Do you want coffee?"

"It's four o'clock in the afternoon, Isa. You're not even dressed."

She hadn't had the energy to dress in days. "I'm taking a day of rest." Or five. "Coffee?"

He followed her into the kitchen where several dishes were stacked in the sink and the coffee pot sat with only half a cup filling the bottom of the carafe. She set the filter with fresh grounds and rinsed the pot.

"Stop staring at me." She just wanted to be alone.

"Have you had anything besides coffee today?"

"Yes."

She had ice cream for breakfast sometime before the sun came up. She didn't have the strength to answer for herself or bear his scrutiny, so she tried not to make eye contact as she loaded the dishwasher.

"What did you need, Lucian?"

He hesitated, the coffee pot hissing quietly in the background as it brewed. His gaze was sharp, scrutinizing every telltale sign of her dysfunctional mind.

"Something was delivered to my office yesterday."

She stilled and shut off the faucet. Pulling a fresh mug from the cabinet, she tried to appear interested, but couldn't muster any intrigue. "Oh?"

"It was for you."

Frowning, she turned to him. "What was it?"

Her personal mail was typically sent to the house, but sometimes her statements went to his office. He usually handled those things.

"It's... Are you sure you're okay? Your eyes are really puffy."

"I'm fine. I'm just tired. I probably caught a bug," she lied.

He grudgingly accepted her word. Reaching into his pocket, he withdrew a white envelope. "Here."

She took the envelope in her hands and stared at it, not recognizing the penmanship. "What is it?"

"I don't know. Someone left it on my desk."

"Who?"

He shrugged. "No one saw who put it there."

There was no address, no identifying seal or even a stamp. "This was hand delivered?"

"Appears so."

Since when did her brother let people near his desk? He was usually obscenely protective of his private space.

Her thumb slid under the lip of the seal and she paused. Maybe she should open it when she was alone.

"Are you going to see what it is?"

She looked at him. "I'm surprised you didn't already peek."

His grimace proved the temptation was there. "It's addressed to you."

"You open plenty of my other mail."

"Statements. This looked personal."

The coffee finished percolating with a steamy fizzle. She slid the envelope into the pocket of her cardigan and filled a mug. "You sure you don't want any?" She asked out of politeness, but hoped he wouldn't linger.

"I can't stay. I just wanted to give you that."

"Well, thank you."

Guilt bloomed, as she was relieved he was leaving, but she pushed it away—too many negative emotions already occupying her heart. She couldn't handle company at the moment. She'd even been deterring Parker from visiting when she could, though he persistently found his way over, even if just to sit silently by her side.

Lucian's forehead creased and he hesitated. She sipped her coffee, staring at him, raising a brow.

He shook his head, eyes troubled. "You know you can talk to me, Isa. If something's wrong, I'll fix it for you."

"Some things can't be fixed, Lucian."

"Does this—" He waved a hand at her disheveled appearance. "—have anything to do with Hughes?"

"Wouldn't you just love it if I said yes?"

His expression appeared wounded. "No. I get no pleasure from watching someone hurt my sister."

She weighed the truth of his words and sighed. In that moment, she wanted to lean into her brother's strength and confess she was breaking on the inside, that a man she gave half her life to was suddenly gone and she was in such despair she could barely move. But she didn't.

She looked at him, seeing his strength, recognizing his need to make everything right for those he loved, and she knew even he could not fix this for her.

The secrets she carried would be her burden for the rest of her life. Sawyer's half added to everything else that already rested on her shoulders.

She was done keeping secrets, done hiding behind lies, but this one was a permanent tattoo on her past. Without Sawyer, it seemed wrong to confess the truth now, like a betrayal to his memory.

Never again would she make the mistake of thinking that deception solved anything. If anything, Sawyer taught her how blemished reality could be when clouded by a lifetime of secrets and lies.

She studied her brother, believing he would never honestly position himself between her and her happiness. She trusted that he loved her enough to let her choose what her heart wanted.

A decade ago it would have been the same, but she'd let Sawyer scare her with his own insecurities. She should have told Lucian what was happening then. Another thing that was too late to change, because telling him now would fix nothing.

She was done hiding. Done waiting for a clear path. Life was too short and she was through wasting time on sadness or concerns for other people's bullshit when her own world was complicated enough.

She put down her mug. "I'm in love with him, Lucian."

He drew in a slow, measured breath. "I know you are."

"I know you don't approve, but ... this is my life. If he asked me to marry him tomorrow, I wouldn't hesitate." She paused, waiting for him to protest, but he remained silent. "Are you going to ask if he loves me?"

"No. I believe he does. You're easy to love, Isa."

She laughed without humor, sorrow cutting her breath into a shallow ache. "Not always."

He scowled at her. "Yes, *always*." Stepping around the island, he turned her shoulders and looked in her eyes. "I want you to be happy. That's all I've ever wanted for you. If Parker makes you so, then I'll try to put our personal differences aside. For you."

Shocked that her brother could not only accept her decision but also clear the path for her future, she struggled to respond. "Thank you."

It was that easy seeing how quickly he surrendered his grudges for her. But she supposed she always knew he would, be it his trouble with the Bishops or this. She just never expected it to be so simple.

When someone loved you they accepted you as you were. No conditions. Lucian accepted her now and he would have accepted her then. It was an untrusted truth she wished Sawyer had been given the time to learn.

Her mouth formed a sad smile. "Sometimes, I think we have to suffer through the crappy parts of life to prepare us for good. Maybe it's sadness that makes us appreciate the value of the little happy moments in between."

His face pinched with concern and she realized her mind had gone someplace he couldn't follow. "Are you sure you're okay?"

Realizing he had no idea what she was talking about, she nodded. "Maybe none of us are ever okay, but when we find the right people, the people we're meant to be with, I think the ups and the downs don't matter so much. All that matters is having someone there to hold your hand—someone who truly gets you and won't let go. That makes things okay."

He still wore a look of confusion. "And you think Hughes gets you like that? You trust he's in this to stay?"

Scattered memories danced through her mind, filling her heart with warmth, smoothing over the broken edges. "He gets me more than anyone in this world ever has. We have no secrets and our flaws only make us stronger, because there's no room for shame when you love and accept someone that completely."

"I get it." He nodded and let out a breath as if he could finally put down a worry he'd carried for a lifetime. "Trust me. I definitely get that sort of love and acceptance. I'm glad you found it."

And she believed he did get it. "He misses Evelyn. Life's too short to let insecurities get in your way, Lucian. Let them have their friendship back."

Letting out a low groan, he rolled his eyes. "Give it time. I'm starting to believe he's over her."

She scoffed. "I should hope so."

He smirked and winked, letting her know he was teasing. His expression sobered. "The other night I was watching him. The way he looks at you when you talk, the way he anticipates and hangs on your every word... There's something right between you two. There has to be if even I can see it."

She smiled. "I know."

He sighed and tapped a hand on the countertop. "I'll work on it. Try to get some rest. If you're not feeling better tomorrow I'm sending Vivian over to check on you."

"Of course you will." She walked him to the door.

She waited until he left to take her coffee to the den. Pulling the envelope from her pocket she tore open the seal.

My Dearest Isadora,

If you're reading this, then I assume I'm gone. I'm so sorry to put you through this, as it has been something I've always feared leaving you to face alone. I never wanted to cause you pain.

You wear your heart on your sleeve and love without reservation—this I know. No one has ever loved me with the unguarded ease that you have. *My only regret was loving you too much and not enough at the same time.*

Yes, <u>I loved you</u>. Some days I loved you so much I couldn't bear the intensity. Other days I loved you enough to push you away, knowing you deserved so much more than I could offer. You put me, along with so many others, before yourself. I only ever wanted to be the sort of man who put you first. Thank you for loving me more than I ever deserved.

I know you're hurting. I know I've been a clumsy fool with your heart and I should have done better. If you can forgive me for leaving you this way, please find it in your heart to remember these simple truths...

I loved you in the beginning. I loved you in the end. And I loved you every day in between. My love will never fade. My heart belongs to you. Carry it with you always and please don't grieve too long. You have a world of opportunities waiting for you.

Do not take life for granted, Isadora. Laugh easily, love fiercely, and go after everything you want. That is my final wish for you. That is what I've always wanted for you.

I love you, now and forever.

~Sawyer

Tears streamed down her cheeks as she held the damp pages to her chest and curled into the chair. Harsh sobs broke from her throat as every emotion she'd tried to stifle over the past week, burst through her defenses and came tumbling out.

She wasn't sure how much time had passed or how many times she reread the letter. She didn't move from that chair until late that night.

When she reached her room, she folded the paper, soft and soggy with tears, and lovingly tucked it into her jewelry box, beside her mother's pearl earrings and her walnut kisses.

Her hand brushed over the note one last time and she whispered, "Thank you."

Everything that letter said, and the secrets tucked between the lines, pulled poetry out of pain and exemplified what true love was. It wasn't the words, but the gesture. Not the closure, but the opening.

From the familiar squiggle of the casual *e*'s to the cleverly positioned *p*'s, she understood everything this letter was intended to accomplish and loved it all the more for failing its purpose.

Resting on her bed, she looked up at the ceiling, wondering if there was a heaven. Her eyes stared at nothing as everything shifted into perfect lucidity.

"I love you." It was the greatest truth she knew. And speaking it aloud seemed to let her heart finally rest. For the first time in days, she slept soundly through the night.

The following morning she showered and dressed, feeling like a weight she'd carried for decades had finally faded away. The letter was perhaps the greatest gift she'd ever received.

To know she'd given half her life to this outcome seemed the saddest journey one could walk alone. But, in the end, she wasn't alone.

She was loved. Deeply. Unconditionally. And selflessly.

The proof of that love mended so many scars. The evidence rested between the lines of the only lie she'd ever let stand between her and Parker, because that lie was perhaps the most gallant expression of love anyone had ever shown her.

He loved her enough to go against all his principles, somehow involve her brother, and pretend to be a man he despised, just to sew up the hole in her heart. Each little word mending wounds that no one other than Parker knew she bore.

She swore she'd never tolerate a lie between them, but he'd found the one exception. In trying to convince her that Sawyer had loved her, Parker only managed to prove how deep his own love reached.

Pulling up at his house, she waited in the car for a moment, willing her nerves to settle. This was her life. This was her journey. And her hero had come out of nowhere, a dark knight who managed to catch a pawn and make her feel like a queen.

She smiled, wondering what she would have done had they never crashed into each other that evening at the opera house. It was now her move and she knew exactly what she wanted, exactly what she needed to do.

Her fingers closed over the key and shut off the engine. As the car rattled into silence, she glanced at her reflection in the mirror and smiled. "Checkmate."

She knocked quietly on his door and he opened it a second later. He stared at her, guarded worry in his green eyes, hidden behind unrefined affection. "Isa."

"I have a question for you and I want you

to give me the absolute truth. I'll know if you're lying."

Fear flashed in his eyes. "Okay, do you want to come in first?"

"No. Not until I have your answer."

His Adam's apple made a slow bob as he swallowed. "I'm listening."

"I'm done being sad. I know grief takes time and it will come and go, but I don't want to put my happiness on hold for something I can't control. I love you, Parker. That hasn't changed, nor will it ever."

He still appeared guarded, but slightly relieved. "I love you, too."

"That's why..." Damn, this was harder than she expected. "That is why..." She licked her lips and drew in a deep breath. She could do this. On an exhale she pushed the words out. "Parker Hughes, will you marry me?"

His eyes widened. "Wh... What?"

"I know this isn't the traditional way it happens, but forget tradition. When I look at you, I can imagine a family—*our family*—and I want that with you. Life's too short for regrets and I'd regret it forever if I didn't tell you, here and now, how I feel. You're *my* person. You're the missing piece I was always meant to find in this world. I believe that with every ounce of my being and every battered piece of my heart, which, by the way, you've made grow so much it sometimes makes me ache."

Out of breath, she sucked in a gulp of air. "I just ... love you. More than I ever knew someone could love a person. And I want to be with you. Always."

As dependable as the sun rises and sets, his arms closed around her, supportive, protective, dependable, and strong. His mouth found hers as he lifted her off her feet and turned their bodies, walking her into the house.

"Is that a yes?" she asked when he finally broke the kiss long enough to let her talk.

"Shh." He kissed her again.

"Park—" His lips demanded all of her focus. "Parker, is that a yes?"

He shook his head. "What is it with you Patrases always stealing my thunder? The guy is supposed to ask."

She shrugged. "I didn't want to wait."

He laughed. "Stay here." Giving her a sharp glance, he pointed to where she stood. "Do. Not. Move."

Unsure what he was doing, she watched as he raced up the stairs and returned a moment later, moving at a slower pace.

"This is *not* how this was supposed to go. I

had a hot air balloon and stargazer lilies in store."

She frowned, unsure how he could have possibly anticipated this was going to happen. They never discussed marriage until this very moment.

He dropped to his knee, unveiling a small velvet box in his hand and her eyes widened. "Oh, my God."

"Isadora, I always thought I knew what love was. Then I met you. You're my shoe that fits, my Oz I've been searching for, my everything. I don't ever want to let you go and I'm prepared to spend the rest of my life giving you reasons to let me stay. You've become my best friend, my lover, my last thought before I go to sleep and my first thought when I wake. Now I want you to be my wife. I want to make a family with you. I want to give both of us the chance at a fairy tale."

He opened the box and a stunning diamond winked in the sunlight. "Will you marry me?"

"When did you get that?"

He smirked. "The moment I realized there would be no living without you."

Her fingers covered her lips as she lost her composure. "Yes!"

He bolted to his feet and kissed her again, this time backing her to the wall and slipping the ring on her finger. She glanced down at her hand, finding the weight comforting, like a steady reminder he'd always be with her.

"It's beautiful."

"*You're* beautiful." He continued to kiss her and then started to laugh.

"What's so funny?"

He chuckled. "I was just thinking... You're going to be a Hughes."

She snorted. "My brother and father will love that."

He arched a brow. "*I'll* love it. Isadora Hughes." His eyes closed as he pressed his brow to hers. "My wife."

As he held her, her heart felt a sense of completeness she'd never known. Sometimes love hurt, but it wasn't always painful.

Parker had shown her that love could be freeing and fun, an unapologetic method in seeking happiness that didn't depend on other people's opinions. He showed her what true love really was and now that she knew, she'd never accept anything less.

She would never tell Parker she knew he wrote the letter. She would read it often, and though he'd signed it with another man's name, it was his love that filled the page.

Sawyer would have called her *bella*, but that wasn't what gave it away. It was Parker's heart behind those words, which she recognized better than her own.

He showed her that the heart could grow and love again, deeper, longer, epically so. That was how he loved her and that was how she loved him. Just the way love was meant to be. Open, in living color, not a single gray area to be found.

The moment she chose her path, time moved swiftly. Days were filled with laughter and evenings were full of sultry pleasures.

That autumn, just before the snow came, they planted the hedges at her home—their home. Over time the yew hedges would grow. By the following spring, they were tall enough for her nephew Keaton to toddle through— though he still was learning how to walk.

Their children would play there one day as well, chasing and laughing with their cousins like children were meant to do, secure, happy, and free.

As she sat on the veranda staring over the blooming gardens, she gazed at the labyrinth in the distance. Of all the crazy twists and turns, she and Parker had found their way home.

Things had certainly changed. Turns out her Master's in English was exactly the degree she needed to figure out her calling.

Her life had never been that interesting. But once she found her hero, everything changed and it became that much easier to save herself. He made her brave, a lioness full of confidence and courage. He made her believe she could achieve anything.

Parker rescued her the day they met and, in a way, he rescued her every day since simply by encouraging her to be exactly who she was on the inside. When he found her ramblings hidden on a file in her laptop, he'd read her words from beginning to end in one sitting. Not a single secret between them.

It was Parker, with his love of literature to match her own, who convinced her she had a story to tell. In the end, other people agreed.

She'd received a letter that September, an offer to buy her story. It had come from years of journaling about the inexplicable patterns of love, but in the end, the heroine became a queen, rescued by a knight, and they lived happily ever after.

She'd always assumed Lucian was the interesting one, Toni the mischievous one, but maybe they all had a love story in them. The sort that proved even the most jaded heart could love again. And happily ever after wasn't just for fiction.

Her hand rested on her stomach, as her eyes found Parker's. He smiled and placed a dish on the bar as he crossed the veranda.

"I see you looking at me," he teased, laughter dancing in his green eyes. "Don't think I don't know what that look means. You want to ravish me. Have your wicked way with me right here in the gardens."

She laughed, pretty certain he was the one responsible for the last ravishing. "Not in front of the company."

His lips brushed hers as his hand gently rested over her fingers. They shared a knowing look. After dinner, they'd share their news.

"I better start the grill," he whispered. "If I don't feed them soon they'll never leave and there will be no ravishing." He kissed her one last time and collected the plate. "Lucian, you gonna prep these steaks or what?"

Her brother turned and scowled. Rising from his crouched position on the stone, he scooped Keaton onto his hip.

"That's your Uncle Parker. He's a real pain

in Daddy's ass. Mostly because he's still upset I beat him up a few years ago. It was a great battle and *I* was the indisputable victor."

"Lucian!" Evelyn snapped. "Don't teach him words like that!"

Lucian tsked. "That's Mommy's serious voice, Daddy's only weakness. Come on. Let's go help Uncle Parker before he burns the steaks."

Evelyn waddled to the seat next to Isadora and sat with a winded sigh. "My ankles are eating my shoes. I'm so over this second pregnancy."

"Stop," Isadora laughed. "You look beautiful."

Evelyn lifted her glass and grimaced. "Between just finishing with nursing Keaton and your brother's potent virility, I haven't had anything fun to drink in almost two years. After this, I'm done."

Toni, ever the graceless one, took the seat between them and poked Evelyn's ankle. "Look at the way the skin stays puckered in. Is that normal?"

Isadora rolled her eyes. "Don't be a brat. One day it'll be you."

Her sister scoffed. "Doubt it. Need a man for that to happen."

Parker called over to the table. "Scout, are you eating meat this week?"

Evelyn made a gagging face. "No. I've been off meat since my second trimester. I'll just have sides."

Parker turned back to the grill and Evelyn swatted Toni's hand away. She glanced at Isadora and smiled. When she looked at Isadora like that it was if she were silently thanking her for bringing Parker into their family, where he belonged.

Sometimes Isadora caught the two of them sharing a look, which ended in a laugh, as if their happiness was all too surreal to believe. Isadora had moments like that too—when she looked at Parker, unable to believe her happiness was real.

They had been married in the summer, a small, private ceremony on the coast. Her father and Tibet had flown in, but didn't linger. Christos danced with her and told her she'd done well for herself. That he was proud of her. But his praise didn't affect her the way she imagined it would. Funny, how when a person goes without something long enough, the significance tends to fade.

Life had taught her that nothing was impossible. Every day, Parker took her breath away then breathed it back into her soul at night. He showed her a love she could depend on, above all else, a love that was real and only grew with time.

He told her he loved her each and every day, never letting her wonder otherwise. But she never doubted his affection. She knew, not just from his words, but his actions.

Their love was a tangible presence in their life, what made their house a home. It was a gentle surrender that led where they had no choice but to follow.

Passionately, fiercely, easily, he cherished every piece of her, even the tarnished parts others had left behind. Their love was so powerful, so epic, all that came before seemed like a child's sketch next to a Monet. Just as someone special once promised love should be.

Sawyer had loved her, admitted or not, a real love now guarded close to her heart. But he could never own her heart because it was meant for someone else.

Parker fearlessly loved her with the truest kind of love. Her heart might wear scars, but he adored every tender inch of her being, accepting her completely, just as she loved and accepted all of him. It was ... *everything* love was meant to be.

THE END

**Want more edgy romance from Lydia Michaels?
Read *BLIND* next!**

Claim your FREE book when you subscribe to Lydia's newsletter!
<u>Click here to sign up for Lydia Michaels' Newsletter.</u>

Are you follow Lydia Michaels?
Stalk her on <u>TikTok</u>, <u>Instagram</u>, <u>Facebook</u>, <u>Goodreads</u>, and <u>BookBub</u>!
<u>TikTok @LydiaMichaels</u>
<u>Instagram @lydia_michaels_books</u>
<u>Facebook @LydiaMichaels</u>
<u>Goodreads</u>
<u>BookBub</u>

Show Your LOVE
If you enjoyed this book, please don't forget to <u>leave a review</u>.

LYDIA MICHAELS' READING ORDER

<u>MCCULLOUGH MOUNTAIN</u>
<u>Almost Priest</u>

Beautiful Distraction
Irish Rogue
British Professor
Broken Man
Controlled Chaos
Hard Fix
Intentional Risk

JASPER FALLS
Wake My Heart
The Best Man
Love Me Nots
Pining For You
My Funny Valentine
Side Squeeze

CALAMITY RAYNE
Calamity Rayne Gets a Life
Calamity Rayne Back Again

THE SURRENDER TRILOGY
Falling In
Breaking Out
Coming Home

RUTHLESS BILLIONAIRES
One Billion Secrets
Two Billion Enemies

<u>MASTERMIND</u>
<u>Blind</u>
<u>Untied</u>

<u>NEW CASTLE</u>
<u>First Comes Love</u>
<u>If I Fall</u>
<u>Something Borrowed</u>

<u>ADDICTED TO YOU</u>
<u>Crush</u>
<u>Bang</u>
<u>Throb</u>

<u>THE ORDER OF VAMPIRES</u>
<u>Original Sin</u>
<u>Dark Exodus</u>
<u>Prodigal Son</u>

STAND ALONES
<u>La Vie en Rose</u>
<u>Simple Man</u>
<u>Sugar</u>
<u>Breaking Perfect</u>
<u>Hurt</u>
<u>Protege</u>

About Lydia Michaels

Lydia Michaels is the award winning and bestselling author of more than forty titles, a certified life coach, and transformational speaker. She is the consecutive winner of the 2018 & 2019 *Author of the Year Award* from *Happenings Media,* as well as the recipient of the 2014 *Best Author Award* from the *Courier Times*. She has been featured in *USA Today, Romantic Times Magazine, Love & Lace*, and more. As the host and founder of the *East Coast Author Convention*, the *Behind the Keys Author Retreat*, and *Read Between the Wines*, she continues to celebrate her growing love for readers and romance novels around the world.

In 2021, Michaels released the groundbreaking, non-fiction series, ***Write 10K in a Day***, to commemorate her career in the publishing industry. She looks forward to many more years of exploring both fiction and non-fiction writing, teaching about the craft, and learning from the others in the author community.

Lydia is happily married to her childhood sweetheart. Some of her favorite things include the scent of paperback books, listening to her husband play piano, escaping to her coastal home at the Jersey Shore, cheap wine, *Game of Thrones*, coffee, and kilts. She hopes to meet you soon at one of her many upcoming events.

You can follow Lydia at www.Facebook.com/LydiaMichaels or on Instagram @lydia_michaels_books

<u>**Read By Mood**</u>
Billionaire Romance
<u>Falling In</u> | <u>Sacrifice Of The Pawn</u> | <u>Calamity Rayne</u> | <u>Blind</u>

Contemporary Romance
<u>Wake My Heart</u> | <u>The Best Man</u> | <u>Love Me Nots</u> | <u>Pining For You</u> |<u>Almost Priest</u>| <u>My Funny Valentine</u> | <u>Side Squeeze</u> | <u>Almost Priest</u> | <u>Beautiful Distraction</u> | <u>Irish Rogue</u> | <u>British Professor</u> | <u>Broken Man</u> (LGBTQ) | <u>Controlled Chaos</u> | <u>Hard Fix</u>|<u>Intentional Risk</u>

Emotional Favorites
<u>La Vie en Rose</u> | <u>Simple Man</u> | <u>Wake My Heart</u> | <u>Sacrifice of the Pawn</u> | <u>Crush</u>
Romantic Comedy
<u>Calamity Rayne</u>

Erotic Romance
<u>Breaking Perfect</u> | <u>Protégé</u> | <u>Falling In</u> | <u>Sugar</u>

First in Series
<u>Almost Priest</u> | <u>Falling In</u> | <u>First Comes Love</u> | <u>Wake My Heart</u> | <u>Crush</u> | <u>Original Sin</u>

Paranormal Vampire Romance

Original Sin | Dark Exodus | Prodigal Son

LGBTQ+ & Menage Romance
Broken Man (MM) | Breaking Perfect (MMF) |
Crush (MMF) | Hurt (Non-Consensual) |
Protege

Sexy Nerds & Second Chances
Blind | Untied
**_Teacher Student, Workplace, and Age-
Gap Love Affairs... Oh my!_**
British Professor | Pining For You |Breaking
Perfect | Falling In | Sacrifice of the Pawn

Single Dads & Single Moms
Simple Man | Pining For You | First Comes
Love | Controlled Chaos | Intentional Risk

Dark Tortured Hero Romance
Hurt

Non-Fiction Books for Writers
Write 10K in a Day: Avoid Burnout